THE BOY ON THE DOCK

A.J. McCarthy

Black Rose Writing | Texas

ISBN: 978-1-68513-743-4
LIBRARY OF CONGRESS CONTROL NUMBER: 2025949824
PUBLISHED BY BLACK ROSE WRITING
www.blackrosewriting.com

Printed in the United States of America
Suggested Retail Price (SRP) $19.95

The Boy on the Dock is printed in Garamond Premier Pro

*As a planet-friendly publisher, Black Rose Writing does its best to eliminate unnecessary waste to reduce paper usage and energy costs, while never compromising the reading experience. As a result, the final word count vs. page count may not meet common expectations.

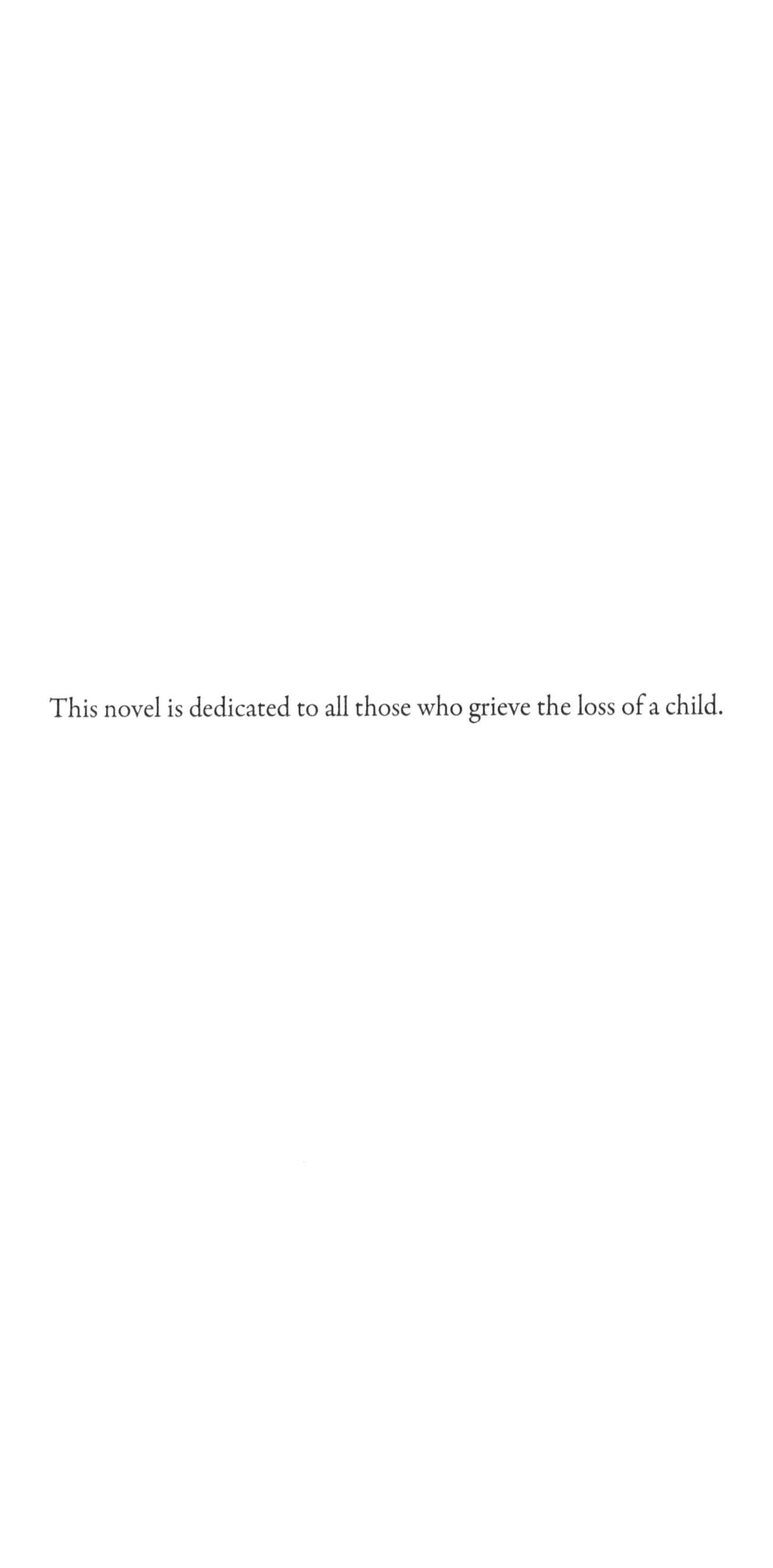

This novel is dedicated to all those who grieve the loss of a child.

Praise for
The Boy on the Dock

"From the opening page, I was hooked by this psychological thriller, rife with foreboding, complex characters, and vivid detail."
–Lena Gibson, award-winning author of the *Love and Survival, Time Slip*, and *Train Hoppers* series

"A masterful psychological thriller!"
–Ruth F. Stevens, award-winning author of *My Year of Casual Acquaintances*

"A gripping psychological thriller that tugged at my heartstrings with every page that I turned."
–Lucille Guarino, author of *Elizabeth's Mountain* and the *Lunch Tales* series

"This is a gut-wrenching, emotional read, where tension screams from the pages as reality comes into perspective."
–Paulette Mahurin, author of literary and historical fiction

"McCarthy's *The Boy on the Dock* is like Shari Lapena's *The Couple Next Door* meets Lisa Jewell's *Then She Was Gone*—psychological tension from start to finish!"
–Cam Torrens, bestselling author of the *Tyler Zahn* mystery/suspense series

"*The Boy on the Dock* was one of my most riveting reads of the year."
–Hannah McNamara, author of *Gut Instinct*

"It is a gripping psychological thriller that lingers after the last page and earns a strong five-star recommendation."
–Michelle Caffrey, award-winning author of *Desire in Dairyland*

"A.J. McCarthy's *The Boy on the Dock* is an atmospheric, page-turning suspense novel steeped in dread, isolation, and the unsettling question of whether the protagonist can trust her own perceptions."
–William Rabbitt, author of *Hanging Rock*

"This is a quiet, atmospheric novel that relies on mood and emotional weight rather than shock. The writing is intimate and unsettling, creating a slow, persistent tension that never fully lets go."
–Jesse Roder, author of *Sirens and Shenanigans*

"A.J. McCarthy shines here with a visceral delve into what the mind will conjure if left unchecked and given a path to travel."
–Paul Jantzen, award-winning author of *Sour Apples*

"A.J. McCarthy has crafted a psychological thriller you won't put down. Highly recommended."
–Karen K. Brees, award-winning author of *The Esposito Caper*

THE BOY ON THE DOCK

First, grief is an ocean that pulls you under.
With time, it becomes a river that you learn to swim in.
But these waves... they never stop coming.

—Unknown

Chapter 1

The boy on the dock would change everything. I just didn't know it yet.

His back to me with his sneakered feet dangling above the water, fog barely masked his thin shape. Something about his stillness and his hunched shoulders sent a ripple of unease through me. I moved my kayak within ten feet of the dock, drawn to him, almost mesmerized. The boy twisted toward me, and the mist shifted, revealing a pale, tear-streaked face capped with short, dark hair. His eyes wide, dark, and desperate locked onto mine. Neither of us moved. Then a faint cry escaped him, sharp and quick, like a baby bird in distress. He sprang to his feet.

I opened my mouth to call out, to ask if he was okay, but he bolted. The soupy fog swallowed him whole.

My pulse hammered as I paddled closer, my eyes scanning the shoreline. Nothing. As if he'd never been there.

Was it my imagination? A trick of the early morning haze? My mind playing games with me?

I knew better.

That image of him, forever tattooed in my brain, always reminded me of his plight, inspiring me to continue. Long after I left the dock, long after I tried to shake it off, it lingered and haunted me in the days and weeks to come.

***

Earlier that morning, I woke to a sharp chill in the air, the kind that crept into your bones and stayed there. Pulling my blanket tighter, I curled deeper into the mattress, eyes fixed on the wall. I should get up. Make coffee. Go outside. Do something.

Instead, I lay still, listening to the silence.

Three weeks. That's how long I'd been here, entombed in this self-imposed solitude. Most days, I barely spoke out loud, except for the occasional comment directed at the furniture. My voice was an unused muscle, wasting away.

I forced myself out of bed, my feet recoiling at the shock of the cold linoleum. The cracks I'd taped closed gaped wider, revealing the darkness underneath through which creepy crawlies could emerge.

The room held little, only a twin bed, a stubborn chest of drawers, and a painting of an eagle perched over an empty nest. The edges curled within the frame, as if trying to escape. Was the eagle mourning lost young? Or watching them fly, knowing they'd never return?

Six-thirty. "Time to start the day."

I slid my feet into slippers, shuffled to the window, and yanked the curtain aside. The lake, veiled in mist, imitated the heavy sky. A loon's distant cry cut through the silence, low and mournful. The sights and sounds used to fill me with something close to wonder. Today, emptiness.

The cottage was small, one step up from a cabin, but it's what I'd wanted. A tiny retreat on Sala Lake, an hour and a half drive from Victoria, far enough from people to have peace but close enough to civilization to function. I didn't need much. Electricity, an internet connection, and isolation. The essentials.

I made coffee on autopilot, the rich scent filling the air. Wrapping my hands around the mug, I settled by the window and stared at the lake. A stretch of dew-covered grass separated the cottage from the water. I eyed it with mild regret. Dan, the cottage's owner, had shown me how to operate the electric mower. I'd used it once, but it needed another pass.

"So do I," I said, tugging at my too-long, brown hair. It once would've sent me running to the hairdresser, but now, I couldn't be bothered. A messy ponytail sufficed. My wardrobe fit in a single drawer. The tiny bathroom held little more than a toothbrush and hairbrush. No makeup. No hairdryer. No need.

Stepping outside with my coffee, I took in the lake's stillness. Most seasonal residents came here for watersports, barbecues, and parties. Not me. I wanted only solitude and my kayak.

Dan, a friend of my ex-husband, had questioned my choice to stay alone when he first brought me here and handed me the keys. "Julie, you sure you don't mind being by yourself?" Dan removed his peak cap and thrust his arthritic fingers through his gray hair before covering it again. "You've gotta traipse through a couple hundred feet of bush to get to your nearest neighbor."

"I know. I'm fine with it."

"This place isn't fancy. Things could break."

I'd toured it quickly. He didn't tell me anything new.

"I'm not worried," I said.

"And if you get bad weather, there's nothing to do. You didn't even bring a TV." Dan's tone sounded incredulous.

"I'll be okay. I have books to read and work to do," I said, hoping he'd soon get over his fears and leave me alone so I could do neither of those things.

As his truck disappeared down the road, I made my way to the dock. Solid, well-built, with its handholds and ramp, it was exactly what I needed. I'd be on the lake every day, unless a storm stopped me.

Something about water drew me like a magnet. Maybe because it was the only place where I felt close to being alive. Or it was the only thing I looked forward to when I got here.

Or maybe, deep down, I still waited for something.

I didn't know what then. I just knew when I was out on the lake, not only was I more in my element, but a sharp sense of anticipation prickled through me. As if the lake knew a secret.

A secret that, when discovered, would change my life.

Chapter 2

The worn leather of my sandals felt cool against my bare feet as I dragged the bright red kayak toward the dock. The life jacket, a faded orange relic over my T-shirt and shorts, weighed heavily on my shoulders, unlike the light, sleek one I'd left behind along with everything else from my old life. With a grunt of effort, I pushed the long, narrow kayak into the water, the familiar resistance a welcome challenge to muscles that showed signs of regaining their strength after three weeks of daily practice.

A stream of sunlight fought through the clouds, struggling to penetrate the thick cover of trees that sheltered the dock. The faint, briny smell of fish and waterfowl mingled with the shoreline's damp, earthy scent. That lone loon called out its desolate cry, its woeful song echoing across the still lake.

I settled into the kayak, pulling on my pink peak cap, its faded logo barely visible after years of use. My sunglasses, scratched and worn, sheltered my dark-circled eyes from the occasional glint of sunlight.

Within seconds, my arms fell into the rhythm of dipping the paddle from side to side. I built up my pace quickly, enjoying the sensation of the kayak slicing through the water, leaving a V-shaped wake in its path.

Three years before, I'd given up competitive kayaking, my passion for the sport dying after close to a decade of training, practicing, and competing. Now, I paddled for peace. I still clung to my treasured racing kayak, sleek and familiar, even if I no longer craved the exhilaration of speed.

Sala Lake stretched before me, long and narrow, almost a kilometer in length, half as wide. Unlike the busier lakes on Vancouver Island, this one remained relatively undiscovered, with less than a dozen cottages surrounding it. At this hour, I had it to myself.

With my rented cottage located almost in the middle of the eastern side, I'd fallen into the routine of a fast paddle to one end to wake my muscles, a slow drift past my cottage to the other end, and a full-tilt trip back.

Most mornings, I absorbed the birds' chirps and calls as I drifted alongside duck families and listened to the frogs croaking. Dark, cold water surrounded me, reflecting the trees and sky like a mirror. Serenity enveloped me, giving me a calming oasis, a chance to clear my mind.

But that morning, the familiar routine held little appeal. The crushing pain of loss, ever-present, seemed sharper in the lake's peaceful solitude. A pain that usually subsided with the rhythmic exercise instead settled on me like a layer of dust. Why was that? Was this the price of a brief respite from the nightmares that usually plagued me? Or was it an omen?

A hawk spiraled overhead. Below, the flash of a fish breaking the surface caught my attention. In a blur of wings, the hawk dove, talons outstretched. A brief struggle, a splash, then it rose again, victorious. The fish, caught in a moment of carelessness, never had a chance.

I looked away. A powerful lesson. One I'd learned the hard way.

As I neared a small island near the lake's end, a strange quiet descended. The birdsong seemed to fade, replaced by an unnatural stillness. I rounded the island with a sense of unease.

Then, movement.

A flash of blue against the shoreline's greens and browns.

Like a bull attracted to a red cape, I paddled harder, my gaze scanning the opposite shore. I didn't know why I cared. It could've been another early riser, a fisherman wanting to take advantage of the quiet. I'd never had a desire to make those things my business. Why change now?

My gaze locked onto a figure at the edge of a dock. A boy.

He sat with his legs dangling over the water, his posture rigid. His dark hair was cropped short, and an oversized blue T-shirt hung from his frame. I guessed him to be about ten years old. Something about him, his thinness, his posture, set my nerves on edge.

I dipped my paddle into the water. A soft splash. The boy's head snapped up.

Our eyes met across the distance, and I sucked in a sharp breath. I expected surprise, but stark fear greeted me instead. In a sudden burst of movement, he sprang to his feet and fled, vanishing into the dense foliage that lined the bank.

I sat frozen, my heart hammering.

Why run? Fear of a stranger? Or fear of something else?

I scanned the shoreline. No house, no cabin. Just trees, their tangled branches creating a thick curtain. The only visible structure, a weathered boathouse, sat to the side of the dock. I saw no sign of an adult.

I hesitated, torn between instinct and logic. Chasing after him was pointless. He was already gone, swallowed by the undergrowth. But the image of his wide, terrified eyes lingered, gnawing at me.

Had he snuck out while his parents were asleep? Was he in trouble? Or had I simply interrupted an innocent morning ritual? It only took a moment for a child to tumble into the water and drown. Why was he unsupervised?

I exhaled, trying to shake my uneasiness. *He'll be fine. He probably learned his lesson about wandering too far.* But the thought didn't comfort me. Because another, darker one followed. What if he'd fallen in? What if I'd come across him struggling in the water? Or worse—floating, lifeless?

A cold weight settled in my stomach like a stone. I let the paddle rest across my lap, my kayak drifting aimlessly. Minutes passed. Maybe longer. I didn't know.

A motor rumbled nearby, breaking the spell. An early morning boater cruised past, lifting a hand in a lazy wave. I blinked, shaking off my cloudy thoughts.

I checked my watch. Almost ten. Later than I thought.

With stiff arms, I forced my paddle back into motion, but my usual rhythm was lost. Every stroke felt sluggish.

The boy's image wouldn't leave me. His frightened eyes, the way he disappeared. I couldn't let it go.

By the time I reached my cottage, exhaustion overcame me. I stumbled inside, my legs shaky, my breath shallow. Collapsing onto the bed, I curled in on myself, arms circled around my stomach.

The boy's face, front and center in my mind, morphed into that of another child, and a tiny, melodic voice rang out in my head. "Help me, please."

Chapter 3

Love filled my childhood home. I remember clutching my worn, stuffed bear as the five of us piled onto the threadbare sofa, listening to Dad's booming voice as he read aloud. Mom smiled, a strand of dark hair slipping from her bun. We didn't have much, but we had everything that mattered.

Will, my older brother, was my shadow and my guide. Only eighteen months apart in age, we shared clothes, scraped knees, and a thirst for adventure. Isabel, our younger sister, longed for frilly dresses, while I was content in patched hand-me-downs, racing barefoot along the rocky shore. Will and I spent our weekends on the water, sailing, water skiing, kayaking, pushing limits, testing strength, believing ourselves invincible.

We lived in Saanich, a suburban area with sprawling neighborhoods, parks, and agricultural land, a perfect blend of nature with residential life. It snuggled close to Victoria, the capital of British Columbia. Like her namesake Queen Victoria, the city intimidated a young girl. Stately and noble, the city boasted well-preserved historical buildings, cultural landmarks, and stunning harbor views.

By the time I moved to Vancouver to study at the University of British Columbia, the water still called to me. I found a part time job at a marina, where the scent of salt water and the rhythm of the waves felt like home. Summers, I worked in kayak rentals; winters, I served tables in the restaurant. That's where I met Keith.

He and his friends were celebrating something forgettable. One of those occasions young men invent to justify a night out. I was their server, uneasy in the face of their teasing. Keith, tall and calm, put a stop to it. Two days later, we went on our first date.

We built our relationship on a love for the outdoors—hiking, kayaking, exploring. Within two years, Keith talked about marriage. I made him wait until I earned my graphic design degree. He'd already made a name for himself as an architect, designing dream homes for Vancouver's wealthy elite.

The day I graduated, I accepted his proposal. Two months later, a simple joy-filled wedding followed, along with the purchase of a modest home that, to us, seemed like a palace.

A few years later, along came Abby. Our perfect daughter, with eyes the color of the summer sky and a giggle that could melt glaciers. We were both over the moon in love with her. Years of trying to give her a sibling failed, and Abby remained an only child, but I promised to replicate the love I'd experienced growing up in a happy home.

Promises are fragile.

***

A defeated sigh escaped my lips as I sank into the creaky porch swing, my laptop landing with a dull thud on the rickety table beside me. The image of the boy and his escape into the woods looped in my psyche like a film reel stuck on repeat. I needed to shut it off, to silence the nagging sensation I should do something. But I suspected it wouldn't fade.

"An hour. I'll give it an hour. Anything more is icing on the cake."

I had awoken that morning to gray dampness and a matching spirit. The newly arrived, golden shimmer of sunlight on the lake gave me a flicker of hope. Maybe the quiet solitude and the sunshine would unlock my creativity. But now, staring at the blank screen, the blinking cursor taunted me. My fingers hovered over the keyboard, unmoving.

I wasn't here on vacation. I needed to work. Money was tight, and the cottage, however humble, wasn't free.

Once, photography had been my dream. I remembered my first disposable camera, gripping its cheap plastic casing like a precious jewel. The thrill of waiting for those prints cemented my love for the craft. Later, with my trusty Canon Sure Shot tucked in my back pocket, I chased that once-in-a-lifetime shot. A grazing deer, otters playing in a stream, Isabel posing in her latest outfit, Will mid-air on his skateboard.

But practical choices steered me toward graphic design. It paid the bills, and for a while, I didn't mind. After Abby's birth, I built my own business, balancing clients with motherhood while Keith's architectural firm kept us comfortable.

In the past three years, my satisfaction had soured. What once felt fulfilling now drained me. Deadlines became shackles. Clients, relentless. Creativity, a trickle. Emails, phone calls, revision after revision were emotional hurdles.

Here, at the cottage, the perception intensified. The idea of designing another logo or branding package made my skin crawl, but walking away wasn't an option. I needed money. And so, the cycle continued. The perfect storm of frustration and creative paralysis.

A sudden splash broke through my thoughts. I turned toward the lake just in time to see a duck skim across the surface before settling in the water. As the ripples faded, another image overtook my mind.

The boy.

Sitting alone on the dock, thin and watchful. Something about him tugged at my heart, something unsettling. A pull I couldn't explain. *Why is he affecting me so much?* Something told me I needed to reach him. But how?

"Tomorrow," I said. "Tomorrow, I'll connect with him to warn him about the dangers of the water. He shouldn't be out there alone."

Yet deep down, something told me the water didn't pose the real danger.

Chapter 4

The following morning, my steps from the bedroom seemed brisker, more determined. The day held the promise of warmth and sunshine, likely to entice people to the lake earlier. To take advantage of the peace and tranquility, I needed to reach the water as soon as possible.

I transferred my coffee into a thermal mug and donned my insulated clothing before heading to the dock, dragging my kayak behind me. With my mug secured between my knees, I pushed off into the open water. The lake sparkled under the rising sun's glow. The air was crisp with the sharp smell of pine needles and moss. Paddling away from the dock, I couldn't shake the feeling something was different. A sense of anticipation, mixed with a hint of unease, settled in my gut.

Despite an urge to veer left, I adhered to my routine and turned right. My leisurely glide back across the lake was quicker today. Glancing at my watch, I estimated I was ten minutes ahead of my usual time, a throwback to my days of training for a competition.

I realized what energized me, but I couldn't fathom why the boy created such a response, just as I didn't understand why I expected to see him again. After all, I'd frightened him off the day before. Probably a one-time event for him, never to be repeated. Yet, the profound need to check gripped me, certain I'd experience a wave of disappointment if he wasn't there.

I circled the island, my heart pounding faster with each stroke. I'd almost convinced myself I wouldn't see him, and I blinked twice when I spotted the slight figure on the dock, legs swinging over the water, head turned away from me. My arms stopped their motion as I froze, the kayak continuing its forward momentum without my help.

As I drifted closer, the boy glanced over his shoulder, his eyes widening in surprise. I expected him to jump to his feet and run away again. But time slowed; neither of us stirred, the only sound the gentle lapping of the waves against the kayak's hull. He finally rose, but with a calm and deliberate motion, unlike his previous frantic dash like a startled deer.

I had a few seconds to assess his height and build, reinforcing my suspicion that he was around ten years old. From this distance, his eyes looked dark, perhaps a few shades darker than his hair. His face was narrow, his limbs long and gangly, with kneecaps that seemed too big for his skinny legs.

I cautiously dipped my paddle to bring myself closer. "Are you okay?" I asked, my voice barely a whisper.

His lips parted, but the sharp bang of a slamming door reverberated through the air, cutting him off. Then a male voice, booming and indistinguishable, followed. The boy froze, his small frame rigid as if the noise turned him to stone. Fear washed across his face, his wide-eyed gaze darting toward the woods. Escaping in a flurry, his thin legs pumped furiously, leaves and branches stirring in his wake as he vanished into the trees.

"Wait." I knew he didn't hear me, and even if he did, he wouldn't stop. Someone far more frightening prompted his panicked run.

The crash of disappointment hit me. I yearned to learn his name and what he was afraid of, but I missed my chance. I might not have another. For two consecutive days, we'd seen each other. Obviously terrified, he probably wouldn't return. The reason for his terror remained a mystery, but I suspected it involved the person we'd heard.

Likely, it was his father, and he'd strictly forbidden the child from hanging out close to the water. This was an explanation I understood, yet something made me dread the punishment he was about to receive.

"Why presume he'll be punished?" I said aloud, scolding myself. "I don't know this boy or his father. I'm projecting things I know nothing about on other people."

A cool morning breeze blew a strand of hair across my cheek as I analyzed my emotions. Two ducks flew overhead, quacking loud messages to each other. Or were they telling me to mind my own business? If so, I should listen to them, but something told me I wouldn't.

Although afraid for the boy, something more made my stomach flip. Something close to excitement, a sensation I hadn't experienced in years. As I pivoted the kayak toward my summer cottage, I thought of this strange new reaction. I wanted to know more about him. I wanted to sit on the dock beside him, keep him safe, and learn about his interests and thoughts. Of all the people I could have chosen to interact with after years of hiding from everyone, it was a young boy.

Upon deeper reflection, those yearnings shouldn't surprise me, but the speed with which they overtook my mind alarmed me. I wasn't normally so reactive to other people, at least not lately. Was this it? Was this the change everyone predicted would come over me? Part of me hoped it was. Another part felt guilty for that hope. Why should I change? Did I really deserve to change? After everything I'd done?

I thought of the hours I'd spent in therapy, sitting in the comfortable black leather chair in Trish's office. With her calming presence, warm smile, and short, naturally wavy gray hair, she gave off an air of wisdom and comfort. It was that aura, more than her professional track record, that made me return. To be honest, I'd noticed only a slight improvement in my mental state.

She'd once explained the many types of guilt, patiently untangling them as if sorting a drawer of mismatched socks. According to her, I carried more than my fair share. She was also a firm believer in the power of change, often reassuring me my time would come.

Maybe it finally had.

***

The day our little family moved into the new house in West Vancouver, it felt like stepping into a new life. Everything about it was bigger, with sprawling rooms, a two-car garage, and an expansive backyard that boasted an inground pool. It wasn't waterfront, but it was a world away from where we'd been. A house filled with possibilities.

Abby sprinted through the hallways, her laughter bouncing off the bare walls. "It's so big," she squealed, darting from room to room, already planning where she'd put her toys, where she'd play hide-and-seek.

I trailed after her, watching with a mix of exhaustion and happiness. Moving was chaos, but seeing her joy made it worthwhile.

"It needs a little work before we can swim," I said as she pressed her hands against the sliding glass doors, staring longingly at the pool.

"When?" Abby said, twisting to face me.

"Not long. And in the meantime, you'll keep up your lessons."

She groaned, but her eyes sparkled. She loved the water. She had my restless spirit, the same pull toward lakes and rivers, toward anything that promised adventure.

That summer, we threw her a seventh birthday party, a pool party, once the water was warm and blue. The house buzzed with the excited shrieks of children and the chatter of parents getting to know each other. We'd invited neighbors, hoping to build roots.

The scent of barbecue filled the air as Keith flipped burgers, his easygoing laughter blending into conversations. I stood at the edge of the pool, watching Abby climb onto the diving board. Sunlight glittered on the water as she launched herself into the deep end, floaties secured around her arms.

She surfaced, gasping and giggling. "Did you see that, Mommy?"

I grinned and nodded, my heart full. This was exactly what I wanted for her. Safety, stability, a home bursting with joyful noise and childhood wonder.

At the end of the night, one by one, parents whisked children away to be tucked into their beds. Abby's small arms curled around my neck when I carried her upstairs. As I pulled the covers over her, she yawned and said, "Best birthday ever."

I kissed her forehead and whispered, "Many more to come."

For the first few months, everything felt like a dream. Weekend hikes in the mountains, knowing winter ski trips would be just a short drive away. I planted flower beds, started a vegetable garden, and Keith built a sandbox for Abby.

Laughter echoed through our home. A perfect house. A perfect life.

Until it wasn't.

Chapter 5

I awoke with an idea, not yet fully formed. Coffee mug in hand, I searched the cottage but found nothing suitable for my plan. Pulling on a hoodie and beat-up sneakers, I ventured into the woods to the left of the cottage.

It had to be something special, something you wouldn't see every day.

My gaze wandered, taking in the trees, shrubs, and mossy forest floor. I tried to think like a ten-year-old boy, recalling the days I roamed similar forests with my brother. In the same way, I sensed this boy and I shared common ground. I focused on what fascinated my brother at that age, which would have equally fascinated me.

Squirrels chattering and scampering across the branches drew my gaze upward. That's when I spotted it. A large nest, likely a heron's, perched high in a bigleaf maple tree. I studied the tree's trunk and decided I could handle it. Many years had passed since my last tree climbing experience, but this one had a lot of hand and foot holds to ease the task. If I found what I hoped for, it'd be worth it.

The early morning sun filtered through the leaves, blinding me as I planned my approach. My first challenge was reaching the lowest branch, which hovered eighteen inches above my head, putting it at just under seven feet high. I jumped and grinned as my fingers closed around the rough branch. I felt like a child again, hearing my mother's voice warning me about the dangers of falling from a tree and breaking my leg.

The wind whistled through the branches above me as I grunted and shimmied my feet up the trunk until I wrapped my ankles around the sturdy branch and dangled like a sloth. I swung my right leg over the limb, grateful for choosing jeans over shorts, saving myself from the bark tearing at my skin. Glancing upward, I saw more accessible branches above. I worked my way up limb by limb, not looking down and trying not to worry about how I'd make it back to ground level.

I climbed until I stood and balanced safely, my arms aching, my breath raspy. Seeing the nest expertly built in an intersection of branches made the effort worthwhile. I stretched and peered into the bird's home, a surge of excitement coursing through my veins. My climb had paid off in spades. I reached across the mixture of branches and mud and removed the treasure from its shelter, safely tucking it into the pocket of my hoodie. It was the perfect gift for a young boy, unique and extraordinary.

"He'll understand. I know he will. I feel it."

Drawing a deep breath, I braced for the climb down, always my least favorite part of tree climbing. My brother had spent plenty of time coaxing me down, sometimes even climbing up to get me rather than endure my mother's wrath. *I'd welcome his calming voice at this moment.*

I lowered one foot after the other to the next branch and the next until the last one appeared in sight, the climb down much slower than the climb up. I sat on the lowest limb, my legs dangling on either side while I savored my accomplishment, before swinging off and dropping with a sense of victory to the soft earth below. Not only had I achieved my goal, but I'd unearthed a cherished childhood memory.

I swiveled to head back to my cottage and yelped in shock.

Chapter 6

A man stood before me, hands on his hips, legs spread wide, and brow furrowed. His slightly disheveled brown hair brushed the collar of his red plaid shirt, and worn jeans stretched over his long legs. His dark eyes drilled into mine, taking me aback as I wondered at his obvious irritation.

"What did you do?" He delivered his question in a growl and didn't wait for my response before firing another one at me. "You meddled with the nest, didn't you?"

His tone made me find my voice and indignation. "I did not. I'd never do that."

"Then what were you doing?"

"Getting something." I placed my hands on my hips, mirroring his stance, my chin thrust forward.

"An egg," he said.

"Not an egg. I'd never take an egg." Who was this guy, and what gave him the right to accuse me of harming a nest? "It's none of your business what I did." I swung toward my cottage, my footsteps thumping as I stormed away, the simmering fire in my chest fueling every stride.

"I could report you to a conservation officer!"

"Go ahead." I waved a hand. "Ask me if I care."

I closed the cottage door behind me and leaned against it, a shiver running through my limbs. I went to great lengths to avoid people, and the abrupt appearance of this man unsettled me. Dan had mentioned a neighbor. Assuming that was him, I hoped it was our first and last encounter. But the meeting ruined the moment for me, dampening my enthusiasm for the small adventure.

I won't let his attitude mess this up. I've gone this long without seeing him. I can make it through the rest of the summer.

I paced around my small abode, inhaling deeply and steadying my nerves until my resolve returned me to an even keel. Glancing at the clock, I realized it was later than I usually started but still early enough to avoid most residents.

The morning air braced me as I gathered my things, shrugged into my life jacket, and hauled the kayak to the dock. Lowering myself in, I paused to double-check everything. Paddle, supplies, and the small treasure tucked securely in my pocket. Satisfied, I pushed off and began my usual circuit, the rhythm of my strokes soothing.

As I passed the cottage next to mine, home to my ill-tempered neighbor, I let the kayak glide while my gaze scanned the area. The windows stared back, blank and lifeless, but an uncomfortable feeling settled over me. I couldn't shake the sensation of someone watching me. Forcing myself to ignore it, I carried on.

When I reached the island, I experienced both disappointment and relief at the sight of the deserted jetty where I'd seen the boy. My anxiety subsided. Had he been there, I'd intended to try to talk to him, promising an awkward and perhaps frightening experience for at least one of us. His absence meant I could go with my backup plan, which required no direct contact, giving us time to adapt to our new relationship, whatever that may be.

Reaching into my pocket, I pulled out a plastic bag and retrieved the small stone I'd brought. The string I'd tied around it earlier dangled loosely, waiting for its counterpart. I attached the string's other end to the treasure.

Satisfied, I paddled closer, my breath steady but my heart thrumming with a strange mix of hope and hesitation. Leaning over, I set the gift on the worn wooden planks. I didn't leave a note. *He'll know who left it.*

Backing away, I let my paddle dip into the water, watching as the blue heron's beautiful feather danced in the morning breeze, twisting and swirling as if waving goodbye. I lingered a moment longer before turning, the ripples of my wake following me back across the lake.

***

As often happened, something—I'm not sure what—triggered memories of that day three years earlier, when fluorescent lights flickered overhead, throwing a sterile glow on the white walls. The cold, hard, plastic chair supported me, but it was as if I floated above it, detached from my body. I could've been anywhere; it wouldn't have made a difference. Emptiness and shock engulfed me. Keith's warm hand clung to mine, but I couldn't work up the strength to return the comfort. My mind was a blank slate, a void filled with deafening silence.

Eventually, I raised my head and surveyed the room. Through my haze, it sank in that we were the center of attention, drawing the curious gazes of others waiting to see a doctor or a loved one. Parents shushed young children who pointed at the small puddle that had formed at our feet. An older man's loud moan shifted people's attention to a different corner. The distant wail of an ambulance signaled another arrival in the emergency bay.

I shivered, my numb fingers clutching the thin, starched blanket closer. The clinging stench of chlorine mingled with the hospital's antiseptic smell, and Keith stifled a sneeze beside me.

A scream balanced on the edge of my lips, but I doubted I could muster more than a hoarse whisper. My chest tightened until a sob finally escaped, a desolate sound that seemed to echo through the cold, unfeeling room. I tried to smother it, but it was too late. Tears flowed, hot and salty, burning my cheeks.

We'd been shuffled out here so the doctors could concentrate on our daughter. But, deep down, I knew. It was a certainty within my soul. An immense piece of me had vanished, my angel taken away. I'd never experience those small arms around me again. I'd never look into those precious eyes or hear her voice or watch her play. My lips would never press against her cheek or heal a scraped knee with a kiss.

Abby was gone. The truth slammed into me with a tidal wave's strength, drowning me in despair. I didn't need a doctor to confirm it. I'd seen it with my own eyes, felt it in the coldness of her small body lying limp in my arms by the pool. My throat ached from the desperate cries for her to hang on. No amount of will or pleading could bring her back.

Abby was gone. My little girl, my baby, lost forever. And I'd never be the same.

The rest of that day disappeared. I remembered nothing. One moment I sat beside Keith as a doctor explained our daughter's death, and the next I woke up in my bed, the room pitch black. Confused, I glanced at the bedside clock. Four fifteen. I sensed I was alone. Reaching out my right hand, I encountered nothing. Keith wasn't there. At this hour? Why not?

Then it crashed down on me. The entire horrible tragedy flashed before my eyes. Abby was dead. Drowned in our backyard. Within feet from where I now lay.

Was it a dream? A terrible nightmare? It must be. I was in my bed, after all.

No. I vividly remembered it. Nothing was more real.

An anguished cry started inside my gut and worked its way up through my throat until it escaped and bounced off the walls. Within seconds, Keith raced into our bedroom, his eyes wide, grief-stricken, panicked.

He bent over me and clasped my arms as if I'd levitate off the bed and he needed to hold me in place. I collapsed into sobs, and he pulled me close, our tears mingling.

He explained I'd lost consciousness when the grim-faced doctor delivered the horrible news, as if I'd fainted. Completely understandable. A few minutes later, I came to, but I remained zombie-like, not responding to questions. Keith walked me to the car, drove me home, and got me into bed, but I remembered none of it. We were later told the trauma had likely caused a blackout.

Understandable.

Chapter 7

Now, my anticipation spiked. Waiting until tomorrow morning seemed impossible. I'd venture out this afternoon, despite the likelihood of sharing the lake with other water enthusiasts. I needed to know if the boy found my gift.

The sun beat down on my face as I eased away from my dock. As expected, the lake bustled with activity. The allure of sunshine and warmth beckoned kayakers, paddle boarders, jet skiers, and motorboaters alike. Those who created waves tended toward politeness and slowed around the non-motorized or smaller watercraft, but it didn't ease the encounters. Not for me. Everyone expected me to smile and wave in a happy, congenial manner when all I really wanted was to paddle my way to the boy's dock as quickly as possible. And return straightaway to my isolated cottage.

Rounding the corner, a grin broke across my face, stiff and unfamiliar, as if it had forgotten how to form. The rock and feather had vanished. I stopped paddling and allowed the kayak to coast toward the dock. My gaze swept across the trees for any sign of a small boy, but if present, he remained well-hidden.

As I lowered my paddle into the water, intending to make my way to the safety and seclusion of my cottage, something caught my eye. My breath hitched. The dock wasn't empty. A pebble weighed down a piece of paper, but a corner fluttered in the breeze. With a racing heart, I dug the paddle into the water and drove the kayak closer until I grasped the dock's rough edge. Splinters dug into my palms, but I ignored them. My fingers stretched, brushing the paper's edge until they closed around it.

Again, my gaze roamed across the shoreline, expecting, hoping to see a pair of eyes peeking from behind a tree. A tiny feather slid out of the folded paper and landed in my lap. It was even smaller than the one I'd given him. I wasn't certain of its origin, but it was a beautiful thing, soft and delicate, with intricate patterns on its surface. It seemed we had a theme.

Another smile spread across my face. The boy found my gift and left one in return. A small but important gesture. Hope filled me.

I glanced at the dock and alarms bells sounded in my head. A muddy footprint, small enough to belong to a child, was on the edge of the dock, surrounded by water droplets. Had he been in the water? Jumped in? Fallen? Was it simply a dangling foot that brushed across the surface? An image flashed in my mind of Abby, and pain shot through me. My vision blurred. I shook my head to clear it.

I frantically cast my gaze around me, searching for him, hoping to catch a glimpse of a young boy, safe and sound.

"Stop it, Julie," I said, admonishing myself. "Stop overreacting. Kids play in the mud. It happens."

I dragged in a shaky breath to settle my nerves before I unfolded the paper, hoping for a message. A few words. Instead, I found a drawing. Rudimentary, it depicted two figures facing each other. A shorter one, probably meant to represent the boy, wore a blue shirt and had a mop of brown hair. A much taller adult faced him, his hair lighter in color.

Alarm bells again. A raised arm hovered over the child's head. Was he hitting the child? He couldn't be. My imagination was seeing evil in every corner. He might be pointing at something, although there was nothing else in the drawing to point at. Maybe he was waving at the boy. Possible.

Think positive. He's sharing a drawing of himself with his father, telling me something about his life. Something important to him. It's a good thing.

The boy and I needed baby steps, a concept that revolved around new beginnings. What could represent it better? Feathers from baby birds and a drawing about him.

I knew the boy thought of it the same way. We'd formed a connection. Small and fragile, but a bridge, nevertheless.

I ran my fingertip across the tiny feather, so soft I barely felt it. Smiling, I carefully tucked the gift inside my shirt pocket and paddled my kayak homeward. More vacationers had crept from their homes to frolic on the water, some with a gentle paddle in a kayak or canoe, others preferring the speed and noise of motorized watercraft. I didn't discriminate. I hugged the shoreline to avoid them all, focused on reaching the cottage and finding the perfect spot for the boy's present.

Where will I put it? Somewhere special. Once landed, I raced across the lawn and into the cottage.

As my eyes adapted to the room's dim light, I realized exactly what I wanted. I'd discovered it on my first day at the cottage. An antique tin, possibly one sold with candy inside, adorned with a painting of a robin perched on the edge of a nest. I dug it out of a cupboard and looked at it with fresh, purposeful eyes.

The bird stared straight ahead, as if watching for predators intending to snatch her little ones away from her. Scratched and bent, it required effort to open the lid and nestle the drawing and feather inside.

I'll find something else for him tomorrow. He'll start feeling comfortable with me, and we'll build a friendship.

I marveled at these thoughts. Three years since I'd sought human connection, and a young boy was the one to fire me up. Why now? Why him? Was it fate? Happenstance? I hoped to find the answers.

I paced the cottage's short width. *What will I give him next? Do I continue with the bird theme or move onto something else? What would appeal to him?*

I ditched my water shoes for sneakers and headed out the door.

Chapter 8

The sun filtered through the trees, forming speckled designs on the forest floor. I opened my eyes and ears to nature. Birds chirped back and forth in the branches as if having an animated discussion about my intrusion in their domain. A passing motorboat filled with summer revelers created waves that lapped at the dock.

Picking my way through the undergrowth and navigating over dead trees and around large rocks, I examined the ground and surrounding vegetation. A glint snagged my gaze. Nudging aside a leaf with the toe of my sneaker, I discovered a white stone nestled on the moss like a diamond on a bed of velvet. I picked it up and inspected it, running my fingers over its pearly sheen and smooth, rounded surface. A beautiful specimen, worthy as a gift.

Happy memories of my childhood flooded me, eliciting a smile. I saw my brother, his pockets bulging with stones he'd collected. My mother grumbled good-naturedly about the mess and how the stones and pebbles disrupted her day, finding their way into the washing machine.

Sometimes, Will tried to convince me to carry them for him, but I saw through his ruse. I may have adored him, but I wouldn't take the fall for his obsessions.

However, this time, the smooth stone took its place in my pocket, and I scanned for more. Another, with a sparkly pinkish tint, slightly larger, joined it. I continued on my path, my head lowered, searching. Soon, a small collection clinked with each step I took, like wind chimes on a summer porch.

Suddenly I noticed it was the only sound. The birds and squirrels had quieted, the wind died, the boats nowhere to be seen or heard. I stopped in my tracks, my chest tight, my nerves pinging.

"Looking for something?"

I spun toward the voice. The man from earlier. My startled gaze darted from him to my surroundings. I stood on the edge of a clearing, obviously his. I'd strayed too far.

I had a different, unrestricted view of his property. A bungalow, much larger and newer than mine, sat several feet away. A well-manicured lawn sloped toward the lake with a dock that stretched out across the water. Two red Adirondack chairs sat on the pier with a fishing rod and tackle box resting between them. I pictured it through a camera lens, the perfect image of summer peace.

My gaze swung back to my neighbor, dressed less casually now, as if he'd returned from a day at the office. Clean-shaven and hair neatly combed, he'd paired his gray button-up shirt and black trousers with dark leather loafers.

Regretting my intrusion, I stepped backward. Our earlier aggressive meeting remained clear in my memory, and I didn't feel up to a repeat performance. I cursed my inattention that let me wander out of bounds.

The man placed his hands on his hips in much the same way as the last time I'd seen him, and I tensed, anticipating another confrontation. A smile softened his features, confusing me. Was it a trap? Soften me up with a smile before coming in for the kill?

"You must be a collector." He glanced pointedly at the bulges in my pocket. "Stones?"

How to respond? I didn't want to reveal my tentative relationship with the boy, but it likely seemed odd for a grown woman to search for rocks in the forest.

"They've always interested me." A lame but safe answer.

"Geologist?"

Curious or sarcastic, I didn't know. "No, a nature lover, that's all."

An awkward silence hung between us for a long moment until he broke it. "I noticed you this morning."

A surge of panic rose within me. What did he see? Me, over at the boy's dock? Finding the note? I didn't want anyone intruding on my delicate connection with the child. Not yet. Perhaps not ever.

"You flew by here on your kayak. You've got a powerful stroke."

Relieved to have an innocent explanation, I shrugged off his comment. "I used to compete. Sprint racing." I felt myself flush, suddenly embarrassed to share a detail of my life with this stranger.

He raised his brows, seemingly impressed. "Not surprising. You look right at home in a kayak," he said. "I was fishing off the dock. Guess you didn't see me."

"Focused on getting back." I shifted my gaze to his dock, searching for a way to end this conversation and return to the cottage.

"I saw that." He paused. "Do you fish?"

"Years ago," I said in a low voice, my gaze returning to his.

His eyebrows lowered with concern. I mustn't have masked the pain in my expression. Sometimes, the simplest of remarks brought on bittersweet memories that haunted me. Fishing was a sport I'd practiced with my father, and we'd only just begun doing it with Abby. I always found it calming, and I wanted her to learn something to turn to when she needed a soothing activity, one involving nature and the outdoors.

"We may have gotten off on the wrong foot this morning. I apologize for that." The man smiled wryly as he extended his hand. "Sometimes, I'm a bit too quick to make assumptions. My name's Mark Webb, by the way."

I scrutinized the offered hand before I reluctantly placed mine in it. I noted his firm, dry grip before I pulled my hand free. "Julie…Hampton." I still hadn't adjusted to using my maiden name again. The quirk of his eyebrow told me he'd caught my hesitation. "I gotta go." A weak goodbye smile, but the best I could muster. I wasn't here to make friends.

I pivoted toward the cottage, shoving my hands deep into my pockets to silence the stones' faint clinking. His apology hung in the air, an olive branch I had neither the energy nor the inclination to grab hold of. My departure was abrupt, bordering on rude, but I couldn't bring myself to care.

The thought of enduring the stilted exchange, grasping for polite words that refused to come, was unbearable. My reserves were depleted, my social battery drained. Self-preservation demanded distance. I quickened my steps toward my sanctuary.

Inside, I leaned against the door and took a deep breath before stumbling toward the couch. "What's wrong with me?" I scrubbed my hands across my face before running them through my hair.

I'd become a stranger to myself. Where had I disappeared to? Before Abby's death, I'd been a social creature, able to converse with anyone. My adventurous spirit from childhood had stuck with me as an adult, always game to take on any activity, whether it be with friends or strangers. Now, I couldn't handle a pleasant conversation with my neighbor without crumbling into a basket case.

Will I ever find myself again? Part of my purpose in coming here had been to deal with my grief, once and for all, and prepare to re-enter life. The isolation I'd seen as a solution wasn't working.

Chapter 9

The wind howled outside, rattling the windows and coating me with an icy chill. I perched on the lumpy couch, staring out at the darkening lake, my mind swirling like the tossed leaves on the lawn. Dinner comprised a dry ham sandwich, its taste and texture barely registering. Since then, I remained still, thoughts stirred by the day's events slowly churning in my brain.

Memories of happier times washed over me. I saw Abby's face, her eyes sparkling with joy as she explored the forest. We spent hours hiking, climbing trees, and discovering hidden trails. She marveled at the simple things we often took for granted. The trees and flowers, the stones and pinecones, the birds and squirrels. Her zest awakened our own childlike wonder.

We'd picnic on the trail, sitting on a rock overlooking the water or the mountains. Both, if we were lucky. We covered most of Vancouver Island, camping in the forest and teaching Abby how to pitch a tent and roll up her sleeping bag. And we sat on either side of her when she dangled her baited hook in a lake and caught her first fish.

A carousel of images revolved past my mind's eye. We were so happy. Our love for each other and our beautiful child filled our lives. I had imagined endless adventures in our future.

Now, the bitter reality of her loss tainted all those happy times. Tears welled up. I still heard her laughter, her voice, her little footsteps snapping branches as she followed us through the woods.

All that was left was silence. A deafening, empty silence, despite the raging storm outside my door. I sat alone in a dreary cottage with nothing but memories and empty arms.

The lights flickered once, twice. I braced for total darkness, but it didn't come. Not yet. Out of the corner of my eye, a curtain moved. I stumbled to my feet and checked the window.

Closed tight. I'd become a victim of my overworked imagination, fueled by the events of the day. I lowered myself onto the couch and pulled a blanket across my lap as if it would protect me from the storm and my thoughts.

The first sob escaped my lips, chased by a torrent more.

I must have fallen asleep. I sat up with a scream in my throat and a vivid image from a nightmare in my mind.

I was in a strange, empty house with no doors or windows, and it was dark and murky. Weak lighting came from somewhere I couldn't identify, but as I wandered around, a child's cry emerged from below me. I looked for a door leading to the basement. After hunting without success for several minutes, the crying guiding me, I finally found it. Flinging open the door, I ran down the stairs, and when I reached the bottom, I encountered a lake instead of a room. Trees encircled it. Searching for a child, cries still echoing in my ears, I plunged into the cold water.

A surprising sight appeared. Abby and the boy were in the water, holding hands. They smiled at me, and I swam toward them, needing to hold Abby in my arms, to save her, to save them both. As I got closer, they waved at me and sank deeper into the abyss until they disappeared.

With fresh pain in my heart, I lay on the couch, curled in a ball, rocking as grief swallowed me whole. Lost, adrift in a sea of misery, I had little hope of ever finding my way back.

The night's blackness encased me like a shroud.

***

My dreams had eased since I'd come to the cottage. Less intense, less frequent. Before, they'd camped out in my mind nightly, making me dread sleep. Initially, I wondered if the stillness of this place had silenced them. If so, it had been a welcome change, even though their absence had left a strange void, as if unwelcome companions had suddenly abandoned me. Now, it seemed like I needn't have worried.

I opened my eyes to the sight of the stones on my bedside table. A shaft of sunlight crept into the room and cast its beam upon them, making them sparkle. Instead of dwelling on the nightmare and the tears that followed, lighter thoughts veered to the boy. I imagined his reaction to my intended gift, creating a tiny swirl of anxiety in my chest as I hoped he'd like them.

It surprised me how much space the child occupied in my thoughts, more than anything else had in the past three years, including my work. As I'm sure my therapist would tell me—or any therapist worth their salt—I'd obviously created a mental connection between my daughter and the boy. But was my desire to bond with the child a way to reunite with my daughter's spirit? Was I looking at him as a substitute? Worse, was he destined to suffer the same fate as Abby? Was that the message from my subconscious? Would he tumble into the lake and drown?

I reined myself in. Despite my brighter mood, I had headed down my well-worn, dark path. Picking apart my dream would drive me crazy with "what ifs." This wasn't the time, and I didn't have the expertise to do it. I'd satisfy myself with the knowledge that establishing a connection with the boy yesterday was a step in the right direction.

"Let's get you guys ready. I've found a new home for you."

The two chosen stones called to me, urging me to action. Ignoring the growl of my empty stomach on my way to the kitchen, I grabbed a sheet of paper, carefully wrapped the stones, and tied them with a piece of twine I'd found in a drawer. The simple act of preparing the gift calmed me, a small offering for the boy who filled my thoughts.

With the stones bundled and my coffee in a thermal mug, I headed to the dock, my movements brisk. Minutes later, the paddle cut through the glassy water in a steady rhythm, each stroke drawing me closer to the boy's world.

It was early, not yet five-thirty. The morning sun painted the sky in hues of pink and orange as I glided across the lake. The water was tranquil, reflecting the sunrise's vibrant colors, my kayak slicing through it like a knife. A gentle breeze carried the lake's crisp scent, most pungent in the early mornings.

As expected, the dock stood empty. I slowed as I approached, letting the kayak coast to the side until it bumped against the structure with a soft thump. My gaze searched the shoreline, not surprised to find it deserted and silent, except for a family of ducks dipping upside down into the water, searching for breakfast. I stretched and deposited the bundle in the same spot I'd found his gift. He'd know who left it. My gaze drifted across the trees again, sending him a silent message, before I shoved off from the dock.

A smile crept across my face as I dipped my paddle, a sense of purpose filling me. I surged forward, my arms straining for speed, a sensation I hadn't experienced in three years. An unfamiliar flare of life and hopefulness glowed inside me, a direct result of my strange interaction with the boy.

After my impromptu sprint, I lifted the kayak onto my dock, noticing it appeared lighter than usual. Was I redeveloping unused muscles? Could I eventually return to the sport I'd loved, experience the thrill of competing against my peers? A rush of excitement thrummed through me. Perhaps, just perhaps, this was a new beginning. *Am I finally transforming? Is it time?*

Chapter 10

I gazed at the small shed to the right of the cottage. My curiosity not strong enough for me to explore it earlier, I suddenly needed to know what was inside. Dan said I was welcome to use anything, but would I discover something worthwhile?

I retrieved the key ring from inside the cottage and rifled through it until I found the match for the heavy padlock. The metal door opened with a loud shriek of rust-coated hinges. A wave of hot, musty air escaped the structure, making me pause as I wondered what creatures called it home.

Peeking across the threshold, I saw a compact and tidy space that stored a variety of mostly useless-to-me paraphernalia. Battered paint cans, assorted hoses and wires, soggy boxes of nails and screws, and a few seemingly broken small appliances sat neatly stacked on shelves.

Bolstered by the absence of scratching noises and tiny scurrying feet, I stepped inside and peered into larger, dust-covered boxes. Gardening tools sparked a tiny interest in me, reminding me of the pleasure of tending my flower and vegetable gardens, watching them thrive.

"What do we have here?" To my left, an old bicycle leaned against a stack of bins, and the spark almost ignited. Swiping aside the cobwebs, I wheeled it outside into the sunshine and decided a good cleaning would give it new life. I checked the tires and wondered if a bicycle pump lurked inside another box.

Returning to the shed, my gaze lifted to the rafters, and a full-blown flame grew.

Another good find. I should've explored this place sooner. I stretched and grasped the end of a fishing rod, carefully easing it down from its horizontal bed. I smiled when I noticed a working reel with a neatly strung line, as if someone had simply set it aside for a few hours.

Now, with a two-fold mission, I searched the shelves for a tackle box and bicycle pump. I found the first in the bottom of another box, but the second remained elusive. I'd pick one up on my next trip into town for provisions.

I carried my fishing finds outside to better inspect the contents of the tackle box in the daylight. It seemed complete. All that stood between me and a trout dinner were a few worms, something easily rectified.

A bit more exploring produced a bucket and a small spade. On the shoreline, I dug into the wet soil and filled my pail with earth and wriggling worms.

Feeling a small sense of achievement, I turned to climb toward the cottage when a noise echoed across the lake, sending chills along my spine. A shrill, high-pitched scream, sounding like a woman in distress. After a slight pause, another one reverberated through the air.

An animal obviously. A bobcat? I'd heard red foxes emitted scary sounds. I took a deep breath and chided myself for acting like an idiot. After all the time I'd spent outdoors throughout my life, a perfectly normal screech of an animal startled me out of my wits.

I checked my watch. Late afternoon, prime time for fishing. Just what I needed to relax my over-worked nerves. I'd gone from weeks of sameness day after day to the excitement of discovering the boy, and it had made me jumpy.

I carried a white plastic chair down to the dock and set up my gear. I'd never been squeamish about handling worms, and within minutes, the first one dangled in the water, awaiting its fate.

The act of fishing allowed my mind to wander and appreciate the peacefulness of nature. Apart from the occasional wild shriek, I thought wryly. But as a trace of campfire smoke reached my nostrils, my mind roamed to the camping trips we'd had with Abby, roasting marshmallows over the fire and constructing our s'mores. The stories we'd told around the firepit always fascinated her. A mantle of loneliness and self-pity descended upon me, enfolding me in a vise-like grip.

The roar of a jet ski, quickly followed by another, shook me from my stark thoughts. Teenagers sneaking a race in before the dinner hour. When the third one rumbled past, I knew my fishing mission was fruitless. I'd put it off until dawn, when most people with an eye for noisy water sports still lay in bed.

As I stowed my fishing gear, I heard the familiar splash of a paddle cutting through the water. In my peripheral vision, I spotted a forest green canoe glide close to my dock, bobbing on the waves.

"Not a good time, is it?"

My head swiveled at the sound of Mark's deep voice. Wearing navy cargo shorts, a white T-shirt under his blue life jacket, and a black cap that read "Rather be fishin'," he fit in with the vacation vibe. His relaxed smile boded well for a neighborly visit. Perhaps he'd forgotten about my rude departure yesterday or at least forgiven it.

I strived for the same mood, despite thoughts of Abby still throwing me off. "Fun seekers are out in full force," I said, suspecting my smile appeared forced.

His gaze moved over my rod and tackle box. "You seem all set."

"Found a treasure trove in the shed," I said, gesturing toward the small structure.

His gaze moved past me to take in the dusty bicycle with skepticism. "Including a bike?"

"I'll fix it up," I said, defensive on the bike's behalf. "It just needs a cleaning and a tire pump."

"I have one if you'd like to borrow it."

I hesitated, unsure how much contact I wanted with this stranger. Another glance toward the bicycle told me to change my attitude. It was only a pump.

"Thanks. That'd be great," I said, attempting to stretch my lips into an appreciative smile.

"I'll bring it over after my run," he said, as he used his paddle to push away from the dock.

I nodded my assent, grateful for both the offer and the fact he didn't hang around too long.

True to his word, Mark returned within the hour, a bicycle pump clutched in his hand. I'd just finished washing the bike, paying particular attention to the rusty rims. With a small nod in my direction, Mark went straight to the bike, pressing tires and running his hands around the rims. His furrowed brow spoke of a man who took his tasks seriously.

Curiosity drew me closer, though I stayed a step behind, watching as he worked. Until now, it hadn't crossed my mind the bike might be unsafe. With a fluid motion, he attached the pump and filled the tires with air. His focus shifted to the gears and brakes. A compact tool emerged from his back pocket. He adjusted, tightened, and realigned, his movements quick and efficient.

"You seem to know a lot about bikes," I said.

"Summer job in a bike shop when I was a kid. Basics are still the same." His shrug said it was no big deal.

"Is this a good one?"

"It's old but in decent shape. You should be all right as long as you're not planning any marathons."

"Not sure of my plans. Just thought I'd ride around here a bit."

He nodded again and returned his attention to the gears.

"Do you know the area?" I asked, surprising myself with my sudden curiosity and chattiness. "Have you rented here before?"

"I own my place," he said, bending over the bike and inspecting the chain. "I'm out here most weekends and a good chunk of the summer."

"Where do you live the rest of the time?"

"Got a place in Victoria."

My gaze slid toward the trees between our properties. I pictured the beautiful home that rested on the other side. "What do you do for a living?"

"I'm an engineer. Have my own business. I can work from anywhere, basically."

I had no desire to become involved in anyone else's life, but his background impressed me. He did well for himself if he could afford a home in Victoria and an upscale cottage on Sala Lake.

Yet despite his relaxed manner, I sensed something in his attitude. Irritation? Avoidance? Was I pushing the limits with my questions? Perhaps he was like me and just wanted privacy. Yet, I had reasons for my inquiries, and my goal dangled within reach. I might not have another opportunity.

"Do you know many people around the lake?" I asked.

He hesitated, pursing his lips. "Some. Most are rentals or owners who only spend a few weeks here." He shrugged and confirmed my suspicions. "I keep to myself."

"Canoe a lot?"

His eyes narrowed, probably wondering how I went from reticent one day to full of questions the next. "Most days. I like to hit the lake around nine. I think you're more of an early bird."

It was my turn to sharpen my gaze. Was he watching me?

"I've seen you a couple of times when I have my coffee on my deck," he said, as if reading my thoughts.

I let it pass. You need to give a little if you want something in return. "Yeah. I'm an early riser."

I hesitated to bring up the property where I'd seen the boy, searching for a way to mention it without seeming like a stalker. I missed my chance when Mark grabbed his pump and tools and patted the bike seat. "You're good to go. Enjoy."

As the thick foliage between the two properties closed around him, it occurred to me he hadn't seemed curious about me or how long I was staying.

Chapter 11

As soon as he left, I studied the bike. Years had passed since I'd last ridden one. I tried to suppress memories of our small, happy family on the bike trails near our home. From the tandem bike to the training wheels and finally to her "big girl" bike, Abby cherished the activity. I pictured her, her face flushed with excitement, as she raced ahead, her laughter echoing through the woods.

This bike wasn't as lightweight as my own, and I was unaccustomed to the squeaks and creaks, but it felt good to pedal along the little-used country road. The sun warmed my skin, and the wind whipped through my hair, carrying the sweet fragrance of wildflowers. Memories of the physical movements flooded me, and I knew I'd be dusting off some little-used muscles.

A few rough paths branched off from the road, but for my first outing, I stuck to the primary route. After half an hour, I wistfully remembered the more comfortable seat on my own bicycle and decided to turn around, leaving a more adventurous ride for another day.

As I meandered toward my cottage, my mind drifted to the boy on the dock and the possibility of him finding my gift. Had he unwrapped it yet? Did he appreciate the gesture? Had he left something for me in return? The hope quickened my pulse, and my pedaling increased to match the pace of my racing mind.

The cottage's gravel driveway came into view just in time. I nearly shot past it. Swerving sharply, I braked to a halt and leaped off the bike, letting it clatter against the shed without a second glance. Restless energy demanded action. My life jacket hung on its hook, waiting like an old friend. I shrugged it on, tugged at the straps, and grabbed the kayak. It scraped against the ground as I dragged it to the water's edge.

The lake sparkled under the waning sunlight, inviting me to take a refreshing dip after my bike ride, but I wouldn't indulge, my focus turned elsewhere. On the dock, on the boy who might be waiting. I wouldn't allow the distraction.

Once settled, my legs caught a break while my arms took over. The slender kayak cut across the water, racing toward the island and the cottage on the other shore. The lake was mercifully quiet, the dinner hour granting me a break from the usual parade of motorized watercraft and noise. The solitude allowed me to focus, letting me push harder. Open water stretched ahead, and I sped across it, my muscles having regained their previous strength and purpose.

My gaze eagerly sought the dock, and as it came into view, I squinted, hoping to see an object waiting for me. The light thump of my kayak against the wooden structure sounded like the death knell of that hope. Nothing.

As I lifted my paddle to press the tip against the dock and push off, my gaze level with the top of the boards, a leaf that lay on the wharf fluttered in the breeze. But it didn't blow away. A pebble held it in place.

"My gift," I said with an overjoyed laugh.

Backpaddling, I reached across and slid the leaf from underneath the rock. I stared at it in awe as it lay in my palm, dwarfing my hand. A perfect specimen, its veins branched out from the central stem like delicate rivers, a marvel of nature. Its smooth, green texture held a faint sheen that caught the sunlight. In fall, it would've glowed red, gold, or orange. The boy had found a flawless gift for me, and its beauty and his thoughtfulness drew tears to my eyes.

Gazing at the leaf, my kayak drifting slowly on the almost deserted lake, I wondered where the boy and I were going with this. My concern about him hanging around the dock on his own still nagged at me. He was too young to be unsupervised. Would he be angry if I spoke to his parents and warned them about what their son was doing? Most likely he'd feel betrayed by the woman he thought he'd befriended. Or was it possible his parents knew and were all right with it?

The memory of the fear in his eyes struck me. Who or what was he afraid of? Strangers? His parents?

I'd never forgive myself if something happened. It only took a split second for tragedy to strike. What if he swam alone in the lake? What if one of those jet-skis collided with him? They moved so fast, and a small boy was difficult to see in the dark water.

I had another thing to consider. Taking the first step with his parents would bring me closer to establishing a proper relationship with him but also with them. The prospect of forming a friendship with strangers made me cringe, knowing the questions they'd ask about my family and background, something I avoided at all costs. But it would ease my conscience if I knew they looked out for their son and he was safe.

My decision made, I beached the kayak, climbed out, and tugged it onto the shore. I stowed the precious leaf inside my life jacket that I tucked deep inside the vessel.

As I pushed through the thick foliage lining the shore, I finally caught a glimpse of the house that remained invisible from the water. The meticulously cut lawn stretched upward, the green expanse interrupted by a path with slate steps that guided me to the side door.

Two stories with enormous lake-facing windows and a wraparound porch, the house was an imposing sight, especially compared to my small two-room cottage. Evergreens and large, leafy trees ringed the house. On the opposite side, gardens lined the long driveway with two neat rows of flowers, one of marigolds and one of white petunias evenly spaced as if standing at attention, awaiting a dignitary's arrival.

My knock remained unanswered, even when followed by a more insistent knock. I turned to take in the surroundings. The driveway was empty of cars, but the house included an attached two-car garage. The vehicles could be in it.

I spotted a doorbell and hesitantly pressed the button. Inside, the chime rang cheerily. Seconds later, a man opened the door. Of average height with closely cropped brown hair and traces of gray at the temples, his age was difficult to determine. Late fifties, early sixties? Was he the boy's father or grandfather? His body seemed fit and muscular underneath a white, tight-fitting T-shirt and olive-green shorts.

Smiling brown eyes regarded me curiously after sending a questioning glance to the driveway, obviously wondering how I came to be there. I glimpsed the hallway's white-walled expanse behind him with its hardwood floors, which seemed to lead to a living area, the corner of a black leather couch visible atop a Persian rug.

"Yes, may I help you?" A soft and melodious voice eased my nervousness.

I introduced myself and explained that I stayed at a cottage on the lake's opposite shore.

"I just wanted to say I've passed your place several times by kayak, and I've seen your son on the dock a few times. He's always by himself, and I thought you should be aware..."

The words died in my throat. The expression of horror on the man's suddenly pale face took my breath away.

Chapter 12

"How dare you!"

His booming voice slammed into me, sharp and sudden, his hands clenched at his sides. I stepped backward as his face turned deep red, almost purple. He sputtered, seemingly searching for words to expose the depth of his anger.

"I..." Taking another step back, I grabbed the porch railing before I stumbled. "I'm sorry. I didn't mean to upset you."

"You didn't mean to upset me?" His eyes bulged like an enraged toad. He lunged forward and seized my arm above my elbow, his grip crushing. "You came here to pry into my life, to meddle in my business? Who are you? What kind of freak would do something like this?" With each word, he shook me. My teeth rattled.

Terror replaced my initial shock. Panic setting in, I struggled to free my arm. "Let me go! I don't understand," I said. I wanted to run from this terrible mistake I'd made and never come back.

He released my arm so suddenly I almost toppled down the steps. I grasped the banister for support.

"You understand perfectly well. Did someone put you up to this?" His right fist came up, and he pointed a long finger at my face.

"No, I saw him on the dock... a few times." Confusion warred with fear. Instinct kept me from mentioning the gifts the boy and I had left each other.

"You did not see my son on the dock! My son drowned ten years ago. Get out of here. If I see you again, I'll call the police."

***

The lawnmower had spluttered and died, leaving a trail of freshly cut grass in its wake. Keith cursed under his breath as he struggled to restart it. He pulled out his phone, a frown etched on his face, as he searched for a fix. Abby, oblivious to his frustration, bounced on the trampoline, her braids whipping and her laughter filling the air. Apart from Keith's mechanical problem, it resembled a typical summer day.

I suggested a trip to the repair shop, but my husband always insisted on fixing things himself. When all else failed, he'd ask for help. I left him to stew over the lawnmower.

We'd invited friends over for a barbeque, thus the need for a neatly cut lawn, but I also had a million things to do in the house and didn't have time to indulge in mechanics.

"I'll be inside," I called out to Keith as I swept a final glance across the backyard and slid the screen door closed behind me.

Pulling salad ingredients from the fridge, I chopped until I remembered the laundry needed transferring from the washer to the dryer. I sprinted to the basement to take care of that task and noticed Abby's toys strewn on the floor. Normally, she put her own toys away, but it'd only take a few minutes to tidy the room.

I shut my office door, making it off-limits for the kids, before I climbed the stairs to the kitchen. Heading to the pantry, I explored the shelves for what I needed for the salad dressing and grabbed a few burger condiments while there.

A blood-curdling scream rang out.

Heart pounding, I dashed to the patio door, only to halt in shock when I saw a soaking wet Keith waist-deep in the pool, cradling our limp daughter in his arms.

Before I could think, I was in motion. The water's cold shock barely registered as I plunged in, my legs churning against the resistance. I screamed Abby's name, my voice cracking, willing her eyes to open as her head lolled on Keith's arm. My trembling hands slid beneath her as Keith and I hoisted her toward the pool's edge.

I scrambled out, slipping and grasping for balance. Together, we laid her on the grass. Keith performed CPR, his movements frantic and desperate as he yelled at me to call 9-1-1.

Panicked, I staggered into the kitchen, my fumbling fingers sweeping across the countertops in a blind search for my phone. Tears blurred my vision, and my hands shook so violently it took three tries to hit the numbers.

"Stay calm," the operator said, her measured tone contrasting sharply with the chaos inside me. "Help is on the way."

"Please, hurry," I said, my voice high-pitched and strained. "She's not breathing." Somehow, the emergency operator deciphered the rest of my desperate words, and the wail of the approaching sirens soon reached me. I sprinted between the pool and the front door to wave down the vehicle, the phone still in my hand and terrified sobs wracking my body.

Uniformed paramedics stormed into the backyard, their faces set with grim determination. "We've got it now," one said as he firmly but gently nudged Keith aside. My husband's chest heaved as the paramedics took over.

Keith and I hovered on either side, our gazes locked on Abby's pale face. I silently begged for a flutter of her eyelids, a cough, a cry, anything.

With brisk efficiency, they transferred Abby onto a stretcher, medical equipment swallowing her tiny body. A paramedic joined her, straddling her frame, and continued the compressions without pause. The ambulance doors slammed shut behind them, and the vehicle roared to life, its lights spraying agitated red and white reflections over the driveway as it sped away.

I sank to my knees. "Please...don't let it be too late."

Chapter 13

In the cold, damp cottage, I curled into a ball on the bed, hugging my knees to my chest, my body trembling with sobs. The curtains drawn, the door shut tight as if to barricade me from the world, the darkness engulfed me, offering no comfort.

The man's face haunted me, his expression twisted in raw anger and pain. It replayed in my thoughts, a hideous loop I couldn't escape. I squeezed my eyes shut, but it didn't matter. The image burned bright and sharp.

The anguish in the man's eyes reflected my own loss, as if I'd been tossed into the past to look in a mirror. The heartbreak, the grief, the long tear-filled nights all surged back at me, a tidal wave of sorrow that made me gasp.

Probably looking like a madwoman, I'd turned from the man and ran without thinking, without looking back. I darted toward the water, scrambling into the kayak, almost capsizing it, kicking my life jacket further inside. I paddled like my life depended on it. Perhaps it did. My heart almost couldn't endure the beating it took standing before that poor man. I would easily have accepted death over one more moment of looking at his enraged, tormented face.

The lake seemed to stretch on forever, a vast expanse of water that looked as empty as I felt inside. When I finally reached my dock, I tumbled from the kayak, lacking any grace or technique. Soaked to my thighs, I hauled it onto the shore and stumbled up the lawn to the cottage. I collapsed on the bed, wet, exhausted, and broken. I lay there, lost in a haze of grief and self-loathing.

Knuckles rapped on the front window, and a voice shouted something indistinguishable. I rolled over, my heart in my throat. Had he followed me here? Did he intend to wreak revenge against me? What to do? I hadn't locked the door.

"Julie, are you in there?"

The voice penetrated my fevered brain. I pushed myself upright in the bed and turned toward the sound, relieved I wasn't in danger but annoyed someone dared to intrude upon my misery. I preferred to suffer in solitude.

Another shout. Mark. Why was he here? His voice sounded urgent, scared. I sat perfectly still, hoping he'd give up and leave. The thought of facing him, facing anyone, was unbearable.

"Are you okay?"

Confused, I wondered what he'd seen. I didn't answer. I couldn't speak. The words stuck in my throat, a lump of despair blocking my voice. Mark persisted, knocking on the window again and again.

Fully yanked out of my stupor, I heard footsteps thud on the wood as he moved on the porch, calling my name. The door creaked open and slammed shut behind him. He was in the cottage. I slashed my hand across my face, wiping away tears, but I knew the ravages of crying wouldn't disappear so easily.

"Julie, where are you?"

He'd find me easily with only three rooms to choose from, and judging by the closeness of his voice, he stood directly outside the one I was in. "I'm fine. Go away, please." The tremor in my voice exposed my lie.

"Bullshit. Let me in."

"Go away. I'll be fine," I said, revising my timeline.

The knob twisted, and the door shrieked on its hinges. Mark's head appeared in the doorway as he leaned in, his brows furrowed. His gaze slid over me, probably scanning for injuries. But the bruises the man had inflicted were hidden from sight.

Apparently satisfied with my physical condition, Mark eased into the room and perched on the edge of the bed. He turned toward me, his eyes narrowed. "What happened?" he asked, his voice filled with concern.

I couldn't look at him. I moved my gaze to the floor as fresh tears streamed down my face. My resolve to hold them back collapsed like a deflating balloon.

Mark reached out and took my hand. "It's okay," he said softly. "You can tell me."

I shook my head, but I didn't pull my hand away. "I want to be alone please." I spoke in the calmest voice I could muster.

"I'll leave you alone, but first I want to help if I can."

"What makes you think I need help? I'm allowed to cry in privacy."

"Are you kidding? You flew by my place like a rocket. The look on your face was pure terror. I thought someone was chasing you."

I imagined my expression as Mark must have seen it. If it was half as scary as the turmoil inside me, it would've been a terrible sight. No wonder he was concerned.

The only way to get him to leave me alone to wallow in my sorrow was to put his mind at ease. I strove for nonchalance. "I had a shock, that's all. It's no big deal. I'll get over it."

"Cut it out. I'm not a child. I've seen grief and pain before, and it's all over you."

I gulped in a huge breath, trying to contain my emotions, but against my best effort, the dam burst again. My trembling hands covered my face as more tears fell in a deluge.

A warm hand settled on my shoulder, and something inside me crumbled. I didn't resist; I couldn't. I leaned into Mark as I surrendered to the simple act of being held. His solid frame felt alien yet soothing, like stepping into the sun after years in a dark prison. I was beyond caring that he was a near stranger.

Mark didn't offer platitudes. I didn't hear, "Don't cry," or, "It'll be okay." He was a presence, someone who held me up when I wanted to fold into myself. I let the tears flow. I cried until none remained, my body exhausted, my soul raw, but the dense knot in my chest had loosened.

Unaware of how much time passed before I regained control, I awkwardly straightened and shifted away from him, brushing my damp cheeks with shaky hands.

"Sorry. I rarely do that," I said, looking anywhere but at him. "Actually, I've never done that."

"No harm, no foul." He hesitated. "You can tell me about it, if you want."

How could I explain something I didn't understand myself? The man's son was dead, so who was the boy on the dock? I didn't even know where to begin.

"Let's take a step back." Mark spoke calmly. "Someone or something scared you. Who or what was it?"

"No. We have to step farther back than that." I looked at him, measuring him, wondering if this was the right thing. "I saw a young boy on a dock a few days ago, on the far shore, across from the island." I nodded my head in that direction. "He was alone, and it bothered me. But, when I moved closer, he got scared and ran away."

I glanced at Mark and saw a spark of interest in his eyes. "I went back the next day, and the same thing happened, so I took him a gift, a..."

"Whatever you took from the nest."

"Exactly, a feather. A heron's feather. That's all it was. And he left me a tiny feather in exchange. The next day, today, I left two pretty stones, and he gave me a beautiful maple leaf." I paused, remembering that, in my frenzy, I'd left the leaf in the kayak. I'd retrieve it later. "We never spoke or got near each other. We just took turns leaving things on the dock."

I shifted my gaze to him. Did he think I was a freak for enticing a young boy with gifts? Was telling him the story a terrible mistake? He didn't appear judgmental, his nod encouraging me to continue.

"I was still worried. He shouldn't be on the dock alone. Anything could happen. I decided the best thing to do was to mention it to his parents, at least let them know he went down there by himself."

I drew a deep breath, bolstering myself for the next part.

"Let me guess," Mark said. "You went to the house, and the parents blasted you and told you to mind your own business."

The familiar lump rose in my throat. "Not exactly. I just saw a man, a furious man. He told me... his son drowned... ten years ago."

I couldn't go on. I looked at Mark and watched his eyes narrow. Was that anger I saw? On my behalf? "Then who is the boy?" His voice held an edge.

"I don't know, but it's not his son. He was so angry and hurt by what I did. His face was…" I clamped my hand over my mouth, trying to stem a fresh wave of misery.

"How were you to know?" Mark's voice softened as he laid a hand on my shoulder. "You certainly didn't do it on purpose. You can't beat yourself up over it."

"You don't understand. It's not just that, although that was horrible enough." I drew another deep, strengthening breath. "I lost my daughter three years ago. She drowned." A sobbing hiccup almost swallowed my last word.

"Oh God."

Those arms came around me again and held me close as I cried fresh tears.

Chapter 14

The sun had dipped below the horizon, throwing the forest into gloom, when Mark trudged home through the woods between our cottages. He'd listened patiently as I told him about Abby and how she'd drowned in our backyard pool, his eyes filled with sympathy. He didn't inquire about Keith and our relationship. It was obvious I was at the cottage on my own. It didn't take a rocket scientist to realize Keith and I had our problems. Mark likely surmised that it'd open another painful wound and I'd had enough for one day.

I wasn't sure if it was kindness or a missed opportunity. Did I want to unload about Keith or was it a relief to avoid the issue?

We'd sat on the porch for a while, watching the sun set in all its glory. I don't know if it was the tears' cleansing effect or if it was Mark's quiet company, but I finally appreciated the sunset's pink and gold kaleidoscope, mirrored on the lake's calm surface. A deceptive calmness. Above water, everything appeared peaceful, but beneath it, the lake could pull you under without warning.

As the shade stretched across the lawn, the air cooled, and with it, another wave of sadness washed over me. A deep, aching emptiness.

"It's okay to cry," Mark said, his voice gentle. Again, he seemed to sense my mood. Was I that obvious? "It's part of the healing process," he said.

Mark's words made sense. I'd heard them a thousand times before, but yet they grated. I knew he meant well, but what did he know about this kind of grief that sat like a stone in my heart? And this numbness that invaded my body?

A breeze whispered through the pines, carrying the scent of mustiness and lake water. It slipped past me, almost unnoticed, like the days that blurred together since Abby was gone.

The conversation drifted to safer, shallow waters. We talked about the weather and how the chill in the mornings was typical for waterside properties. Mark mentioned the lake's water level, gesturing toward the shoreline with a vague wave of his hand, and I nodded as though I, too, had kept track. He brought up a neighbor's boat, how it was left unattended too long and now was in desperate need of repairs.

It was a conversation that made silence preferable, but we kept going, as if afraid of what would happen if we stopped. Each word filled a space between us, a feeble attempt to block unspoken thoughts. My gaze wandered to the lake and its glassy surface. The slight ripple of wind across the water seemed more significant than our words.

I tilted my head toward him and studied his expression. A familiar one I'd seen before on the faces of my husband, family, and friends. Doubt mingled with concern. Mark didn't speak the words aloud, but I sensed he questioned the boy's existence. Or was I projecting my own thoughts onto him? Perhaps he was thinking about what he'd eat for breakfast tomorrow.

Was the boy a figment of my imagination? Had my subconscious made him appear as a replacement for Abby? If so, why didn't that subconsciousness choose a girl instead of a boy? Or someone who looked like her? That would have been more effective.

Mark's voice pulled me back from the odd trajectory of my thoughts. "So, where exactly is this house?" he asked, dipping his toe back into the snake-infested waters of the conversation we'd left behind.

"Left," I said, with a wave of my arm. "I go down to the little island, circle it clockwise, and it's on the opposite shore."

He squinted his eyes, sharpening the vision in his mind. "What's it look like?"

I described the man's home as best I could.

"And him?" he asked. "What did he look like?"

I wondered why it mattered. His anger and grief were the same whether he was short or tall, skinny or fat. How would it explain the mystery of the boy? Did he think the whole thing was a hallucination? Was this a test? No house, no man, no boy?

Fatigue swept over me. I didn't have the energy to question his interest. I gave him all I could, but it was very little.

After Mark disappeared behind the trees, I remained standing on the porch, watching the moonlight reflect on the water. A wolf howled in the distance, a lonely, chilling sound. Fitting.

As I turned to go into the cottage, I thought a shape moved along the tree line. A trick of the darkness, I told myself. But the unease clung to me, following me inside like a ghost. I stared at the closed door and did something unusual. I locked it. Then I pulled the curtains closed, blocking out the darkness, burying myself in solitude again.

My mind revisited the day's events, and the anguish resurfaced. Nothing could hold it at bay, so I let it take over. It was the only path to the other side, to battle through the grief.

I curled up in my bed, fully dressed, pulling the blanket tight. The gloom swaddled me. I closed my eyes, trying to shut out the world with all its dangers and fears, its pain and despair.

Abby's face floated in the darkness behind my closed lids, her smile wide, her eyes filled with trust. I wanted to hold on to that image forever.

Just as sleep pulled me under, I heard the faint, impossible sound of water splashing, as if Abby were still there, waiting for me.

Chapter 15

The rain hammered against the windowpane, a constant pulse that echoed in every corner of the cottage. I pulled the covers over my head, trying to block out the noise, or the day, I wasn't sure which. My body ached, and my mind was a fog, the tattered remains of the emotional storm the previous day, a storm that continued throughout the night. Not surprisingly, Abby invaded my dreams again.

Underwater in a lake, I desperately swam toward a small hand just out of reach. Abby's fingers stretched toward me, but every time I strained to grab them, they slipped away. Her voice called me. In an instant, the water turned dark and murky. I pushed myself upward, needing air and light, but I surfaced underneath a wooden dock, the smell of damp wood and algae overwhelming. I gasped for breath, choking, and screamed when a hand emerged from the black water and clamped around my wrist. But it wasn't Abby's hand. It belonged to a man.

My heart raced as I sat up straight, the room pitch black, the nightmare fresh and vivid. Whose dock was that? Mine or the boy's? And who did the hand belong to? Mark or the grief-stricken father? I didn't want to return to the dream to find out.

I drew calming breaths and tried to talk myself into going back to sleep. My efforts were more or less successful. I dozed off and on until daylight, when I forced myself to get up, knowing I couldn't hide from my problems, no matter how much I wanted to. As I looked out the window, I saw the lake's usually calm water roiling in the wind and rain. It reflected my restless, disturbed mood. An indoor day might do me good. Keep me away from the dock at the lake's other end, an area that churned up memories better pushed aside. Perhaps I'd advance on my work projects.

"Okay, Julie, time to get at this," I said, pulling out my best cheerleading voice.

I sat down at my computer, coffee mug in hand, determined to focus on my clients. But my rebellious thoughts returned repeatedly to the man and his story. The more I thought about it, the more convinced I became something wasn't right. I couldn't push aside the belief the boy was real and in danger. I needed to discover the truth.

I researched drownings on Sala Lake ten years ago. My search came up empty. Gazing out the window at the black storm clouds, I realized that just because the man lived here now, it didn't mean he'd lived here then and his son had drowned in this lake.

"Set it aside. It's none of my business, and looking into it will only cause me more pain. I don't need that. It won't change what happened yesterday, and it won't bring back any children." I paced as I berated myself.

But, like worms in the soil, thoughts kept digging and squirming through my mind, unwilling to leave me alone. *Fine. If knowing more will rid me of the worst of it, that's what I'll do.*

I needed information. Mark didn't seem close to any other residents, but Dan, the owner of this cottage, struck me as someone who'd know everyone. I'd pay him a visit, but given the storm that raged outside, it'd wait another day.

In the meantime, I struggled through three hours dedicated to a client.

***

Needing to further develop my bike legs, I pulled the bicycle from the shed to visit Dan. I'd been meaning to drop in on him for weeks just to work on my neighborliness but always found an excuse to put it off. Now, I had a reason to see him. I hoped, if Dan had lived here for at least ten years, he'd know the story of the boy who drowned or at least a little about the boy's father.

Dan had left me detailed instructions on how to reach him if I needed anything, and I easily found his home further down the lake. I'd passed by and admired it several times on kayak without realizing who it belonged to. As I approached the cottage, its beauty struck me again. A charming bungalow, white with nautical blue trim and a colorful front garden, nestled among imposing trees overlooking the lake. Off to the side, Adirondack chairs and a swing seat circled a fire pit.

The previous day's rain had rejuvenated the greenery, and the bright sun highlighted the flowers and immaculate lawn. Swinging off the bike, I kicked down the stand and left it to approach the front door. My raised hand froze before it knocked.

"You dug out the old bike. Good for you."

I turned to see Dan lumbering toward me, a wide grin on his face. I returned the smile. "Yes. Mark, my neighbor, filled the tires and made the adjustments for me."

"He's a pleasant lad, that one." His smile dimmed. "How are you getting along? That storm didn't do any damage, did it?"

"No, not at all. Everything's fine."

Dan waved me over to two chairs that offered a perfect view of the lake. "Can I get you something? Coffee or a cold drink?"

I refused his offer as I settled in the chair. My nerves had suddenly shifted into overdrive, and I didn't think I could stomach anything. I needed to dive in.

"I'm curious about some residents and thought you might know the history," I said, aiming for an indifferent tone.

He waved a hand. "Oh, sure. I've been here thirty-five years. I know everyone and everything that ever happened. Is it Mark you want to know about?"

Dan's slight look of distress piqued my interest, but I'd come here with a purpose, and I wouldn't let myself get sidetracked. I'd file it away for later.

"Actually, I'm most curious about the people in the house to the west of the island." I cringed inwardly at my clumsy attempt to be stealthy, but fortunately Dan didn't seem to notice. He squinted his eyes and gazed at the treetops, as if the island's map was displayed there.

He nodded. "It's not people. It's person. Name's Graham Peller. Lives alone. Ex-military guy." He gave a sad shake of his head. "Terrible story. Lost his boy years ago. Drowned."

Despite already being aware of that fact, the words made my gut tighten. "Here? In this lake?"

"Oh no, somewhere else. In Manitoba, I think. Used to live there."

"He told you about it?"

"Yeah. He was real broken up. Tragic."

A troubled look crossed Dan's face as if suddenly realizing the conversation's turn. Keith had likely filled him in on our own tragic past. But I'd already steeled myself against that possibility, determined to stick to the reason behind my visit.

"Are you sure he lives alone? He doesn't have any other children? Or a wife?"

Dan's eyes narrowed as he focused on my face. "What're you getting at?"

I needed to tell him at least part of the truth. "I saw a child alone on his dock. It seemed dangerous, but obviously it wasn't his child. Probably a neighbor or someone visiting." I raised my brows, as if asking him a question, encouraging him to take the bait.

Dan frowned and rubbed his chin. "He never has visitors that I know of, and there are no children on that side of the lake. There's some on this end, but it'd be strange to find them over there. Are you sure it was his dock?"

"There's only one in that area."

Dan nodded. "Pretty odd, if you ask me."

"Yes, it is."

***

With stiff knees, I eased off the bike. More new muscles to work on, I thought.

"How'd it go?"

I spun toward Mark as he emerged from the trees. It took me a moment to realize he referred to the bike ride and not my interrogation of Dan.

"Fine. Like riding a bike."

He chuckled politely at my lame joke. "Did you take the trails?"

"Not this time. I went to see Dan."

The gravity in my voice and expression must have clued Mark in that my meeting with Dan was more than a social visit.

"You asked him about the boy." It wasn't a question.

"Kind of. And the man. His name's Graham Peller. His son drowned somewhere in Manitoba years ago." I hesitated. "And, according to Dan, there aren't any other children close by who could be on his dock."

"Peller," he said slowly, an expression crossing his face that was hard to define. Anger? Frustration? "Dan must be wrong. There's gotta be someone."

His belief in me bolstered my spirits, but I still needed to know who the boy was, and I wasn't sure how to do that. "I don't know where to begin," I said.

"We'll find a way. The Manitoba lead is useful, and you have a name. All it takes is a little web research."

Yes, of course. I need to be logical. I smiled my thanks at Mark, but a concerned frown marred his face.

"What else did Dan talk about?" he asked.

"Nothing. That was it." What was he getting at? The memory of Dan's cryptic question about Mark popped into my head, but I didn't want to pursue it. Now wasn't the time.

"You have an internet connection?" Mark said.

I swung toward the cottage. "Follow me."

Chapter 16

The computer screen projected an eerie glow in the cottage's dim light. My fingers danced across the keyboard as Mark sat beside me, watching intently while I searched for information on Manitoba drownings. Narrowing our parameters to one province and a date of approximately ten years ago made our search easier. We came across a surprising number of drownings, mostly children, in that year.

"There it is," Mark said, pointing to a news article, a note of excitement in his voice despite the find's morbidity. "Nathan Peller. Drowned in a lake near Winnipeg."

I enlarged the write-up and read on. The son of Graham and Annette Peller, the boy was ten years old at the time of his death, putting him at twenty now, had he survived.

The article filled me with a creeping fear. I scanned it for details. The boy had fallen off the pier at a rented lakeside cottage, his body recovered from the water the next day. Losing their only child devastated the parents.

The parallels unsettled me. My concern for the boy on the dock was exactly that. I worried he'd slip off and perish. My daughter, also an only child, had drowned. And I estimated the boy's age at ten years old, Nathan Peller's age when he died. I took a deep breath, struggling to suppress the horrifying memories and disturbing thoughts.

"We don't have to do this, you know."

I opened my eyes to meet Mark's concerned gaze. "I'm okay. Strangely enough, I expected worse."

It was true. The mere thought of another child drowning usually plunged me into the abyss, but my emotions remained subdued. Or my encounter with Graham Peller had worn them to a frazzle.

"So, now we've confirmed the circumstances of Nathan's death," I said, forging on. "But it doesn't explain the boy I saw."

"Do you mind?" Mark gestured toward the computer mouse.

I pushed my chair aside and gave him access to my computer. He clicked through a series of websites until a photo appeared on the screen. A young boy of about eight years old stood between Graham Peller and a woman I assumed was his wife. The boy's face was narrow and thin. He had short-cropped brown hair and hazel eyes. His smile showed white, slightly uneven teeth that would likely need braces in a few years.

"Does he resemble the boy you saw?" Mark asked.

"It's hard to say. They have the same hair color, and the boy I saw is thin, but I never got close enough to see his eyes or other features. Besides, this boy is dead," I said, pointing to the computer, confused. I knew the boy I'd seen was not Nathan Peller. He couldn't be.

I leaned forward to peer closer at the photo, zeroing in on Graham Peller. His haircut was even more severe in the picture, with no evidence of gray. He stood straight and rigid, his expression serious beside his wife and child, whose smiles lit their faces. There was something vaguely familiar about Peller, although the woman and boy didn't strike any chords. I hadn't noticed it during the confrontation at his house, but this older photo sparked an elusive memory.

"I thought a relative, a nephew or something." Mark jolted me from my thoughts. "A family resemblance."

"It's possible," I said, returning to the problem at hand. "But if he had a nephew visiting, why not mention it? How could he not realize it was him I saw?"

"He might not be well. Maybe his wife is taking care of the child," Mark said, obviously grasping at straws.

"I didn't see anyone else, and Dan said he lives alone. Can we check his marital status somehow?"

Mark nodded and started on another round of web surfing while I prepared two cups of green tea and found a package of cookies in the pantry. By the time I set the cup beside him, Mark wore a triumphant smile.

He waved a hand toward the computer screen that displayed an official-looking document. I didn't know how he found these things so easily.

"Divorced," he said. "He and his wife split up four years after Nathan drowned."

Another marriage that fell apart after a child's death and another eerie connection. "So, he's probably living alone, like Dan claimed," I said.

"Probably. Unless he's got a girlfriend or someone else living with him. Not something I'd find on the internet."

I slumped into my chair. "I guess that's it. Apart from peeking through his windows, I have no way of knowing if a boy is living there or if someone is sneaking to his dock from somewhere else."

"Unless you face him with proof the boy was there."

I chuckled. "All I have is a feather and a leaf. Not very convincing evidence. Even with the drawing."

"Drawing?"

"He gave me a drawing with the feather." It occurred to me Mark might have a different interpretation of the boy's artwork. "I'll show you."

Mark's brow furrowed when he unfolded the paper I placed in his hand. "This is disturbing," he said.

"You think?" Had my first instinct been right? Was the boy telling me someone hit him?

"Hard to tell," Mark said. "It might be innocent, but I don't like the look of it."

Something fluttered within me. Anxiety? Urgency?

"What can we do?" I asked.

"Get proof. A photo of the boy would be best." A gleam glittered in Mark's eyes, like a kid trying to convince his friend to get into mischief.

I mulled over his suggestion, staring out the window as if the clouds would send me a message. The idea held merit, but it meant staking out the dock, waiting for the boy to appear. I hadn't seen him in two days. What if he was scared and never came back?

Mark seemed to read my mind. "You'd need to entice him with another gift or something. We'll keep watch. When he shows up, we'll get a picture."

A tiny spark of enthusiasm ignited inside me, Mark's eagerness contagious. "Yes, I could leave it and wait. But what would I give him?" Another thought occurred to me. "How would he even know I'd left him something?"

"He knew the other times. Maybe he can see the dock from the house."

We sat for long minutes, both thinking about what might appeal to a ten-year-old boy. I'd already given him a feather and rocks.

Mark snapped his fingers and grinned. "How about a book? I have one at my place full of animal and nature photos. That'd be a prize, wouldn't it?"

"Absolutely," I said, a smile slowly spreading across my face. It felt good to have an ally.

***

I left the cottage as the sun rose and burned away the lake's thin veil of fog, revealing a mirror of oranges and pinks. I pushed off from the shore, the kayak slick and cold, its surface damp with morning dew, as I paddled toward Peller's dock. The boy also seemed to rise early, and I hoped the dawn trip worked in my favor, giving me a glimpse of him. With deliberate quiet, I sidled up to the deserted wharf. My breath hitched as I placed the book, a battered hardcover wrapped in paper, on the weathered wooden planks.

I glided away, paddling to the island's shadowed side. There, hidden among the trees, I wedged my kayak between two low-hanging branches that dipped into the water. The suddenly cool air made me shiver. From my waterproof backpack, I extracted my Nikon D3500 and aimed the lens at the dock, using the book as my focal point. My pulse quickened as I imagined the boy discovering it.

The morning chill seeped through my light jacket, but I ignored it, willing myself to remain still. A breeze whistled through the branches, creating faint ripples on the lake's surface. My toes curled in my shoes, cold and cramped from my rigid position. I'd left behind my usual thermos of coffee, a sacrifice to avoid the nuisance of having to pee, the duration of my wait uncertain, as was the outcome.

Minutes stretched into an hour, the camera growing cumbersome in my hands. Doubts crept in like the sun's warming rays. The lake would soon awaken, disrupted by the hum of motors and the noise of summer vacationers. A woman alone, lurking in the trees with a camera would draw attention, and not the kind I wanted. I'd wait just a while longer. At the first sign of stirrings, I'd figuratively abandon ship.

A splash behind me shattered the quiet. My breath caught, and I spun in my seat, the kayak wobbling. Mark's canoe emerged through the mist, and he pulled alongside me.

"No luck, I guess," he said.

"It's still early, but I can't stay here once people are out on the lake."

"I can take over, if you'd like a break."

"Thanks for the offer, but..."

I broke off as I spotted movement amongst the trees near the dock. Someone approached from the direction of the house. My heart thumped as I lifted my camera to my face and waited for the boy. Mark perceptibly tensed beside me.

Denim-covered legs and booted feet came into view, and I jerked in surprise.

Chapter 17

This wasn't a child. It was Graham Peller, his anger palpable through my lens. He marched to the dock and only hesitated a moment before seizing Mark's book. I witnessed his fury as he ripped off the paper and scowled at it.

His head shot up, and he scanned the lake, obviously looking for the source. I froze as his gaze swept across our hiding spot. Convinced our meeting remained as vivid in his memory as it did in mine, I knew he pinned me as his prime suspect. Finding me lurking in the trees wouldn't go over well.

When he swiveled and marched up the steps toward his house, I realized we'd lost our chance to see the boy today. He wouldn't receive the gift, which Peller would likely throw in the trash, and if the man was truly aware of the boy's existence, he wouldn't allow him to come to the dock again.

My shoulders slumped in defeat as I turned toward Mark.

"It was worth a try," he said. "We'll come up with another plan."

"I should just give up. I mean, what's the point, right?" I threw my hands in the air. "He's just a boy, a stranger. What he does or what Graham Peller does, is none of my business. I've got enough to handle. What do I have to gain from this?"

Mark's steady stare remained fixed on me as I vented. When I heaved a breath, he answered my rhetorical question.

"I think you've already gained a lot."

"What?"

"Those were the most passionate words I've heard from you. Even though we haven't known each other long, I'm certain those are the first words of true emotion about another subject that you've spoken since your daughter passed. The grieving woman is disappearing, and one with a clear purpose is taking her place."

My head jolted in shock. He was right. I hadn't been this fired up over anything in three years. Grief still lived in me like an unwelcome houseguest, one who had claimed squatter's rights but now had to share a bed with someone else. The boy. My worry about his welfare lit a fire under my maternal instincts.

I'm not just wallowing anymore. I'm planning, considering, acting. I looked at Mark, his stare a silent challenge. "What now? Do I dress in black and break into Peller's house to find the boy?"

"Drastic, not to mention dangerous. Let's try to come up with something else first."

***

I wrapped my hands around my cherished cup of coffee, thankful for both the warmth and the java's kick. The aroma filled the air, a comforting smell that reminded me of simpler times.

We had settled on rattan chairs on the porch to drink our brew and come up with a plan. Mark tapped his foot and nodded to a rhythm only he heard, as if a band performed a private concert in his head.

"Is it good?" I asked, amused.

He stopped moving and frowned at me. "The music," I said, tapping the side of my head.

"Oh, sorry. It drove my wife crazy. I often listen to music that isn't there."

I nodded. I guessed it was no worse than me talking to inanimate objects, a habit that annoyed Keith.

"I'm Alright."

"Yeah, it's fine," I said with a dismissive wave. I wasn't one to judge another person's habits.

"No, the song. Kenny Loggins. A classic."

I smiled as his words kicked in. "You're divorced?" I realized I needed to know more about this person I'd hitched my wagon to.

He nodded. His gaze shifted to the darkening sky, not offering more insight into his life. I recognized the move, one I'd used several times in the past three years. Avoidance.

The wind stirred the leaves, carrying the smell of rain. It felt like the entire sky was on edge, waiting to explode with lightning. The lake would turn treacherous in minutes. We would've needed to abandon our surveillance anyway. Even with a new plan, we were stuck here on the porch for the time being.

"Were you born and raised in B.C.?" I asked.

His jaw flexed as he shook his head. "Not really from anywhere. We moved around a lot."

I tried to absorb this information. In my view, the place where you were born was the place you were from. I'd never considered the alternative of having nowhere as my hometown.

Mark's gaze pivoted toward me, and the hard glint in his eyes took me aback. "You?" he asked. "Divorced?"

"Same." My turn to avoid his gaze, I shifted it to the rapidly moving dark clouds heading our way. A subject neither of us wanted to explore, he'd turned it on me almost like a defense weapon. I struggled to refocus. "Anyway, back to the subject at hand. Our plan this morning fell through, and I'm reluctant to knock on Peller's door again. Next time, he might have a shotgun aimed at me."

"I could do it somehow."

My eyes widened as I looked at Mark. The thought of him standing face-to-face with Peller made my stomach twist. What if things went wrong? What if Peller actually had a gun and didn't ask questions before pulling the trigger?

"We could wait for him to leave the house," I said, searching for a safer option. "Then we can peek in."

"That could take forever," he said, with a shake of his head. "Maybe he never leaves. It'd be impossible to get in."

"You want to get in?" I asked. *Is he talking about breaking and entering?*

"We'd know for sure if a boy is there and in danger."

On a certain level, his calmly spoken words made sense, but uneasiness crept over me. Why was Mark so willing to help me? Most people would have backed out by now. But not Mark. And that made me wonder. Was he looking for something else in the house besides the boy? And why was he so reticent to share his past with me? Was I signing on with a criminal?

Chapter 18

My mind raced as Mark returned to his cottage, claiming he needed time to think through some ideas. The thought of gaining access to Peller's house filled me with anxiety. I knew deep down Graham Peller would never voluntarily allow us near his house, and doing it on the sly could land us in hot water. However, on the opposite scale sat the boy, perhaps in danger. Saving him would justify the rest, wouldn't it?

Tea mug in hand, I nestled into my workspace, determined to make a difference, laptop open, client files at the ready. The faint aroma of cedar drifted through the open window, and suddenly, I was in our backyard, watching Keith build the swing set for Abby. The thud of a hammer on wood. The giddy squeal of our daughter's laughter. And then, like a light switch, the memory vanished, leaving only silence and loss.

I stared at the laptop screen, trying to focus. But the cursor blinked like a heartbeat, steady and relentless. Abby had a steady pulse, too. Until she didn't.

I opened the project folder and scrolled through client emails, forcing my brain to engage. But my thoughts tumbled like pebbles down a hillside. Mark's avoidance. Peller's glower. Abby's small shoes by the door that last day, Keith's pained expression every time I looked at him. I shut the laptop and pressed my hands to my face, as if I could thrust the memories away.

Memories of love and happy times. Memories of a broken home and moving into my brother's basement rather than walk by Abby's empty room.

No final fight. Just silence and distance.

We signed the papers, sold the house, moved on. Three months ago, Keith told me he'd met someone. I smiled and said I was happy for him. But the words tasted like bile. I wanted to mean them. Instead, I felt nothing.

***

I awoke in the cottage's small bed. Despite my sleepless night, I felt rejuvenated and prepared to tackle the day, an unusual sensation after three years of dragging myself from sleep. Although an early-morning chill lingered, the forecast promised a hot and humid day. I opted for black sweats and a T-shirt topped with a light, black jacket, guessing I'd be home before the heat crept in. I smiled as I recalled my joke to Mark about wearing black to sneak into Peller's house.

As he'd suggested, my plan was similar but not as drastic.

I prepared my backpack and hoisted it onto my shoulders before I unlocked the shed and wheeled out the bike. Climbing on, I took the road that skirted the lake. Likely because of the early hour, I didn't meet any sign of life along the way. I pedaled past Peller's house before guiding the bike into the woods and concealing it within the dense underbrush.

Pulling my camera from the backpack and slinging the strap around my neck, I kept low as I crept through the trees toward the house, my feet sinking into the rich, loamy soil. Once in range but well-hidden, I settled on a rock and watched for activity.

The air smelled of damp earth and resin. I swatted at a mosquito buzzing near my ear as the rock's coldness seeped through my clothes, making me shiver. Every crack of a twig, every breath of wind through the trees seemed magnified in the stillness.

Checking the time, I acknowledged that, at six-thirty, it was early for someone to be outside doing chores or playing. In for the duration, I retrieved the thermos from the backpack and sipped my coffee, my gaze scanning the house and the surrounding area for movement.

At seven, I thought I detected something in the kitchen, but the sun's angle on the windows made it impossible to see who or what it was. I remained poised with my camera.

Fifteen minutes later, I spotted a slight movement to my left, a flash of white near the lake. It had to be the boy, but the trees obscured my view. I edged closer to the tree line, crouching low, trying to be inconspicuous. I chose my steps carefully, sticking to the mossy patches to avoid snapping branches or crunching leaves, all while attempting to keep the wispy form within my sight. No simple task.

Reaching the edge of the trees, I lowered myself onto my belly and propped my elbows on the soft moss, the camera to my face. The fog swaddled the dock like a thick veil. Each time the figure seemed to shift, I questioned whether I'd really seen him, or if the mist played tricks on me.

Is the boy looking for me? Did he hope to find another gift on the dock? I'm certain he never received the book, and I regretted not bringing something with me. *Should I approach him? Call out?* I couldn't be sure Peller wasn't out here too. Having him find me on his property wasn't an option. I needed to stick to my plan.

My camera clicked and whirred softly as I snapped shot after shot. I willed the fog to dissipate to give me a clear photo, but I was allowed only a vague impression of the boy's presence. I had faith the lens would capture it.

A noise to my right startled me, making me lower the camera and prepare to escape. A door slammed, and I heard heavy footsteps on a wooden deck. The figure reacted. Like a mouse fleeing from a hawk, he dashed from the dock and vanished into the brush lining the riverbank. The bushes rustled followed by an eerie silence.

Chapter 19

I lay still for several long moments, thrilled with the opportunity handed to me, but disappointed it ended so soon and with so much anxiety for the youngster.

I didn't dare budge. Graham Peller's boots thumped as he walked to the end of his deck and stood with his hands on his hips. He didn't speak or call out. He stood much as the boy had, staring across the misty lake, his larger, darker silhouette more visible through the fog. Was he also looking for me? Wondering if I'd come back with another gift for him to destroy?

He moved his gaze across the forest where I hid, but my choice of clothing must have served its purpose. He returned to the house, the door creaking shut behind him.

My breath shallow, my pulse loud, I counted the seconds. A hundred. Two hundred. The ache in my arms spread to my back, but I didn't move. *What if Peller returns? What if he sneaks up on me?*

I wanted to run to my bike and get away from this creepy house, but the thought of Peller spotting me held me back. I waited. How long, I can't be sure, but the dampness infiltrated my jacket and pants, making me shiver, and my entire body cramped in pain.

At last, I eased into a crouch and crept slowly through the trees toward my bike. As I passed the house, I averted my face, in case he was outside and on the lookout for a suspected prowler.

I retrieved my bike without incident and headed the long way around the lake, not wanting to pedal past his house. The ride gave me time to gather my thoughts and compose myself. I was excited about the photos, but I needed to recover from the anxiety of my success.

As I biked past Mark's place, I slowed and thought I glimpsed him sitting on an Adirondack chair by the water. I backtracked and steered toward him. He stood as he heard me approach, setting his fishing rod aside. Hardly waiting to come to a stop, I jumped off the bike, eager to show him my findings.

"What's up?" he asked with a smile. "You look like the cat that swallowed the canary."

"Almost. I think I snagged some tail feathers."

He glanced at the camera hanging from my neck. In my rush to leave, I hadn't bothered to shove it in my backpack.

"You got a picture?" His expression reflected his surprise and excitement.

"Not his face. Peller interrupted me." Catching Mark's concerned frown, I explained further. "He didn't see me, but he came out onto the deck and the boy ran off."

Mark narrowed his eyes. "Why would he run away from Peller?"

I shrugged. "Not sure. He always runs away. Maybe he's been told not to go out there. Or he doesn't live with Peller. Like we said, he could be a neighbor. We haven't figured that out yet, but this should help," I said, gesturing to the camera.

"Let's see," he said, reaching for it.

With a grin, I slid the device from around my neck and handed it to him. As he powered it up, I studied his face. His fingers moved over the buttons, and his brows lowered into a confused frown. Wringing my hands, I moved to his side to get a view of the screen. The first picture showed the dock barely visible through the mist.

"That one's not clear," I said. I grabbed the camera from him, eager to find one that had the boy more in focus. But as I clicked through the dozen shots, my heart sank in disappointment and disbelief. I had contest-worthy photos of a lake and dock obscured in a cloud of fog, but no discernible images of a boy within that cloud.

"What happened?" I said in a low voice. "He was there, but we can't see him."

"The fog's pretty thick."

Mark's words hit me like ice water. The same pitying tone I'd heard too many times before from doctors, friends, even Keith. That slight, dismissive smile. They didn't take me seriously. Grief muddled my mind. That's what they all thought. My hands trembled as I gripped the camera. I wouldn't let him see how he affected me. Not now.

"He was there. I saw him." I heard the strident cry in my voice. I inhaled a deep breath, trying to calm myself. I couldn't believe the camera had deceived me.

Maybe the fog was too thick, or my camera adjustments were off. Or... he was never there at all. *No. I can't think like that. I can't let this slip through my fingers.*

"I understand," Mark said. His hand hovered near my arm, but he didn't touch me. "Sometimes we see what we want to see."

I pulled away, his words stinging me. "I know what I saw."

He raised his hands in surrender. "Okay. I'm just saying... the fog..."

"It wasn't the fog." I hated my cracking voice. But Mark's pity was worse than any fog. It choked me.

I found it unbearable. The same brush had painted my interactions over the past three years, and it made me sick to think Mark, someone who seemed different, treated me the same way.

My mind flooded with disturbing images. Sympathetic clients telling me they had to take their business elsewhere. Alarmed parents reacting to me approaching their child on the street, a little girl with a chilling resemblance to Abby. The faces of neighbors and friends who slowly distanced themselves from the zombie-like woman who couldn't get on with her life.

I blinked and returned my attention to Mark, thinking he was too quick to shrug it off. Like the photos didn't matter. But they mattered to me, so much I could hardly breathe. I studied his face, searching for a hint of doubt or concern, but found only that same infuriating patience and understanding.

I swung away from him, grabbed my bike, and mounted it. My exit may have been graceless and wobbly, but I ignored his apologetic tone as he called out to me. Within minutes, I arrived at the cottage.

I dropped the camera on the kitchen table and glared at it like it had betrayed me. Why didn't it catch what my eyes saw? Did Mark erase the best photos somehow? No. That was crazy. What possible reason did he have?

But doubt coiled around my brain like the fog around the dock. I powered up the camera and flipped through the images again and again, hoping one would change. But nothing did.

This was supposed to be proof. Proof I wasn't crazy. Proof the boy was real. But all I had were mist-covered images of a dock.

***

I paced the floor several times before deciding I needed to leave the cottage. I had to put physical distance between myself and Mark. Knowing my fridge was almost empty of anything fresh, I grabbed my purse and car keys.

Warm air greeted me when I wrenched open the car door, but once on the road, I lowered the windows and welcomed the breeze that sent my hair flying in every direction. The closest town was Namima, a village really, but it had a few shops and a wonderful fresh vegetable stand.

Within ten minutes, I pulled the car to a stop in the gravel parking lot, glad to be the only customer at this hour. It was a small, open-air building with large baskets of produce to select from, based on what was in season. Behind the counter, fridges preserved pies, juices, and other homemade goods.

I recognized the women on duty from other occasions, but we'd never gotten to know each other. I presumed she was the business owner. Now, she greeted me warmly as I made my way to the counter, my recyclable bag slung over my arm.

I gave her my warmest smile while avoiding direct eye contact. Instead, I examined the selection in the baskets and wondered how I had sunk so low that all traces of my past graciousness had vanished.

I chose two tomatoes and three potatoes, placing them on the counter as my gaze swept over other vegetables, calculating how and what I needed to get through the next few days.

"I have bags of potatoes over here, if you prefer," the woman said.

"I don't need that many. I live alone." I stifled a wince. Why had I shared personal information?

"You must be a summer resident. I know all the permanent ones." The woman chuckled.

I'd fallen into the trap of idle conversation. Being the only customer had turned against me. "Yes, just here for a few weeks," I said.

"On Sala Lake?"

I nodded as I picked up a large zucchini.

"Do you know the stories about that lake?"

My head shot up to meet her gaze. "Stories?" I said, unable to stop myself.

"Well, it's more local lore, I guess."

She'd caught me on her hook. Could this somehow help me in my research on Peller?

Encouraged by my evident interest, the woman continued. "Actually, it's an old First Nation's tale." She raised her eyebrows as if asking for permission to recount it. After my nod, she continued. "It's the legend of the Shadow Waters. They say that, long ago, a woman called the Shadow Woman lived by Sala Lake and protected the children of her people. But invaders stole them away. Her heartache turned her into a restless spirit bound to the lake for eternity. On quiet nights, some say they hear her grief-stricken cry calling to children, luring them to the water. Some said they saw the image of a woman rising from the mist, her arms outstretched."

I stood frozen to the spot, mute. The story, told in a soft, sing-song voice, both entranced and frightened me. The memory of the cry entered my thoughts like an arrow, that strange shriek I'd assumed came from a bobcat or a fox.

"Families used to tie red ribbons on trees or leave gifts to keep her away, but rumors circulated about kids who disappeared near the lake. Sometimes they came back, claiming they'd been cradled in the arms of a woman beneath the waves."

The dreamy look in her eyes transformed into a concerned frown. My reaction to the story probably distressed her. I cleared my throat and attempted to school my expression.

"Have any children disappeared recently?" My voice came out in a croak.

"Oh no, dear. I'm so sorry. I shouldn't have told you about it. I don't think sometimes." Her warm hand reached across the counter and closed around my forearm. I flinched but didn't pull away. "I've never heard about children disappearing, and I've lived here forever."

I knew she meant to comfort me with her smile, but my mind raced through the ties between myself, the boy, and the lake's legend. I hurriedly paid for my purchases and left the vegetable stand behind me, perhaps never to return. The excursion did little to improve my state of mind.

***

"C'mon. Get out of there." I spoke through gritted teeth, pressing the knife as hard as possible without causing actual damage. "Damn you, I'm going to get you, whether or not you like it."

I jabbed the knife in the grimy dishwasher track, perhaps with more force than necessary, the blade scraping against the stubborn filth. At first, I told myself I was just cleaning, but I needed to have control over something, anything. It gave me a slight sense of power, yet the dirt didn't let loose.

I exhaled sharply, stepping back and gripping the knife tighter before setting it down with a clatter. The grime wasn't going anywhere, not without proper tools, and that meant a trip to the store, an excursion I couldn't stomach right now. After my earlier experience, the thought of fluorescent lights, casual chatter, and strangers surrounding me was unbearable. It could wait.

My eyes darted around the kitchen, searching for another outlet for my frustration, something productive to pour my restless energy into. My gaze landed on the window, the patchy lawn outside catching my attention. The grass had grown in the past few days, enough to warrant another swipe with the lawnmower.

About to slip into my sneakers, movement caught my eye. Mark emerged from the woods, striding at a deliberate pace toward my cottage. My hands fell to my sides. So much for losing myself in chores. Whatever he wanted, I doubted I could ignore it.

I studied his expression while he couldn't see me. What if he'd come to apologize? Or worse, what if he'd come to deliver that infuriating concern people always showered on me, the kind that made me feel like a child with a scraped knee? No, I wouldn't give him the satisfaction of thinking I needed his pity. Had he rehearsed a speech to "calm me down?" If so, he'd be in for a surprise.

I tensed when he rapped on the door. Should I ignore him? That'd be childish. He knew I was here. No, the air needed clearing.

I didn't force a smile or offer him a fake greeting when I opened the door.

"Do you want to hammer out a plan?"

His upbeat tone made me wonder if he'd forgotten our argument. Did he not only hear music in his head but suffer from memory lapses?

"What plan?" I said, my tone hesitant and wary, playing along for now.

"To get closer, get a better picture."

I didn't know how to deal with this man, and my dilemma must have shown on my face.

"Look," he said. "I know you're pissed at me, and that's fair. But I won't grovel or change who I am. I decided long ago that people need to either accept me, warts and everything, or not at all. It's fine either way. But you got me interested in this boy, and I'd like to see it through."

It was a straightforward speech, and I sensed a certain honesty. *Besides, who am I to judge? He's not the only one with warts.*

However, most people didn't just show up to help, not without expecting something in return. What did Mark want? And why did he care about the boy? I hated how my mind twisted his presence into suspicion, but after everything I'd been through, I couldn't help it. I wanted to ask him if he really believed the boy existed. But didn't the fact he was here and ready to help speak for itself?

"What's the plan?" I asked again, skepticism edging my voice. His smile was too easy, too relaxed, like he'd already decided I'd forgiven him. Did he really think it was that simple?

The smile morphed into a quick grin, filled with excitement for the hunt. Perhaps it was more about the hunt than the truth we might uncover. Should that worry me?

"We'll go together," he said. "Two different angles. We'll have better luck."

"Early tomorrow morning?" Despite everything, his fervor caught me up, building my enthusiasm, knowing I wouldn't be alone this time.

"I thought tonight, once it's dark enough for the house lights to be on. We'll see what's happening inside."

I nodded, thinking it through. "By water?"

"Why not? We'll have a better chance," Mark said. "Less risk of someone spotting us sneaking around."

"And what if he's outside?" I asked, my mind flitting through all the scenarios where something could go wrong.

Mark shrugged, as if the possibility didn't faze him. "We'll figure it out."

"It's dangerous," I said. "Peller could catch us, and if the boy's out there, he might run off again."

Mark tilted his head, considering. "That's the thing about risks. If you don't take them, you get nowhere."

I nodded again, but I had a sinking sensation that once we crossed the lake tonight, there'd be no going back.

As Mark stepped away, I caught a glint of something in his expression, something that looked too much like glee. Was this simply an adventure for him, a chance to play spy like in the movies? Or was he as invested in this as I was? Had I dragged us into something we weren't ready for?

I watched Mark disappear into the woods, a hard lump forming in my stomach. I sensed we'd devised a plan that only sounded good in the light of day. Something would go wrong. I just didn't know what yet.

Chapter 20

Dark clouds swirled across the sky, creating a spooky backdrop for our late-night espionage attempt. The air seemed charged, from both the incoming storm and the impact of what we were about to do. I wasn't sure which would hit harder.

We'd considered postponing our excursion until the next day, but neither of us wanted to wait. We hoped to accomplish our mission before the rain started, although all depended upon which came first, the storm or viable proof of the boy's existence.

Mark and his canoe led the way across the lake and around the island. We relied on memory and the brief intervals when the moon peeked around the clouds to create a slice of white over the water, but most of the time, I followed the faint sound of his paddling.

We arrived at Peller's property and maneuvered our watercraft into a shallow area near the house, securing them to trees while steering clear of the dock or any areas where he might spot us. We crept through the thick underbrush, branches and brambles snagging on dark clothing that masked as much white skin as possible. Despite the covering, the damp, cold air raised goosebumps on my skin.

Remaining quiet was difficult, yet I hoped the distant rumbling of thunder would cover any noise we made. We attempted to stay on mossy ground, but the moon only offered a dim light, and we couldn't risk using a flashlight.

Reaching the tree line, the house loomed before us. Through the immense windows, its warm lighting showcased white walls, contemporary furniture, and upscale appliances. The open-concept floor plan displayed the entire kitchen, eating area, and living room that offered a front-seat view of the water. Two rooms, presumably bedrooms, had lake-facing balconies on the second floor.

Graham Peller worked at the kitchen counter, seeming to chop something. He wore another tight-fitting white T-shirt that highlighted his muscular physique. I was certain an indoor gym occupied one of those rooms.

I crouched and brought the camera to my face, zooming in on the house's interior. Nothing out of place. Matching cushions sat symmetrically at each end of the couch. A coffee table had a tasteful centerpiece of dried flowers in a bowl. The kitchen counter held a minimum of clutter—the only appliances a toaster and a coffeemaker. No visible sign of a child's presence, and no one else in view. Did he prepare a meal for one or two?

"Stay here. I'll circle around to the other side."

I nodded in response to Mark's whisper, my throat dry. The plan seemed fragile, as if one wrong move might shatter it.

"We'll text each other once we get what we want or decide to give up," I said, keeping my voice soft and even.

He gave me a thumbs up before slipping out of sight, bending low as he disappeared amongst the trees. My pulse thudded against my ribs like a war drum. Alone in the forest's gloom with the swish of leaves and the hum of insects, I returned my attention to the house, my grip firm on the camera.

Movement caught my eye. Peller. He lowered his knife onto the counter and turned halfway, his posture tense. His head tilted, as if listening to someone behind him. I raised the camera, my finger hovering over the shutter button. I clicked once, twice, capturing the scene, as I waited for the boy's appearance. I hoped Mark got the same shot, or better, with his phone from a different angle.

Is Peller talking to someone or is he simply looking at something or listening for a sound? Did Mark make a noise to alert him?

Peller's arm shot up, gesturing toward the front door. My pulse spiked. He wasn't alone. He spoke to someone I couldn't see. He turned back to his chopping, the blade flashing in the light, but his lips moved, his gestures with the knife deliberate.

I held my breath, every nerve in my body taut with anticipation, not wanting to miss this crucial shot, like an assassin poised for the target to enter his sights. But instead of bullets, I had a digital camera with unlimited ammunition to capture a photo, every frame evidence that might tip the scales in my favor.

Click.

I took another shot, and then another, the shutter sounding like the flutter of a duck's wings as it lifted off the water. But the boy wasn't visible, not yet.

Come on. Show yourself.

There! A glimpse of a skinny arm in the hallway behind Peller. My finger pushed the shutter button repeatedly like a miniature jackhammer. I hoped I'd caught it, but I didn't hazard a glance at the screen.

"Please, let me get this," I said, unsure who I pleaded to. The need to prove the boy's existence to Mark drove me, coupled with the need to help a boy who might be in distress.

Thunder rumbled closer. Peller's body language changed, tensed like a wildcat catching the scent of prey. He set the knife on the counter with almost ceremonial care and stood perfectly still, listening. Then he turned, slowly, as if he knew someone was out there. *How could he?*

Chapter 21

A breath of relief escaped my lips when Peller retrieved a flashlight and what appeared to be candles from a cupboard. He prepared for a power outage, a common event on the island. Trees blew onto power lines, and electrical transformers were susceptible to lightning strikes.

I knew Mark and I needed to return to our cottages as soon as possible, but seeing Peller's lips move again rooted me to the spot. I was certain the boy would appear soon, perhaps looking for comfort from the oncoming storm.

A flash of lightning lit up the lake, the trees, and everything trying to hide within the area. I froze. The likelihood of being seen was slim, but I couldn't control the lightning or the storm, just like I couldn't control what we might discover inside the house. *Where's Mark? Is he well hidden?*

As the first raindrops fell, Peller strolled to the immense lake-facing window and stood like Zeus surveying his domain. His head turned in my direction, but barring more lightning flashes, he wouldn't see me. Moving his gaze to his right, he tilted his head as if something caught his interest. I prayed it wasn't Mark.

The skies opened, and the rain poured in sheets, the cold drops slicing through the tree canopy like needles. I pulled my coat's hood over my head and hunched forward. My fingers slipped on the camera, and I barely caught it before it hit the ground. Stashing it in a plastic bag, I wiped my eyes and squinted at the house, but everything blurred through the swaying branches and the raindrops glistening on the windows. Peller's figure wavered like a ghost behind glass.

I shifted my attention between Peller's movements and the rest of the house, hoping to catch another glimpse of the boy. I yearned to check the photos I'd taken, but I couldn't risk missing another opportunity to see him.

As Peller's gaze seemed to zero in on the area to his right, another lightning strike tore through the sky, with a booming thunderclap on its heels. He pivoted and marched down the hallway, obviously with a purpose in mind. Had he spotted Mark? Where did he go?

My phone buzzed in my pocket. I used my left hand to dim the screen's glow as I read the text.

COMING BACK TO U.

I wouldn't risk sending him a response.

A rustle to my right announced Mark's arrival. He almost lost his footing in the slick mud, only his face visible in his dark, hooded raincoat.

"What happened?" I said, raising my voice over the racket of the rain and wind.

"Not sure. He could've spotted me in the first flash, but I think I was well-hidden in the second." He squatted beside me, breathless. "We need to leave. With this storm…"

"I can't go yet. I saw something." If I didn't get this picture, everything would fall apart. Mark's belief in me, my chance to prove I hadn't lost my mind, and most of all, the boy's safety. If I left now, I'd abandon him to whatever fate waited behind those walls.

"Where?" Mark said, his intense gaze swinging toward the house.

"Inside. I'm sure it was the boy."

"Did you get a shot?"

"I don't know. I'll check later, but Peller was talking to someone. Did you see him?" I asked, seeking validation. Had I really seen the boy's arm, or had the storm and gloom conspired to show me what I wanted to see? I wanted to believe it so badly my mind might have conjured it. But what if it hadn't? What if I'd missed my only chance to save him?

"No. I couldn't find a place that wasn't directly in front of his window. You had the best spot here."

"We can't leave now anyway. It'd be stupid to be on the water during a thunderstorm." I grasped at any excuse to stay close to the boy, and it was a good one.

The rain dribbled down our faces and pounded against the leaves, a relentless drumbeat that muffled our voices but couldn't hide the concern in Mark's.

"We have to go," he said. "Now."

"Not yet." My eyes locked on the dark hallway where the boy had disappeared.

Another flash of lightning split the sky.

"We can walk home and come back for the kayak and canoe tomorrow." Mark's tone was insistent.

"You go, if you want. I'll wait it out, and this spot is as good as any."

"You're crazy if you think I'll leave you alone in this."

I wondered how close he was to the truth.

***

The fleece sweater clung to skin that was coated with a dampness I couldn't shake. The shivers came in waves. Not just from the cold, but from the knowledge sinking into my bones. I had nothing left to cling to. My life was a series of failed attempts. Failed marriage, failed career, failed photographs, failed mind.

I clasped my arms around my knees. Tears trickled down my bare legs.

Mark and I had huddled in the underbrush as the storm raged past us. I tensed with each lightning bolt and thunder crash, not a big fan of storms. But I found the alternative of sitting on the water like a soldier alone in an enemy field far more daunting. And Mark's suggestion to walk home appealed less than remaining close to the house, hoping for another glimpse of the boy.

As the storm headed toward the mainland, we pushed through the drenched woods, each step accompanied by the squelch of water in our shoes, the mud clutching our feet as if trying to hold us back. The icy wind sliced through my soaked clothes, making my teeth chatter, the cold sinking into my bones.

When we reached the shoreline, the kayak and canoe lay where we'd left them, wet and glistening in the distant flashes of light. I climbed into my kayak, every movement stiff and awkward from the chill. Hunched against the biting wind, I gripped the paddle in my icy fingers.

Mark took the lead, his silhouette barely visible in the darkness. I followed him across the churning lake, the water black and restless. Each stroke of the paddle felt heavier than the last, mirroring my spirit that sank lower with each additional meter between me and the boy. My dock's familiar outline emerged in the night's murkiness. We pulled up and clambered out, the boards slick beneath my feet. Fumbling with frozen fingers, we secured the kayak and canoe to keep the still fierce wind from carrying them away.

Inside the cottage, I tossed Mark a towel and excused myself as I closed the bedroom door. I peeled off my soaked clothes, my thoughts turning to what my camera might reveal. I grabbed sweatpants off a chair and yanked a fleece sweater over my head. As I opened the bedroom door, I spotted Mark toweling his hair, his chest bare, his wet jeans clinging to him.

"Want a coffee?" I asked, averting my gaze.

"No thanks. It'll keep me up. I'm good."

Grateful for the lack of delay, I pulled my camera from the sealed plastic bag and powered it up. Mark peered at the screen from behind me.

A sense of dread settled in my stomach as I scrolled through the images. Nothing. No trace of a skinny arm, no glimpse of the boy. I'd captured Peller looking over his shoulder, but no evidence he spoke to anyone.

"We'll have better luck next time," Mark said in an even tone.

Next time? Can I handle another failure?

I restrained the urge to hurl the camera across the room. Instead, I gently lowered it to the table and crossed to the kitchen sink. Turning on the tap, I let it run as I stared out the window, wanting to scream in frustration. Why couldn't I get my timing right?

A hand reached over my shoulder and shut off the tap. "We'll find another way," he said.

"No. I'm done." Those three small words held all the despair of the past three years. All the grief, the letdowns, the failures.

A long silence followed, and I turned, braced for an argument.

Mark slung his towel over a chair, and for a moment, he stood still, his gaze intense on my face. I sensed the words on his tongue, words that never came. Instead, he cleared his throat. "All right. I'll get going then. It's late." He pulled on his wet sweatshirt, collected his things, and mumbled a goodbye as the door closed behind him with a soft click.

I filled the kettle to brew a cup of tea. Even after I turned off the tap, the sound of water running filled my ears, an echo that wouldn't stop. Or maybe it wasn't water, perhaps the boy's voice murmured just out of reach.

I moved to the couch and clutched the blanket around me. Tears started, fueled by frustration and fear. Frustration over my botched attempts to get proof of the boy, over my ineptitude. In the past, I'd captured split-second shots of ducks touching down on the water, squirrels soaring through the air from tree to tree, a fish leaping from a river to capture a mosquito. Why couldn't I get a shot of the boy?

Yet, despite the depth of my frustration, fear overshadowed it. Was this it? Had the trauma I experienced three years ago sent me into a downward spiral, ending in this fiasco? Had I finally lost my mind?

Did I imagine the boy? Peller insisted his son was dead. Mark found the documentation to confirm it. No one else had seen the boy on the dock. Only me. The pictures in the fog showed no hint of a person, someone I'd supposedly seen with my own eyes. I was the only one to witness Peller talking to someone tonight. The only one to see a small boy's arm. Did my eyes deceive me? Had my brain finally tipped the scale, plunging me over the brink into madness?

I couldn't count the number of times I'd thought of Abby since her death, reminisced about her, dreamed of her, heard her voice in my mind. But I'd never seen her as a ghostly spirit. I'd never imagined her spectral presence amongst a crowd, or in a schoolyard, or on a dock. My sanity had seemed intact. Why these doubts now?

It could be easier to leave Abby in the past, safe in my memories, safe from the mess I'd become. But this boy had clawed his way into my thoughts, dragging my grief out into the open. Real or just another cruel twist of my mind? Either way, he stirred something in me, something I couldn't control. I let myself fall into a horizontal position on the couch, the tears dry on my cheeks.

I'd experienced an emotional upheaval with the divorce and the subsequent move from my home. Could that have sparked these episodes? Were the changes, including Abby's death, too much for me? Was this what insanity looked like, felt like? Was it even possible to recognize insanity in yourself?

What if I'm already well on my way? What if this is how it starts, the blurry images, the ghostly visions, the desperate need to believe in things that aren't there? Was this a variation of the blackout I'd had that fateful day? How did you know when your mind turned against you? Did you notice it happening, or did you only realize it after it was too late?

The familiar sensation of sinking into a depressive state surrounded me. An emptiness expanded inside me as fatigue took hold. What was the point of my life? I had no one. The daughter I adored was gone forever. I'd driven away the husband I'd once loved so deeply. My career seemed unsustainable. My friends had distanced themselves. Mark, the one friend I seemed to have, was clearly done with me.

Rock bottom had jumped up to meet me, slapping me in the face. My psyche resorted to creating imaginary children in need of rescue by a washed-up, grief-stricken woman. It couldn't get much worse than this.

I collapsed inward, my body caving under the sorrow. I half-hoped morning wouldn't come.

Chapter 22

At first, I thought the banging came from inside my head, like the echo of thunder carried over from the night before, until I realized it didn't make sense. My heart leaped into my throat as I sat upright, disoriented, scanning the room for a source. The pounding came again, this time from the front door.

Mark. It had to be Mark.

With a quick glance out the living room window, I saw the early morning mist coating the lake, resisting the sunrise's efforts to shove it aside.

Unprepared when I swung open the door, I lost another precious moment when I failed to immediately recognize Graham Peller as the man who glowered at me from my porch. He reeked of sweat and dampness, his jaw clenched so tight I imagined his teeth grinding. His eyes, bloodshot and wild, locked onto mine with a hatred that pinned me to the spot. He waved his fist in front of my face, and for a brief second, I thought he intended to hit me with his bare knuckles.

"I've had enough of you," he bellowed. "I know it was you on my property last night."

I blinked at him, too taken aback to reply, but he never gave me the opportunity. I recoiled to avoid a blow as he brandished a flashlight at me.

"Admit this is yours." Red splotches covered his face, and his chest heaved with each labored breath.

The flashlight swung dangerously close to my head again, and before I could react, Peller took a step forward, his boots heavy on the wooden floor.

Not just shouting from the threshold anymore. Inside my bubble, he crowded me, his coffee-scented breath warm on my face. My pulse hammered, and I stepped back, the edge of the kitchen table pressing into me.

I could push past him and run. Would he chase me? Would I get away? If I stayed, could I outwit him? My muscles locked, refusing to commit either way. My thoughts took the same path. I didn't respond, recognizing the flashlight as mine but choosing not to share that information.

His hot breath slapped my face again. "I don't know what's wrong with you, but you better stay away from me and my property. I warned you last time, and I'll warn you again. I'll call the police. You're a nutcase."

I held my tongue. I'd already come to the same conclusion the night before. He told me nothing new.

He was right. I had no business sneaking around his house. But what if I was right? What if the boy was real, and I was the only person who cared enough to save him? I wanted to argue, to confront Peller about the boy, but the look in his eyes told me any word I said might shatter the thin barrier between his rage and control.

"I've put up with enough crackpots in my life to recognize one," he said, unabated. "It's enough to lose a son." His voice cracked for the briefest second before the fury returned. "But someone like you poking around, stirring things up... do you know what that does to a man? You think you know everything, don't you? Well, I know things too, and I know exactly what to do with them."

The mention of his son knocked the wind out of me, as if he'd reached into my chest and ripped out something raw and aching. It clouded everything else he said and did, taking over my mind.

I knew what it was to lose a child. The circumstances were somewhat different, but that didn't make the pain any less real. I almost wanted to tell him I understood, but the hatred and pain in his eyes told me he wouldn't hear or care about anything I said.

Before Peller turned to leave, he leaned in close, his lips almost brushing my ear. "Back off, if you know what's good for you." Menace filled his voice. "Or next time, you won't walk away."

He stepped back, gave me a long, hard look, and walked off the porch. I stood frozen, watching him disappear into the morning mist. A chill ran down my spine but not from the cold; I sensed I'd missed something, something important and dangerous, and whatever Peller was hiding would only get worse the closer I got.

I locked the door behind him, testing the deadbolt three times just to be certain. My knees gave out, and I sank to the floor, my hands shaking uncontrollably. The adrenaline buzzed under my skin, but I couldn't move off the floor. All I thought about was the look in Peller's eyes, the look of a man who'd already decided what he'd do next.

Chapter 23

I sank onto the couch with wobbly limbs. Despite my pride in standing up to him without breaking, the confrontation took its toll on me.

Graham Peller didn't need to worry about me trespassing again. I had no desire to go anywhere near his place. The few times I'd met him had already driven me to the brink of madness. I didn't need a final push over the edge. I swiped my hands over my face. No, I'd stick to the real reason why I was here. To find peace and prepare for a new life on my own.

I dug deep within myself and made a mental list of all I had to be grateful for, a practice recommended by my therapist, and despite the shortness of the list, it helped. My night's sleep, even with the rude awakening, had also improved my inner state. After some deep breathing exercises and an attempt at meditation—another recommendation—I felt ready to set aside my thoughts of the boy and get on with my life, such as it was.

"I'll give my clients more attention, enjoy leisure time on the water, and discover the bike trails," I said, making a vow to myself. "When my stay here is over, I'll move into my apartment and begin a new life." Saying it out loud felt more like a commitment, hopefully one I'd respect.

But first, I needed to shed some guilt. I'd treated Mark badly. I would apologize, explain my decision to withdraw from our project, and we'd both move on. If we remained friends for the duration of my rental, that was fine. If not, I'd get along perfectly well on my own.

After reaping the benefits of a strong coffee, I made my way through the woods toward Mark's cottage. I noticed we'd created a path that hadn't existed when I'd first arrived here. It would likely return to its natural state after the summer.

When I emerged from the cover of trees onto his property, my gaze instinctively slid to the dock, expecting to see Mark perched upon it, fishing rod in hand, the image of calm I'd come to associate with him. The pier stood empty under the hazy sunlight, and a pang of disappointment struck me as my eyes shifted toward the driveway. His car wasn't there.

He could've gone for groceries, or work might've called him away. The explanations did little to soothe the frustration of not fulfilling my task. He'd be back, but I'd have to muster the courage to face him again. With a sigh, I turned and retraced my steps to the cottage.

Grabbing my paddle and kayak, I decided a circuit around the lake would ease my agitation. I avoided the island and Peller's dock, steering toward the quieter waters at the far end. Each dip of the paddle chipped away at my frustration. By the second lap, a sense of calm settled over me, the rhythm of my strokes steadying my thoughts.

After a light lunch, I fetched the bike from the shed and set off for the trails. As I wheeled past Mark's cottage, I slowed, glancing toward the windows. Still no sign of him, the driveway empty. Where was he? I pushed the question aside with a shake of my head. He'd surely be home by the time I returned.

Two hours later, exhilarated from the trails and sticky with sweat, I rolled back into the driveway. Again, my gaze strayed toward Mark's place as if drawn by some unseen force. Nothing. And, most importantly, why did I care? I'd known him a few days. He wasn't obliged to report his whereabouts to me, just as I did as I pleased when I pleased. I needed to shrug off whatever dependance I'd developed. In a matter of weeks, I'd be gone, and our paths would likely never cross again.

Early evening, after a day of languishing without a moment dedicated to my work, I relaxed on the dock's edge, legs dangling in the lake's cool water. The approaching dusk attracted hordes of mosquitoes who claimed the space as their own, their incessant buzzing and biting driving me to admit defeat. The water's surface rippled with fish snapping at the tiny invaders. I pulled my legs from the lake, relinquishing the battle and my spot to the pests.

Pivoting toward the cottage, I recoiled in shock, my hand to my heart. "Oh God, you scared me," I said.

"Sorry. I thought you heard me." Dressed in long, beige chino pants and a button-up shirt, Mark looked like he'd been working.

"You're back. I guess you went to the office." I felt the heat in my cheeks as I realized I'd admitted looking for him.

"I visited a client in Victoria. Took care of some other things at the same time."

I narrowed my eyes at his smug expression. He was hiding something. And proud of it.

"What's up?"

He chuckled and gestured toward the chairs on the porch. "Sit. I'll explain."

My curiosity piqued, I scrambled up the bank and followed him to the porch.

"Like I said, I went to Victoria." Mark settled into a chair and leaned back, his manner relaxed. "Got a friend there, Dustin, a journalist. He's got access to all kinds of software and connections. I asked him to dig around for me."

I suspected the digging concerned Graham Peller. My earlier resolve to abandon everything to do with him and the boy vanished like smoke in the wind. I moved to the edge of my seat, eager for Mark to continue.

"He uncovered the same details we did about the drowning in Winnipeg. The belief is that the boy slipped off the dock, hit his head, and drowned. It split the couple apart; they divorced. But what we didn't know is Peller and his son had a strained relationship."

"Strained? What do you mean?"

"Peller believed in strict discipline. The boy lived a military existence. Up at the same hour every morning, his bed needed to be made just so; he had to eat every speck of food placed before him, do his many chores to perfection. All of this from a very young age."

"How did Dustin find all this?" I asked, narrowing my eyes.

Mark shrugged. "He has his ways. Journalists know how and where to dig. Who do you think taught me how to find all that info I got?"

Images of a young boy standing at attention beside a military cot flooded my mind, causing the knot to return to my chest. No child should live like that.

"His wife had been on the brink of leaving Peller but was worried about custody," Mark said, snagging my attention. "She didn't want her son left in his care, even part time. When the boy died, she had no reason to hang around."

"Do they suspect Peller of killing his son?" I almost choked on the horrible words.

"No proof. Ruled it an accident. I'll send you the file. You can read it for yourself." Mark's tone was casual. Was it because he didn't feel the same horror, or he'd had more time to absorb the information?

I leaned back in my chair, my mind racing. The hand-drawn picture the boy gave me shot to the forefront, quickly followed by the image of Graham Peller raging at my front door that morning, capable of violence, and yes, even madness. Or was I attributing those traits to him, now that I'd heard Mark's story?

"There's one thing Dustin mentioned I found strange," Mark said, rubbing his neck. "Peller's son hated the water. His mother said he'd scream if anyone tried to get him near a lake or a pool."

A wave of dread crept over me. The boy I'd seen hadn't seemed afraid. He'd stood on the dock, staring out at the water like it called to him. But it wasn't the same boy. I needed to keep that straight. Nathan Peller was dead, not the boy I saw.

I pinned my gaze on Mark. "What's your take? Do you think he's a criminal?" I shook my head, not allowing him to answer, throwing my hands in the air. "But that doesn't explain the boy. All it does is make me worry more. If a boy is in that house, he's in danger."

Mark's eyes narrowed. "If? You saw him. We know he's there."

I desperately wanted to believe Mark. His words were like a life preserver in a storm, dragging me through the water toward some version of sanity.

But what if he was wrong? What if I'd imagined it all, every flash of the boy's face, every movement he'd made? Peller told me I'd lost my mind.

Tears welled up, and I struggled to hold them back. Mark spoke with such conviction, a conviction I'd almost lost. I curled my fingers around the edge of the chair until my knuckles ached. The tears burned hot in my eyes, and I couldn't decide whether I wanted to cry or scream. My chest ached, like I'd held my breath since the boy first appeared, waiting for something to prove my sanity.

"I'm the only witness," I said. "You didn't see him. He didn't show up in any pictures. I just don't know anymore."

"You don't know? You know what you saw, and I believe you."

I met his steady gaze with my tear-filled one. "Thank you. You don't know how much I appreciate the vote of confidence, but I decided this morning I'd back off." I scoffed at the memory of Graham Peller using those very words. "He visited me this morning."

"Who? Peller?" Mark's voice held a trace of alarm, his eyes wide as he faced me.

"He found a flashlight on his property this morning. I guess he already suspected someone was there last night and went searching for proof. I don't know. Anyway, he correctly assumed it was mine and that I spied on him last night. He wasn't amused. Actually, he was furious. Threatened to call the police."

Mark inhaled a deep, steadying breath, his jaw clenching. "He better not try that again when I'm around. After my talk with Dustin today, I'm certain we're dealing with a dangerous person, maybe even a murderer."

The word murderer hit like a stone. My stomach somersaulted, and for a moment, I couldn't breathe. If Mark was right, the boy wasn't just at risk, he was in imminent danger. The powerful realization sank in.

A clarity surged through me, cutting through the fog of doubt and fear that had clouded my mind. I believed in the boy again, not as a product of grief, but as something real, someone who needed help. I believed in the urgency of saving him. Most surprisingly, I believed in myself.

***

That night, I endured yet another episode of insomnia. My mind was a whirlwind, thoughts flitting from the boy, to Mark, to Peller, and as usual, to Abby.

Tired of tossing and turning, I got up and pulled on my sweatpants and a light jacket to ward off the chilly post-midnight air. Hands buried in my jacket pockets, I strolled to the dock, my sneakers squeaking on the dew-coated wood.

The full moon reflected on the water, the lake's stillness transforming it into a mirror. Such beauty amazed me, as nature often did. We took so much for granted, but taking the time to admire the world around us made us appreciate what we had. I loved this spot, despite the cottage's near dilapidation. I'd miss it when the time came. Yet, even with its current condition, a place like this wasn't affordable for me. Waterfront properties were worth a fortune. Only sheer luck and Keith's connections allowed me to rent this place for the summer months.

I lowered myself into a cross-legged position on the dock and tuned into the symphony of crickets chirping and bullfrogs croaking. An owl hooted from a tall tree. Everything was motionless without even a breeze to cause a stir.

I relished this tranquility that my suburban apartment would never give me. My new symphony would be the near-constant movements of neighbors and vehicles, the shrieks of young children, and the cheery shouts of adults. I'd have difficulty recreating this peacefulness.

A bone-chilling scream shattered it.

Chapter 24

My heart thudded as I wondered what creature emitted such a horrible sound. It was even more dreadful than the one I heard a few days ago. If it was a bobcat, surely another, larger animal had captured it.

The Shadow Woman's story popped into my mind. Was the legend true? Was she calling the children? I couldn't imagine a sound so eerie and frightening being used to lure children. It had to be an animal.

But when it pierced the night again, I recognized it as unmistakably human. A prolonged, "No!" stretched along the lake's length.

Every muscle in my body tensed. Sounds echoed and bounced off water and trees. It could come from any direction. Yet, my instincts told me it came from Graham Peller's house. And it was the boy's scream.

Like a gunshot had fired at the start of a race, I jumped to my feet and dashed across the lawn and through the woods. I landed on the wooden porch with a thump a split-second before I banged on the door. A wide-eyed, disheveled Mark stared at me in confusion when he swung it open.

"What the hell? What's going on?"

"I heard a scream. I'm sure it's him." I pointed a shaky arm toward Peller's house.

"Who?"

"Him. The boy." I bounced on the balls of my feet, desperate for Mark to wake up and help me. "Something terrible happened. He needs help." I wanted him to come with me, the memory of Peller's raging threats still fresh in my mind.

Mark ran his hands through his already-mussed hair and glanced down at his bare feet under pajama pants, his torso bare. "Give me a second," he said, finally getting the message. He disappeared into the cottage while I paced on the porch, ears straining for more screams. Was the silence a good sign? My imagination ran in circles, picturing the boy lying dead or injured, too injured to scream anymore.

Mark barreled outside, now in jeans and a T-shirt, a jacket clutched in his hand. He slammed the door behind him, the sound reverberating through the night air.

"We'll take my jeep," he said, leaping down the steps two at a time.

I didn't argue. My heart thundered so loudly, I didn't trust myself behind the wheel, especially on these pitch-black country roads. I slid into the passenger seat and fumbled with the seat belt, my fingers trembling. Mark didn't wait. The moment the door slammed shut, he floored the accelerator, tires spinning on loose gravel before gripping the road.

My hands clutched the dashboard as he tore around corners and over hills, the jeep's engine growling in protest. Every twist and turn seemed sharper, every bump more jarring, but Mark didn't ease up, his sense of urgency overriding everything.

He swerved to the shoulder near Peller's driveway, the jeep skidding to a stop, gravel crunching beneath the tires like bones snapping.

I didn't wait for the engine to die before throwing open the door. Cold night air hit me as I scrambled from the jeep and sprinted toward the house, anxiety drowning out every rational thought. Mark's footsteps pounded behind me.

"Wait," he said, gasping. "We can't barge in there if we're not sure."

I swung around, fury raging inside me. "Don't you dare say it's in my head. I'm sure of what I heard. A child's scream. It came from here."

"What if it didn't? What if it came from somewhere else?"

I clasped my fist to my chest. "I've never been surer of anything in my life."

"There's nothing now." Mark studied the house, veiled in darkness, only one outside light illuminating the yard. "No sign of anything."

I didn't stop to second-guess my actions. I stalked to the door and hammered it with my fist. "Open up, Peller," I shouted.

An interior light flashed on, and footsteps thundered on stairs, growing louder until the door swung open. Graham Peller stood before me, his expression shifting from confusion to shock to fury in an instant.

"What..."

"Where is he?" I said, stepping closer, my voice sharp. "I heard him scream. We're going into the house."

The shock flashed across his face again before the mask of fury returned. "You're crazy. What are you talking about?"

He took a menacing step toward me. Before I could react, Mark moved, just a shift in his stance, but it was enough. Peller's attention darted to him, his gaze narrowing as if he'd only just registered Mark standing there. He froze in place.

"Get out of here," Graham said to me, his voice thick with malice. "I've already warned you."

"I heard him scream," I repeated.

"You're delusional. You think you can barge in here and throw crazy accusations around? I'll call the cops."

"Go ahead. I'll be happy to wait for them." I crossed my arms over my chest in which my heart slammed fiercely. The tension crackled between us like a live wire.

Graham changed tacks and shifted his attention to Mark. "Who are you? I suggest you take your deranged friend and leave."

I sensed Mark moving closer to my side, but my gaze remained on Peller's face. A trace of fear crossed his features. Did Mark frighten him? With odds of two against one, I guessed we could handle him if it came to blows. Or did his fear stem from the fact we may have discovered his secret?

I transferred my gaze to the house, searching for a small face peering through a window, pleading for help. Peller shifted to block my view.

"Leave me alone." His voice registered as a low growl.

I swiveled and headed toward the jeep, slipping my cell phone from my back pocket as I walked. I clutched the device with slick palms, my fingers fumbling across the screen as if I'd lost control of them. The man answered on the first ring.

"What is your emergency?"

"I heard a child screaming. I believe he's in danger."

Gasps of surprise and anger rose from behind me. I wanted the police to come, search that house, and find the boy. The only solution. I relayed my location to the 9-1-1 operator and said I'd be present when they arrived.

Peller's chest heaved with rage as I faced him. "You'll regret this," he said, a quiver in his voice. "They'll lock you up."

Mark and I lingered in the shadows of the tall, majestic elm trees as Peller retreated inside. The earthy scent of damp leaves and lake water surrounded us, but all I could focus on was the house. My eyes never wavered, scanning every window searching for movement, every room for a change in lighting. Each second stretched on forever, my mind ricocheting between doubts.

What if I'd imagined the scream? What if it was just an animal, after all? Or worse, a hallucination, another symptom of my crumbling mind? But no. The scream had been real. It had to be real. I needed to believe that.

Peller emerged from the house, his figure hunched as he settled onto the steps. Mark touched my arm and guided me toward a garden bench nestled in the shade of some evergreens. I couldn't sit. My legs vibrated with restless energy, and I paced as Mark's patient gaze followed my movements. No one spoke aloud, but I whispered under my breath, begging the authorities to hurry. My fear for the boy's well-being increased with each second that passed.

Then, distant but unmistakable, came the flash of red and blue lights cutting through the darkness. Relief and dread battled within me as the white RCMP vehicle navigated the driveway, its tires crunching on the gravel. The officers hadn't used their sirens, perhaps because of the late hour, but the sense of urgency in their arrival was evident.

I moved into view, eager to tell them about the endangered child in the house and the fact his life was at stake. The two officers stepped from the vehicle, their hands poised on their holstered firearms as they scanned the area and the trio involved in the standoff.

"Ms. Hampton?" the older officer asked, looking at me. Tall and slender, his short, graying hair reflected the lights from their vehicle.

I stepped closer. "Yes. I made the call."

"You reported a child screaming? Where is he or she?"

Peller descended the steps and rushed toward the cop, his face flushed with anger. "Officer, this woman is…"

"Stand back, sir. We'll get to you." The other officer's muscular physique and combative stance stopped Peller in his tracks, but the curling of Peller's lips made clear how unpleasant he found it to submit to someone else's authority.

The first cop turned back to me and nodded, urging me to continue. I explained where I lived and what I'd heard.

"What makes you think the scream came from here?"

"Yeah, explain that to him please," Peller said with a sarcastic sneer and a dismissive gesture. "She wanders the woods at night, spying on people. A grieving woman, imagining things…you can't really blame her, I guess."

His taunts hit their mark, exposing my fears and insecurities to everyone. I took a deep breath and gathered my resolve. "I saw a boy on the dock here, twice, but he always runs away. And no children live nearby. He has to be in the house." A hint of doubt crossed the cop's face. "He refuses to let us in to see if anyone's there." I waved a hand in Peller's direction.

"These people are trespassing, and it's not the first time. She snuck around here late last night. She's a nutcase. Insists I have a child here, and I don't." Sarcasm gone, rage re-entered Peller's tone.

The cop studied Peller for a long moment before facing me. "Any chance you made a mistake?" the officer asked, his polite words clashing with the irritation in his tone. I saw a trace of a condescending smile, a warning that he thought I'd wasted their time.

"I know what I heard." I spoke through gritted teeth, barely holding onto my patience, tired of walking down this road. "Could you look, please? He could be hurt or worse, and we're just standing here, doing nothing."

The cop held up a hand to block my outburst and addressed Peller. "Do you mind if we look around?"

Peller's answering smirk grated on my nerves. "Not at all. Feel free."

The infuriating man watched me in a certain way, as if he knew exactly how to push me to the edge. Like he enjoyed seeing me unravel. I fought to hide my confusion. *What is he doing? Did he hide the boy so well they had no chance of finding him?*

I took a step to follow the cop inside with Peller, but his partner shook his head and waved for me to wait with him. I paced again, feeling the situation slip through my fingers, the boy drifting further out of reach.

The wait stretched into an eternity, each second undoing my confidence thread by thread. I imagined the boy huddled in a corner, just out of reach, praying for someone to find him before it was too late.

Chapter 25

My frustration level reached an all-time high. Two brutal laps around the lake in my kayak hadn't burned through it. Neither had mowing the lawn at a breakneck pace. The flower garden was next. Then I planned to bike until my legs gave out.

Following the debacle at Peller's house, I'd fallen asleep around four in the morning, exhaustion overtaking me after I replayed every detail. The cops had emerged from the house with grim expressions, declaring they'd found no trace of a boy or anyone else.

Peller, with a triumphant sneer and smarmy arrogance, graciously agreed not to press trespassing charges against us, provided we stayed off his property. The police officers did their part by giving me a stern warning to obey that condition, as if I were a child incapable of understanding the simplest things.

I clenched my fists when they gave Mark a look that said, "Keep the little woman in check." My back stiff, Mark steered me toward the jeep with a hand on my elbow. Tears of anger filled my eyes, but I refused to let them fall. I shot one last glance at Peller standing smugly alongside the cops as we left the driveway.

In the jeep, I bristled to vent my fury, but my thoughts were so jumbled and my rage so hot I couldn't voice anything coherent. Instead, I sat in strained silence, my body trembling. The engine hummed, but it wasn't enough to drown out the roaring in my ears. Mark kept his eyes on the road, reminding me I wasn't alone, but it did little to soothe me.

I finally blurted, "You don't believe me." I shocked myself with the statement. After everything that'd happened, from hearing the scream to the condescension I'd gotten from Peller and the police, my first reaction was to lash out at Mark.

"I didn't say that." His tone held an element of anger, but I didn't know who he directed it at.

"It's obvious."

"No, it's not. You're angry and frustrated. I get that. So am I. I don't know how to handle this. I've got a lot of thinking to do."

I blew out a long breath. "Fair enough. Me too."

We conducted the short drive in silence, exchanging nods and weak smiles when he dropped me off at my cottage. I hadn't seen him since. My heart and spirit were at a loss. Where did the scream come from? I had to believe the police combed the house and found nothing. Surely, if it existed, they would've found evidence of foul play. My mind scurried in every direction, and I couldn't calm it. Thus, all the activity to burn off frustration and organize my thoughts.

I yanked off my gardening gloves and grabbed the bike from where I'd left it leaning against the cottage, swinging my leg over to mount it. I steered onto the main road and headed for the trails. The tires' hum on the pavement and my legs' rhythmic effort gave me focus and a break from my churning thoughts.

As I passed Mark's cottage, I glanced toward his driveway. His jeep was gone again. Probably another day with clients. A small lump formed in my chest as the memory of last night and our disastrous episode with Peller and the cops threatened to invade my thoughts again. I shook it off and pushed harder on the pedals, heading toward a trail Mark had told me about, one that wound through the woods, demanding and rarely used. My mood was ready for a challenge.

I veered off the main road onto a narrow trail of hard-packed earth with trees and brush lining each side, needing to keep my eyes open for rocks and roots that dotted the terrain.

My thighs burned as the path steepened, and the bike wobbled with each push. At the summit, I stopped, chest heaving, sweat dampening my shirt. I guzzled water as I took in the view. The Pacific Ocean stretched endlessly into the distance, a vast expanse of shimmering blue that met the sky at the horizon. The air was crisp and bracing, filled with the scent of sun-warmed trees. I noticed the slow release of my tension.

I eyed the path, a sharp descent ending in a curve. I considered turning around. After all, I'd have to make that climb on the way back, but I decided to forge on, no longer interested in half measures. I had energy to burn.

My fingers gripped the handlebars, and I pushed off. The first section began with a slight decline, followed by a sharp dip, along with a few rocks and roots that kept me focused. I felt a twinge of regret about my decision to continue but intended to see it through.

As the hill steepened, I gathered speed, and that regret intensified. I squeezed the brakes and noticed them responding, until there was a sharp, metallic snap. The handles went slack in my hands. My heart lurched as the bike shot forward, gaining momentum with every split second.

"Damn it!" Panic laced my voice as a blur of green and brown filled my vision. I gritted my teeth, steering frantically to avoid jutting roots and rocks. The tires bounced hard on the uneven ground, jolting me from my seat as my feet lifted off the pedals. My hands gripped the handlebars in desperation.

Ahead, a towering tree loomed, an immovable reality. The trail veered to the right, but I'd never make it. I twisted the handlebars sharply to the left and prayed for control. The bike skidded sideways. The back tire hit a boulder, and I was airborne, the ground vanishing beneath me. My arms instinctively covered my head. I heard myself scream as I prayed to avoid crashing into solid wood or rock.

Chapter 26

A tangle of brush cushioned my fall. Branches clawed at me as I descended toward the ground, but a rock waited for me at the end, my left hip taking the brunt of the collision, the impact wrenching a strangled cry from my throat. Somewhere behind me, the bike landed with a metallic crash. I lay still, lungs heaving, my body buzzing with sharp stings and throbbing aches.

Motionless, I let the terror ebb and began a slow, cautious inventory of my battered body. Fingers flexed. Toes wiggled. My arms and legs responded, though every movement caused a dull ache or sharp pain. Nothing seemed broken, but I expected several bruises, scrapes, and sore muscles. I thanked my lucky stars. It could've been much worse.

I groaned as I braced my arms to push myself upright. Pain flared through my hip, sharp enough to bring tears to my eyes, but I stood, albeit hunched and unsteady. Each step sent jolts of pain through my limbs.

The bushes that saved me proved an unexpected challenge as I scrambled out. Thorny branches clung to my clothes and scratched fresh lines across my arms as I forced my way through. By the time I emerged, panting and sweat-soaked, it seemed as if I'd fought a battle. And lost.

My gaze drifted down the hill to where the bike lay crumpled against the massive tree I'd avoided. I'd fared better than it. The handlebars were twisted at an unnatural angle, the chain dangling limply. The frame looked warped and beyond repair.

I limped toward it. My scraped palms stung with each brush of movement, and my breaths were so shallow they barely filled my lungs. I bit back curses with each crunch of gravel under my feet. Muscles burned and bruises throbbed, but I refused to stop.

I stood over the bike's wreckage and grimaced. It wasn't mine, but most importantly, I wanted to know what went wrong. Was it the brakes? The trail? Me? Pain shot through my hip again as I bent to inspect it. I didn't want to leave it here. I needed to sort this out.

A tree supported my weight as I contemplated my return to the cottage. A definite challenge. The faint rustle of leaves and the snap of a twig seemed loud, intensified by the forest's emptiness. Even the breeze had died, creating a strange stillness. I felt alone and exposed, as if dark spirits in the trees watched and waited for my next move. I swept my gaze around me, peering in the bushes, wondering if an animal or human lurked there.

A desperate need to escape filled me, to return to my safe, decrepit cottage. I shoved myself away from the tree, gripped the bicycle's twisted handlebars, and studied the path ahead.

As I pushed off, climbing the hill seemed like scaling a cliff, each step unbearable. My hip throbbed like a drumbeat, and the bike seemed to have gained weight. Its warped frame caught on roots and rocks, creating resistance. Sweat trickled down my face, stinging the scratches, but I gritted my teeth and forced myself onward despite my trembling legs.

My water bottle lay on the trail, confirming I was headed in the right direction. With shaking hands and a groan, I scooped it up and gulped greedily, the lukewarm water soothing my parched throat.

The hill loomed ahead, taunting me with its steep incline. My body screamed for rest, but I wouldn't surrender.

The slope eventually gave way to flat ground, and I staggered toward it with a final, shaky push. The moment I reached the crest, I nearly dropped the bike from sheer exhaustion.

The sight of the main road brought tears to my eyes. I aimed toward my cottage with shaky limbs.

The sound of crunching gravel behind me jolted me from my dazed trek. I looked over my shoulder to see Mark's jeep pull to the roadside. He slid from the vehicle and jogged toward me, his expression concerned.

"What happened?" His gaze moved in astonishment from me to the mangled bike. "Are you okay?"

"I lost control on a hill. Nothing's broken. Just really sore."

He peeled my fingers off the handlebars and let the bike tumble to the ground with a crash. "C'mon. I'll drive you home." His gentle hold on my elbow guided me toward the jeep.

"I don't want to leave the bike," I said, even as I realized I held irrational concern for the scrap metal.

"I'll come back for it," he said, not slowing his forward motion. "No one'll steal it."

I winced as I lifted my aching leg to step up into the jeep. My fingers gripped the doorframe, knuckles white. When I sank into the seat, I let out a shuddering breath, the soft leather hugging me.

Mark climbed into the driver's seat and threw me a quick glance containing equal parts concern and reassurance before slipping the jeep into gear. It eased forward, slow and careful as if one sharp bump might break me. I stared out the window, watching the passing trees, and concentrated on holding myself upright.

Minutes later, the jeep rolled to a stop outside my cottage. Mark came around to my side and opened the door, leaning across me to unfasten my seat belt.

"Easy," he said, his voice low and calm.

I winced again as he helped me out, his arm braced under mine, steadying me. The short climb to the porch steps felt like a mountain, but Mark matched my halting pace.

By the time we reached the door, my body shook from exhaustion. He guided me inside and lowered me onto the couch.

"Made it," he said, a small smile flickering across his face.

I let out a long breath and sank back into the cushions.

"Where does it hurt?" he asked, kneeling before me as I emitted a low groan.

"Almost everywhere, but my hip took a beating. Nothing broken, though." I hoped he'd leave soon. I wanted to suffer alone.

"I'll take you to the hospital. You need x-rays."

"I'm good. I need to soak in a hot bath and lie down. I'll be right as rain."

"Julie…"

I held up a hand. "Honestly. I won't spend hours sitting in a hospital waiting room to be told to go home and take a hot bath and lie down."

Mark's touch was gentle as he examined my scratches and bruises, his brow furrowed with genuine concern, but a part of me resisted, stiffening under his touch. I didn't want to see the tenderness in his gaze. And was there something else? A trace of guilt? A hesitation? Was he holding back, wanting to tell me something, or was I reading too much into it? The trust between us was new and fragile.

"Can I get you anything?" He stood, wringing his hands, as if uncertain what to do.

"The bike, please. I want to know what happened."

"What do you mean? You said you lost control." His voice rose slightly in alarm.

"Yes. Because I had no brakes."

His eyes widened. "I checked the brakes. They were fine."

"Not today they weren't."

He jumped to his feet and headed out the door, his stride determined. I let out an enormous groan of pain, relieved to have a brief period to wallow in my misery alone.

Ten minutes later, Mark returned, letting himself into the cottage. I hadn't budged from my spot on the couch. I didn't think I could.

He carefully lowered himself beside me, and I anticipated the words that would come out of his mouth. "It looks like someone tampered with the brakes."

I nodded, his revelation not surprising me. "I wonder who."

Chapter 27

Anxiety ate at me, clawing at my mind. Were we overreacting? Had I sped too fast, or was it just a fluke, a one-in-a-million mechanical failure? But the word "coincidence" tasted like poison.

A muscle tightened in Mark's jaw, and his eyes narrowed. "I have something to tell you." His tone made my tension inch upward. "I met with Peller's ex. She had a lot to say."

Mark's voice was low, disturbed. He seemed to avoid my gaze, his hand fiddling with his key chain. What exactly had he learned? I remained calm, but a bad feeling settled in.

"Like what?" I asked. "We already know Peller was a control freak with his son."

"Yes, and she confirmed that. His abuse extended to her as well."

The word set off alarm bells. "He beat her?" The thought shocked me, but it shouldn't come as a surprise, not after my run-ins with Graham Peller.

"I believe it was verbal abuse. Bad enough."

The room seemed to grow smaller, the walls pressing in. My heart thudded as I absorbed this news. I knew firsthand how words could tear a person apart without leaving a visible scar. I pictured Peller with his icy stare and twisted smile exerting that kind of power against his wife and child. My stomach curdled at the thought of being married to such a man.

I studied Mark's worrisome expression. "What is it? What are you not telling me?"

He sighed. "I got some of Peller's history. He's ex-military. Did some missions in Bosnia and other war-torn countries. Suffered PTSD and was discharged."

Graham Peller wasn't just a man with a bad temper or a cruel streak. He'd been trained and something broke him along the way.

"So, he's dangerous," I said quietly. My mind spiraled through every encounter I'd had with Peller. I thought of the boy, of the scream I'd heard. Evidence that somewhere in that house, someone suffered. I didn't know how Peller hid him from the police or how he'd silenced him, but nothing the cops said would convince me the boy wasn't there.

I empathized with people who had mental health issues, but did that justify treating your son like a small soldier or abusing your spouse? Could his symptoms have driven him to kill his son?

Peller's history didn't give him a free pass for abuse. His wife had a choice to leave the relationship. His son didn't. And my biggest fear was that another boy was his next victim.

***

The reflection of the swirling clouds turned the lake into a churning black void. Mist clung to the trees, to the ground, to every surface, seeping into the cottage's walls as if nature wrapped me in a damp cocoon.

My computer screen provided the only light in the room, but my unfocused gaze fell past it to the lake. It had been too dismal a day to spend outdoors, and I still ached from my biking trauma the day before. Bruises bloomed on almost every part of my body. It took several minutes of groaning and shuffling around the cottage to ease my stiff muscles, and I still walked with a slight limp.

No, today presented me with an opportunity to put in a few hours' work. Yet my spirit dragged my mind away to reflect on all I'd learned about Peller so far, worrying about the boy, trying to untangle the mystery surrounding him. Those reflections ate up the last hours of daylight.

I jolted when my cell phone jangled beside my elbow. I so rarely received calls, preferring to communicate by email or text. A full three seconds passed before my brain recognized Keith's number on the screen.

I frowned. I'd made it clear I planned to sequester myself here for the summer. He had no reason to disturb me, and this was the first time I'd heard from him.

"Hey," I said, attempting to hide my surprise.

"How's it going?"

I recognized Keith's fake attempt at a light and even tone, which meant what would follow was anything but light.

"Great. Why are you calling?" Rude, I knew, but I wanted to rip off the Band-Aid and get it over with. The long sigh I heard convinced me the Band-Aid was oversized.

"I don't think it's a good idea for you to be shut off from the world out there."

My shock at his unexpected words made me hesitate until I regrouped.

"A- I'm not shut off from anything, and B- I don't see what it has to do with you. I'm a big girl, and I can do as I please." My tone echoed the one we'd adopted since the beginning of our marriage breakdown.

"You're not safe there."

His remark jumpstarted my alarm. "What? How do you know if I'm safe or not? Are you spying on me?" My gaze shot to the darkness outside, half-expecting to see him skulking on the porch.

"Of course not. I just heard…"

"Heard? Who did you talk to? What did you hear?" I didn't control my strident tone. My ex-husband with inside information about my activities sent my anxiety into overdrive.

"Who doesn't matter. It's what I heard that counts."

"And what would that be?" Sarcasm battled with fury.

His hesitation told me the dropping bomb was substantial.

"You're having delusions. Seeing things that aren't there." His words tumbled out in a rush. "Julie, it's obvious where this comes from. Abby, the water, all of that. You need help."

My fingers dug into the table's edge as I listened, my whole body taut as a pulled wire. His voice buzzed in my ear like a wasp, "delusions" and "seeing things" stinging, burrowing into my skin. I could hardly breathe.

"You don't know me anymore, Keith. Stay out of my life." I spit out the words.

"Are you taking your meds, Julie? You know you can't stop them, don't you?"

I disconnected the call, cutting off the rest of his words. But his voice lingered even after I hung up, curling through my mind like smoke.

My phone flew across the room and landed on the couch. It was a testament to my control that it didn't wind up in the lake.

Fury drove me from the cottage, rain and pain be damned. I barely registered the cold and wet seeping through my socks as I stood at the end of the dock, my hands clenched into fists. What right did Keith have sticking his nose in my business? Telling me I'm delusional, seeing things, reminding me to take my medication like I'm a child.

The fact we were married once upon a time didn't give him permission to question my sanity. I did that perfectly well on my own.

I yearned to be out on the water. I needed the burn in my arms and the sound of the water against my kayak to soothe my anger, but the skies created their own tempest with flashes of lightning and rumbling thunder. I might be angry, but I wasn't stupid enough to venture onto the water in a thunderstorm, and the sky was rapidly darkening.

Instead, I breathed in the fresh air tinged with a damp, murky lake smell. The wind that carried the storm toward me cooled my flushed skin and blew my hair across my face, reminding me of the good things in this world.

I could almost hear Abby's laughter, high and pure, drifting in the air. She was there, part of the water, the trees, and the growing wind. She always would be, and maybe that's why I chose this place, why I needed isolation to keep her close. So much was here that she would've loved, reminding me of her.

"I won't let him get to me. His meddling is too much." I heard the anger in my tone. I'd try to ignore Keith's interference, but it needled me all the same. Who was his source? How did he know about the boy and my supposed "delusions?"

Could it be Dan? He and Keith were friends, but how would Dan know what happened between Peller and me? No, it had to be Peller. Somehow, they knew each other and conspired against me.

But what if it was Mark? They might be acquainted. Maybe my neighbor reported to my ex, keeping him informed.

I took several deep breaths, breathing in through my nose and releasing through my mouth, as my therapist had taught me. Yet, as the anger and anxiety faded, a new emotion constricted my throat. Doubt.

Was it true? Was I on the brink of insanity? Was it possible I imagined the boy?

A sense of urgency swept over me. I spun around and bolted for the house, desperation driving me forward. The dock's wooden planks rattled under my racing feet. Leaping from the dock onto the lawn, I slipped on the wet grass and crashed to my knees with a jarring thud. My injuries from the day before sprang to life and screamed at me. My palms pressed into the slick grass as I groaned and scrambled to my feet.

I raced into the cottage, my shoulder bumping into the doorframe as I barreled through. My pulse quickened, every beat reminding me of what Keith had said. His words snaked through my head until I could barely think. Was I losing my mind?

I dropped to my knees on the bedroom floor, ignoring my protesting muscles as I clawed under the bed for the tin, dragging it out from its hiding place, the ancient metal scraping against the floorboards. I sank back onto my haunches and clutched the cold box to my chest.

"Come on," I said, my voice hoarse.

This unassuming little thing held the last vestige of my sanity. My fingers trembled as I forced the lid open, unprepared to see the proof I both needed and feared. I grabbed the paper-wrapped feather and clutched it tightly, as though it was my salvation.

"It's real," I said, but even to my ears, the words sounded hollow.

I hadn't imagined it. He'd given me this gift. It was proof.

But was it? A baby bird's feather folded in a paper with a drawing. No message. No signature. Nothing to confirm the boy gave it to me. My gaze snagged on the leaf covering the tin's bottom. Perfect, thoughtful, appropriate, but also not backed up with proof.

Had I imagined them on the dock as a gift from the boy? Had I found them elsewhere and my infirm brain convinced me I got them from Peller's dock?

And what about the photos? Nothing appeared in them. No boy, no arm, no shirt. Nothing. I only had the memory of what I'd seen. And how dependable was that? Had Abby's loss affected me so much that I imagined children everywhere I looked?

But why now? Abby died three years ago. If I was going to lose it, it should've already happened. Was it the lake, the proximity to water? I searched my memory for the times I'd spent near water since her death, and there weren't many. I leaned back against the bed, legs sprawled out, my thoughts in turmoil.

This was my first foray into isolation. Before, I'd lived in suburbia, surrounded by families with children. A slice of normality, despite how painful it had been to see them. Everywhere I turned I saw children, many of them girls of Abby's age. Unavoidable.

But here, I saw none of that. I'd limited my contact to Dan, Mark, and Peller. The other people around the lake were strangers zipping by in their boats or other water vessels. Their only influence on me was to make me stay away from them. I saw no children. Did I create the boy to fill that void? Did I miss children? But, if so, why a boy? Why not a blonde-haired girl who resembled Abby?

Would that be too difficult, too hard for my psyche to handle? Maybe I needed something, but not too much.

As these thoughts rushed through my mind, the lump in my stomach grew until it moved into my chest, making my lungs constrict. My breath came in brief spurts, building in speed and intensity. I reached a trembling hand to my forehead, damp with sweat, and tried to catch my breath. My vision blurred. I didn't know how much time passed before the panic attack faded.

I thought I heard Abby's voice, a high, lilting sound drifting through the mist outside the window. I froze, heart thrumming, barely daring to breathe, but then... gone, leaving only the empty, crushing silence. Another product of my imagination? I hugged myself, but the chill hung on.

My gaze slid to my right hand where I clenched the small piece of paper between my fingers. I forced my mind to release it, and tears ran down my cheeks as I laid it on the floor and tried to flatten it with shaky fingers. One of the few pieces of evidence I had, feeble as it was, and I almost destroyed it.

A jagged bolt of lightning lit up the room, a clap of thunder hitting at the same time, making the floor quiver beneath me. The lights dimmed once, twice, until I was doused in darkness.

I levered myself off the floor and rolled into bed with a groan, pulling the blanket over my head, the last of my strength seeping away as I lay with the tin clutched to my chest. For a moment, the rain let up, and I thought I heard a noise outside. Footsteps? Another rumble of thunder? The skies opened again, drowning out any sound or movement. I was too tired, too broken, to care. Sleep took me.

Chapter 28

In the morning, the cottage's silence and gloom hovered around me, broken only by the rain beating on the roof. I lay alone with my fear with no one to turn to. That's exactly what they wanted, what everyone wanted.

My fingers dug into the blanket, twisting the fabric in a death grip as I imagined Keith and Peller plotting against me. Or worse, Mark sharing information with Keith, each word a betrayal. My stomach roiled, and my jaw clenched. This was my safe space. No one was supposed to follow me here. My careful plans for the summer lay in shreds.

I stared at the paint peeling off the ceiling and pulled the blanket to my chin. My newly awakened mind circled around to the same unanswered question. Who talked to Keith? The list of suspects was short—Mark, Peller, and Dan. How on earth had Keith met Mark or Peller? Granted, his job as an architect put him in touch with plenty of people, and he was a friendly sort who knew someone wherever he went. Countless times, we'd met his acquaintances in restaurants, or airports, or on the street in a strange city.

Dan, always so polite, had never shown an interest in my activities. I'd never shared my fears and suspicions, only commenting in passing about a boy on a dock. I'd downplayed it, making it nothing worth mentioning to Keith. And certainly, nothing warranting the amount of drama my ex displayed.

Peller's shifty eyes had studied me with such smugness, almost gleefully, like he enjoyed seeing my pain and anger. Yet, something told me that's all it was. An evil, abusive man reaping joy from the agony of others. Hadn't he done the same with his wife and son? It made him feel powerful, in control. Given the impression I had of Peller living like a recluse, the chances of him knowing Keith were slim, weren't they?

A sudden recollection came to mind. That night, at his place, with the police staring at me like I'd escaped from a madhouse, Peller referred to me as a grieving woman. How did he know about my grief? Had someone told him? Did he research me online? Again, another triangle created with Peller and me, and someone else who stood at the other point, connecting us.

Keith? Dan?

I'd confided in Mark, feeling secure that my confidences would remain between us. He'd never mentioned knowing my ex-husband, something that surely would've come up in our conversations. But it was Keith who'd found this cottage for me, through Dan, conveniently placed next door to Mark. Was that the plan? To put me near his spy? My mind drifted to Mark's absences when he visited clients and threw in an extra visit with a journalist friend and Peller's wife. Had he also visited Keith?

Another thought raced to the forefront of my mind. The bike. Someone tampered with the brakes, expertly, unobtrusively. Someone with experience. And who had worked in a bike shop? Mark. Who lived next door with easy access to the bike? Mark.

The cards were stacked against him. And why had he closed down when discussing his divorce? Was there more to that story than just reticence to discuss a painful subject? Did he have violent tendencies? Is that why his wife left him?

The familiar churn of anger in my gut returned. I'd trusted Mark, opened up despite myself, and now here I was, back to square one, unsure of who was friend or foe. Had he told my ex-husband I imagined a boy on a dock, imagined the gifts from him, imagined him running away from me? What was his end goal? Why would he do that? I could understand Keith's satisfaction at having me declared insane, as retaliation for my treatment of him despite being unaware of everything. But Mark had nothing to gain.

What if everyone thought I was losing it? Each glance, every offhand comment. They could all be building some grand plan to prove I was as crazy as Keith claimed. It's what he wanted, what he'd always wanted, to paint me as unstable, a woman falling apart. Like he needed that to justify the breakdown of our marriage.

Ironically, the more I thought of it, the more I came undone.

I threw aside the blankets and sought the living area's relative spaciousness, catching sight of the wind and rain agitating the lake water. There, I paced, my bare feet thumping on the wooden floor, my limp barely noticeable. My mind circled around the same images, over and over again.

My heart finally slowed, anger cooling into a hard, unbreakable resolve. They thought they could control me, shape my reality. But I wasn't a puppet, and I wouldn't be pushed around. If they wanted to see what I was capable of... well, I'd show them. I wouldn't let anyone gaslight me again.

***

After a long, miserable housebound day of fretting about Keith, Mark, Peller, and the possibility of losing my mind, the next morning, I embraced the sunshine with unusual fervor. I felt like a sun-worshipping vacationer as I took to the lake in all its summer glory. Should I credit this newfound enthusiasm to stir-craziness or a new, improved me fueled by determination and anger?

The kayak slid easily over the damp grass as if also relishing a dip. Although barely past dawn, the sun warmed my back as I climbed in and pushed off. I needed to purge a full day of inactivity from my body, so I leapfrogged over my slow warmup to full-out paddling. I'd pay for the burn in my arms, but the sensation of the kayak skimming across the lake made it worthwhile.

The water rippled underneath me, and a cool mist clung to my skin and clothing. Sunlight danced on the surface, turning the lake into a glittering, welcoming expanse. My paddle sliced through the still water, breaking the silence with each stroke.

Like a swimmer in an Olympic-style pool, I reached the far shore, swiveled the kayak, and used my paddle to push off and gain momentum. In what seemed like minutes, the island came into view, and I was suddenly upon it. Circling around, I allowed myself to drift as I gazed at Peller's empty dock.

I scanned the trees standing sentinel on the bank. No sight of the boy or any other sign of life. It was early but not too early for him. *Is he okay? Did Peller take out his anger on him and forbid him to go to the dock? But if he's in that house, who is he?* A mystery I couldn't explain. The boy's image, bound to the house, trapped and hidden, filled me with a dark urgency.

Relieved, I realized my thoughts revolved around the boy's existence and not my mental capacity. Deep down, I knew I was right about him. But on my own to prove it.

As I dipped my paddle in the water and maneuvered the kayak around the island, a slight movement caught my eye. A flutter. I swung back to the dock. What was it? Just a bird or something else?

I swept my gaze over the shoreline, my eyes searching the murkiness beneath the trees. No trace of movement. No small figure waiting near the dock. Just an empty, cold expanse.

No. There it was. Something blue flapped on the dock. I swung left and paddled to the wharf, my arms moving like a locomotive. My gaze scanned the area for onlookers, especially Peller with a weapon, as I pulled alongside the structure and frowned at the object hooked on a nail. It was a piece of fabric, seemingly from a T-shirt. The color struck a chord in my memory. The shirt I'd seen on the boy the first day. It was this color, a deep blue. I gently pulled it from the nail and stuffed it into my pocket. No time to examine it. I couldn't risk being spotted by Peller, not again.

I froze. A soft sound carried across the water. A whisper? A small voice? The wind? My hands clenched tightly on the paddle as my gaze darted over my surroundings. Was someone hiding in the trees? The sensation of being watched clung to me like a rotten smell.

Was it Peller? If so, why didn't he confront me, raging and ready to fight? Or was it something else? The Shadow Woman sending me a warning about following in her footsteps?

I shook off my fanciful thoughts and shoved away from the dock. I barely noticed the return trip to my own dock, my thoughts racing as I attempted to focus on the implications of my find. Something or someone could have torn away the fabric accidentally, or he'd left it as a message, a breadcrumb leading me to some terrible truth.

Inside the cottage, I held the fabric between my fingers, the worn softness hinting at months of wear. My thumb brushed over a frayed edge, and a vision of the boy flashed before me, his skinny arms, his wide, scared eyes. The more I stared at it, the more convinced I was it came from the boy's shirt. But how had it ended up there? Torn in a struggle? Or deliberately left for me? The questions curled around my mind, twisting every thought.

Could this scrap of fabric be proof, or was I reaching for meaning where none existed? I crushed it in my fist, refusing to think I'd read too much into something trivial. No, he was real. I was certain of it.

I pulled the tin from under the bed and carefully laid the fabric beside the other treasures, tracing each object with my finger as if they held secrets only I saw. These gifts were fragile connections to reality, evidence I wasn't seeing spirits. They were my talismans against everyone's disbelief. A quiet promise formed. Whatever it took, whatever lay between the boy and freedom, I'd break through it. I'd be the boy's protector, his way out. Even if it meant facing Peller myself. He'd see what I was willing to risk.

***

At a leisurely pace, I steered the kayak toward the cottage, enjoying the lake and fresh air. Once I'd completed my reflections and made my decision to fight for the boy, I needed a second tour around the lake. With my demons exorcised, my frame of mind found its strength, if not its peacefulness.

Behind me, a jet ski engine roared to life. The vacationers were awake earlier than usual. Soon, the lake would resemble ants on a tablecloth at a picnic, everyone trying to make up for yesterday's lost day of fun in the sun.

Thankful I'd evaded the worst of it, I continued my slow paddle home. As the engine sound advanced closer, I maneuvered my kayak toward the shore to avoid the waves they'd create. I frowned as I heard the machine approach my port side, gaining speed. I turned to share my annoyance with the driver when the rocketing machine broadsided me.

Chapter 29

The moment the jet ski hit, a jolt shot up my spine, as if my bones splintered. The kayak catapulted into the air, hurling me deep into the chilly lake water. I struggled to the surface, lungs begging for air, not having time to prepare for the cold shock that stole my breath. Treading water, I fought to stay calm as the jet ski raced away, a rooster tail of water lifting high behind it.

As I sputtered and wiped water from my eyes, my only impression of the driver was of a tall, lean figure dressed entirely in a black wet suit. I opened my mouth to scream after him, but only a hoarse whisper escaped. No one was around. No boats, no vacationers, just the jet ski's faint roar disappearing around the bend.

My attention swung to my kayak that was rapidly sinking into the lake. My arms pinwheeled as I swam in desperation toward it. I grasped on and fought to drag it to the surface, my feet searching for purchase in the lake's mucky bottom. By the time I reached water shallow enough to stand in, exhaustion weakened me.

I waded back to shore, focused on dragging the broken kayak onto the dock, but my mind was a mess of jumbled thoughts, and the best I could do was haul it onto the bank.

Was it deliberate? Did someone try to hurt me? The logic escaped me. What reason could anyone possibly have? I felt like I stood on a cliff, teetering between insanity and fear of some nameless person, unsure what was more dangerous.

I sprawled in the mud, catching my breath, the musty reek of algae filling my nostrils, staring at the gaping hole in my kayak as if looking at a wound that'd never heal. This wasn't just an ordinary vessel. It was my salvation, my release.

I'd held Abby in front of me as a toddler as we kayaked in calm waters. It helped feed her love of the outdoors and water. This kayak followed me from one competition to the next, a friend and comfort for many years. I felt as if someone had struck down a beloved pet.

I wanted to scream, to curse the person who'd done this, but I swallowed it down. My emotions were all over the map. Fatigue tamped down my initial reactions of fear and anger, but they simmered beneath the surface.

I lifted my gaze to stare across the water. *Who would do such a thing? It was no accident. Someone deliberately attacked me. To kill me? Warn me?*

I struggled to gather my thoughts and remember exactly what happened. He'd come from behind me, from Peller's direction. Was it him? He'd disappeared around the curve and hadn't returned. Was it someone living on that side? But I hadn't seen or heard it coming from that direction. How did he go back and forth? Was Peller hiding the machine over there? I'd never seen it at his dock. Then again, I'd seen no watercraft there. Did he keep a jet ski in the boathouse?

With a newfound sense of determination, I leaped to my feet and ran to the cottage, water dripping from my T-shirt and sweatpants, mud squishing between my toes. I dumped my soggy clothes on the bathroom floor and grabbed fresh, dry ones before towel-drying my hair and snagging the keys to the car.

With only one route, it made it impossible to get lost, even with my mind tangled up in fear and suspicion, and the empty road was a blessing with no impatient drivers to push me.

I crept along, my foot hovering over the brake as I scanned every yard and driveway, searching for the slightest hint of movement. At times, the lake came into view, the water rippling under the sunny sky, but more often, solid walls of trees and cottages obstructed the shoreline. My gaze darted between the dense woods and the houses, and I felt like a prowler in broad daylight, on the lookout for any sign of a jet ski or someone dressed in black.

Unfortunately, the machines were plentiful, making it impossible to distinguish one from the other or know which one had hit me unless I got close enough to examine it for damage. As for black-clad men, I found none. He could be in any of these cottages, and I didn't relish the idea of another visit with the police if the owners complained about a woman harassing them. Same went for snooping in the bushes or on the docks. I'd soon find myself dragged off to jail or a mental institution.

The road formed a circle around the lake. I followed its path to return to my cottage. As I passed Peller's house, I slowed and peered into his yard, wondering if I'd catch him weeding his garden in a black wet suit, but I spotted no sign of life on his property.

Disappointed but not surprised, I drove on. Yet, I couldn't thrust aside the sense of being watched. A flutter of movement in a yard made me brake, my heart hammering, finding only a stray branch bobbing in the breeze. A little farther on, a figure stood on a dock, too far to make out clearly, but his heavyset frame didn't match Peller's or any other person I'd seen around Sala Lake. Was he staring at me? Difficult to tell with the bright sun backlighting him.

"You're being silly, Julie," I told myself. "Letting your imagination run out of control, seeing bogeymen in every corner. Get a grip."

Despite my lecture, my eyes darted repeatedly to my rearview mirror, half-expecting to spot someone following me. How many accidents could I ignore before acknowledging the ghouls around me? First the bike and now this.

Pulling into my driveway, the sight of my disfigured kayak lying on the grass met me. My shoulders slumped in despair. The lack of a kayak over the next few weeks would definitely push me over the edge into crazydom, and finding one of that caliber wouldn't happen overnight.

Still in the driver's seat, my gaze drifted to the cluster of trees separating my property from Mark's cottage. I'd never seen a jet ski at his place, but I'd never done a thorough inspection of his boathouse. I couldn't afford to leave a stone unturned.

I shut the car door with a soft click and crept toward the trees. Remembering how Mark had appeared out of nowhere on a few occasions, my gaze swept my surroundings to make sure no one watched from behind a tree. As I neared the cottage, the sun glared off his car. My head swiveled from side to side, looking for him, trying to plan my approach.

I could knock on his door and ask him if he'd gone jet skiing on the lake, or I could find an excuse to search his cottage for a wet suit. Another option was to tell him what happened and gauge his reaction. But I doubted I could act naturally around him, not with suspicions lurking in my mind. He'd realize something was up.

I squinted and tried to sneak a look at his dock without revealing myself, but trees stood in my way. I took two cautious steps and leaned forward, searching for traces of dampness on the wharf, or better yet, a recently used jet ski. Nothing.

"Looking for something?"

I jumped, my hand to my heart, startled again by this man's stealthiness. Caught off guard, my mouth opened and closed like a fish freshly removed from the hook.

He'd approached from the direction of his house. Clothed in shorts and a T-shirt, sandals on his feet, he didn't look like someone who'd recently struggled out of a wet suit, but he'd had plenty of time to change clothes while I drove around the lake.

Mark's eyes narrowed. "Everything okay?"

"Someone ran into my kayak. On purpose." The first words that came to mind burst from my mouth. Having revealed my hand, without permission from my brain, I needed to play it by ear now.

Mark's gaze shifted over me with concern but also with something else, like he was piecing together a puzzle I wasn't privy to. "That's strange," he said, scratching his head. "Are you sure it wasn't an accident? The lake gets crowded, and…" His voice trailed off, leaving me defensive. Why was he questioning me?

"Of course, I'm sure."

Mark's eyes narrowed on my face. He must have caught my irritation because his attitude shifted from disbelief to growing annoyance.

"Who was it? What was he driving? Is he crazy or what?" With each question, his anger increased.

"I don't know, a jet ski, and yes, he's probably out of his mind."

"A jet ski?" His eyes widened in alarm. "He hit you hard?"

"Hard enough to demolish my kayak and send me flying into the water. It's a fluke I'm not hurt."

Mark ran a hand through his hair, his expression shocked and bewildered. "What makes you sure he did it on purpose?" Mark pressed me again, his gaze steady. "Could be a reckless vacationer who didn't see you in time," he said. "People don't really mean harm."

I realized his words were meant to comfort me, but I caught something else in them—the suggestion I'd imagined the intention behind the incident. That was the question I'd considered since it happened, but it hurt to know someone else doubted me too. I swallowed my pride. "If it was an accident, don't you think he would've stopped to see if I was okay? It had to be on purpose. But why and who?"

Mark shook his head and gazed over the lake as if the perpetrator would appear. "I don't know. It doesn't make sense. I'd say Peller, but what does he gain by hurting you?"

I shrugged. "Satisfaction. Because he hates me. He seems like the type."

"You could've been badly hurt or even killed. A dangerous way to get satisfaction." Mark's tone held a level of disgust I'd never heard before, as if he'd built up his own hatred for Graham Peller.

"We've already established he's not stable." I adopted a mollifying tone, unused to this version of my neighbor, angry and tense.

"First the bike, and now this," Mark said, flinging out his hands, his expression grim.

Yes, we still must consider the bike. Is Peller as at ease with a bike's mechanics as Mark is?

Chapter 30

The phone's jangle jolted me from my trance. I'd been staring out the window as the lake's tranquility worked its magic, lulling me into a quiet peacefulness, making me forget about the laptop and my client's to-do list at my elbow.

The call cracked the silence, a reminder that life outside this place wanted a piece of me. My first thought was that said client called to demand a status update, but with a glance at my screen and the sight of Will's name, I softened, happy to hear from my brother.

"Hi," I said, my cheery voice sounding strange, even to my ears. It showed how much I appreciated the distraction.

"Hey, how's it going?"

Will strived for the same cheer, but it sounded forced. The second I heard the edge in his voice, a familiar tension swept over me, as I prepared for whatever he had to deliver. Will had always been protective of me, playing his big brother role to perfection. Even though we hung out almost like best pals, he always stepped in to defend or include me as a brother would. I loved him for it.

When Abby died, both my siblings were there for me. My father had passed away in his late fifties from heart disease, and my mother, suffering from early-onset Alzheimer's, lived in a long-term care facility. The rest of us banded together, with Will being the most steadfast. Even when our lives slipped into as normal a routine as possible, he called or dropped by regularly. He dragged me from the house to hike with him or to get out on the water, trying to revitalize my spirit. But my spirit had disappeared. It lay in the grave with Abby.

Although it was not unusual to receive a random call from Will, his tone normally lacked the troubling edge.

"Great." I tried to maintain my cheeriness, although it strained my limits. I didn't want Will to worry about me.

"Really? Are you sure?"

This made me pause. I couldn't respond. What was up with this? Digging for something?

"Of course. I should know how I am." Too late, I realized I sounded defensive, a sure giveaway something was wrong.

"That's not what Keith said."

Heat rose through my body, and blood pounded in my ears. "What? What did he say about me?" I couldn't believe my ex-husband had resorted to gossiping with my family. How dare he.

"Back down, Julie. He's concerned. We all are."

"Why? There's nothing to be concerned about."

"You're holed up by yourself in a cottage on an isolated lake. You're imagining a child that doesn't exist..."

It was too much. My hand slammed the table. "I don't believe this. I'm perfectly safe here. Totally safe. And Keith is the one who found this place, so he has no right to say anything about it." I sucked in a deep breath, trying to lower my blood pressure. "And I imagined nothing. I saw a boy. I know I did. Whether he belongs to that man or to someone else, I don't know, but he exists. And I won't let you or Keith or anyone else make me feel crazy."

"Julie," Will said, his voice soft, as if treading over broken glass. "I don't want to dismiss what you're saying. But sometimes... sometimes grief can do strange things. You know that. Just... there's a chance, however small, that what you saw might not have been real." The silence was intense, filled with things he wasn't saying.

"You think I'm crazy?" My voice, sharp as a razor, sliced through his attempt at calm. "Keith has you thinking I'm fragile, hanging on the edge, seeing things that don't exist. Well, guess what, Will, I'm stronger than that, and I don't need either of you making me out to be some pathetic crazy person."

"Julie," Will said in his soothing tone, "it's perfectly normal after what happened to Abby."

There he was, my faithful big brother, the same person who'd helped me pick up the pieces after Abby died. And yet, his words sounded foreign, like they didn't belong to him but to someone who'd lost faith in me.

I fought to match his tone but spoke through gritted teeth. "*If* I was imagining him, it wouldn't be normal, but I'm not, so you can leave me alone."

"All I'm saying is that you might need... help. Talk to your therapist."

My therapist. As if that solved everything. I'd done my time in her office, staring at blank walls while she coaxed memories of Abby to the forefront, just to have my spirits shattered again once I returned to an empty house. If "moving on" was the answer, then she didn't understand the question.

"I've spent a huge amount of time with a therapist for three years and guess what—Abby is still dead. I still don't have her with me, and I never will." My voice broke.

Will sighed. "I know that, and believe me, I feel for you every day. But you're alive, and you can't go on like this forever."

Did they really believe I was seeing things? I wasn't hallucinating. My brain told me so. I'd seen him. I traded gifts with him. But Keith and Will had planted a tiny, unwelcome seed of doubt.

What if they were right? What if this was grief in a new, twisted form? Was I following the path of the Shadow Woman, so consumed with sorrow that I drowned in it, forever living my life searching for children to save? I forced the thought away, steeling myself against it. Abby's absence haunted me enough. I couldn't let anyone else chip away at my sanity.

The thought of Keith digging into my life and stirring up Will's worry made my blood boil. He probably told Will I'd acted erratic, alone here with no one to watch me. He'd never been one to understand that solitude didn't mean suffering. The next time he stuck his nose in my business, he'd regret it.

I drew a breath, digging deeply for patience. I realized Will had my best interest at heart, and my beef was less with him and more with my ex-husband for putting troubling thoughts into my brother's head. I'd deal with Keith later.

"I don't intend to go on like this forever," I said. In fact, no matter my words or intentions, I didn't know what my future held. My immediate goal was to put Will's mind at ease. "That's why I came here. To clear my head, to relax, and to plan how to go forward. Okay, so I saw a boy on a dock. Big deal. I've taken several steps forward. You should be happy."

"Great, but if…"

"There's no 'if.' Everything's fine. I'm fine. Keith is the one who's making a big deal out of nothing. Ignore him. You, of all people, should have faith in me."

A long hesitation followed, and I knew Will weighed my words. I hoped for a positive response.

"I get it, sis. You know I love you, and I only want what's best for you. Call me any time, night or day, if you need anything. Even if it's just to chat for a bit."

Though Will's voice comforted me, I hated the idea Keith had orchestrated a "team intervention" and enlisted Will. That's why my brother's words seemed more scripted than spontaneous. Even his reassurances that he was here for me sounded like an afterthought, a line he'd rehearsed to make sure I wouldn't shut him out entirely.

"I appreciate it, Will. We'll chat soon."

I ended the connection, gripping the phone until the edges bit into my fingers. They could believe whatever they wanted. I knew what I'd seen, what I'd experienced. But as I stood there, alone, their disbelief and doubts felt like worms, trying to wiggle their way inside me. For a fleeting moment, I wondered if I'd lost my grip on reality.

Another surge of anger flooded me, and again I resisted the urge to throw my phone across the room. It was my only means of communication, and I couldn't risk breaking it. But breaking a few bones in Keith's body wasn't out of the question.

Why did my ex care so much now anyway? After putting distance between ourselves, why did he take such a sudden interest in my recovery, or lack of it? Had he created a way to swoop in and "rescue" me, to put me under his thumb again? Or worse, he might truly believe I'd lost it.

As I glanced outside at the lake, its peaceful surface now seemed ominous, like a trap laid just for me. Was I the only one who saw the undercurrents shifting underneath? Like people who posed as friends and loved ones but who didn't have my best interests at heart? Why couldn't they let me be?

Right or wrong, I'd decided to impose this isolation on myself. In retrospect, it may not have been a brilliant decision. Perhaps throwing myself into a place filled with people and distractions would have been a better choice, but I was determined to see it through.

The knowledge of what I'd seen vacillated between a buoy that held me up and an anchor that pulled me under.

I shivered, as if eyes watched me from just beyond the trees, waiting. For what, I didn't know. All I knew was that, alone out here, I needed to watch my back.

Chapter 31

I normally encountered a strange sense of comfort as day gave way to dusk, a calming respite after a long day of struggling with my thoughts and memories.

But tonight, the darkness seemed different. I felt on edge, watched. Friend or foe? Unfortunately, most people around me seemed to lean toward the latter.

My thoughts went full circle again and led me to the root cause of my angst. The boy. He'd given me purpose, allowing me to push aside thoughts of Abby, however temporarily. Had my imagination created him for that purpose? Was my psyche trying to outsmart me, giving me an imaginary friend to help me get over my daughter's loss?

Perhaps.

Should I thank my psyche for the effort? Or ask it to leave me alone? My emotions didn't need the extra workout. They had enough trouble dealing with one child. Why throw another into the mix for me to fret over?

As I thought of the boy, Abby's face danced at the fringe of my consciousness, as if the two were connected, intertwined in inexplicable ways. Abby's laughter used to light up the darkest room. But now, all that remained were reminders of what I'd lost and what I couldn't allow myself to lose again, even if it meant clinging to a stranger... or a ghost.

But if the boy was a conjuring of my mind, why would someone try to hurt me or scare me away? Someone deliberately tampered with the bike's brakes. Whoever hit my kayak did it on purpose. Why? What danger was I to anyone? If I had an imaginary friend, who cared?

The idea of the boy, imagined or real, lodged itself in my brain like a splinter, and I didn't know if yanking it out would heal me or bleed me dry. I could just leave him be, let him fade. But whenever I convinced myself he wasn't real, something happened. A voice echoed across the lake or a specter appeared in the trees, and it pulled me back to the vision of him standing on the dock, just as solid as Abby ever was.

I'd come to Sala Lake to escape, to piece myself back together, but now it seemed I was breaking apart even faster, tiny bits of me floating away with every hint of doubt. It was a bitter irony. This cottage was supposed to be my haven, yet now I'd become a prisoner, cut off from safety, trapped in my own swirling thoughts, with no one to turn to.

I stood and paced the room, turning on a light as I crossed back and forth and scrolled through my list of suspects behind the attacks against me.

Peller was easy to picture as the culprit; his thin-lipped sneer and hostile glances clear in my mind. He had secrets. Dark secrets, I was sure of it. He clearly disliked me. But did his hate stretch far enough to harm me? Or was I just a nuisance, an annoying female, an easy victim? His military experience could've turned him into a bitter, vindictive man. He might target me to vent his frustrations. Maybe he feared I'd discover his secrets. And what were they? They involved the boy, I was sure, but proving it was difficult. I'd already had my share of run-ins with him, and the cops were involved. Accessing his house seemed almost impossible.

Peller was definitely at the top of my list but not the only one to consider.

Mark's kindness and understanding had seemed like a warm hug, yet now it left an aftertaste. He'd been helpful and willing to believe in me. But he had the means and the proximity to hurt me. He was always there, wasn't he? Showing up unexpectedly, lingering near enough to make me wonder if his kindness was part of a master plan. I'd read enough to know even a pleasant man could hold a weapon behind his back, evil at his core. I needed to watch myself around him.

Dan? Unlikely he was behind anything sinister, but he might be the source of gossip, a pawn in someone else's game.

Which led to Keith, the recipient and distributor of gossip. The deliverer of thoughts that wrestled their way into my brain and made me doubt myself. The man who once vowed to protect me but now insinuated himself in ways that seemed anything but protective. Was he capable of hurting me? Did he hate me that much? What did he gain from scaring me? Did he think he could frighten me into sanity? Or was he the only one who knew what it took to push me over the edge? A part of me still trusted him, the man I'd married, but another part wondered if I even knew who he was.

The lamp I'd turned on generated more gloom than light. I heard the lake lapping outside, the sound usually comforting, but now it sounded sinister. The quiet didn't soothe me. Every small creak, every settling noise reminded me no place, no matter how secluded, was safe. *Where does the real danger lie? Outside or in my mind?*

Frustration bubbled over, pushed by the determination lying underneath. Did they think I'd break, like glass under pressure? But they didn't know me, not anymore. I wouldn't sit here, helpless, wondering who lurked in the darkness. If they wanted me afraid, they'd have to work harder. I'd find the person behind this.

I needed answers. No more spinning in circles, pacing the floor until the boards wore down. I'd stop being the victim and let them know I wasn't some fragile, grieving wimp.

I turned off the light and let the room slip into blackness. In the morning, I'd face my demons.

Chapter 32

The lake reflected the sky's colors, and small waves lapped against the canoe's side. The stillness seemed to increase the tension between us. I felt exposed out here, as though something could turn against me at any moment.

"I have an idea."

The sunlight dimmed quickly, the clouds strong-arming their way across the lake, as if to set the mood. It occurred to me that Mark's face, hidden behind sunglasses and cap, looked like a mask, his intentions unreadable. Was he on my side or simply playing a part?

I returned my concentration to my paddle, moving it through the water. A different animal from a kayak, I nevertheless easily transitioned to a canoe and appreciated Mark's offer to use his extra one. I set aside my suspicions about him for a chance to be back on the water, an indication of how easily I could be bought. I also believed the adage of keeping your friends close and your enemies closer. If I wanted to find out what thoughts circulated through his head, I needed to be near him.

Undeterred by my silence, Mark shared his idea. "We need to know if the boy is in the house. See if there's a place Peller could've hidden him. I'll try to get in."

Surprised, my gaze spun to my side, but Mark focused on his canoeing. "How? He'll never let you in," I said.

"I'll disguise myself as an evaluator for the municipality. He won't suspect."

Mark delivered his plan in a calm voice, not even looking my way, keeping his gaze straight ahead. Was he avoiding my eyes? A pang of apprehension gripped me. My fingers tightened around the paddle. Was he hiding something, or was I overthinking it?

"He's seen you," I said. Despite everything, my heart raced with excitement at the idea, knowing it was a good plan, but I searched for spokes Peller could throw in our wheels.

"Thus, the need for a disguise. Besides, it was dark when he saw me."

"What if he checks with the municipality to see if you're legit?"

"That's a risk I'll take."

The only sound we heard for several seconds was the splash of the paddles.

The rush of enthusiasm at his suggestion mingled with something colder. Doubt. Here I was, trusting a man I hardly knew, agreeing to a plan that felt flimsy at best. Mark was helpful, maybe too helpful. Was he genuinely invested in helping me, or did he nudge me toward danger? He was still a suspect in the attacks against me. Why trust him now? Then again, he'd assume the risk. I'd remain a bystander.

"It works in the movies," I finally said, even as my mind raced to find holes in his plan. Deep holes I could fall into.

Mark snorted a laugh. "Yeah, we've copied a few movie scenes lately."

"They didn't work out." My tone was wry as I remembered the unsuccessful session trying to get a photo of the boy and the nighttime visit to Peller's house.

"Yet. We're due for something to work."

To anyone else, his tone emitted confidence and trustworthiness, but what if he led me into a trap? The idea crept in uninvited and tried to take root in my brain. His steady gaze, his willingness to jump into risky plans— loyalty or deception? I tried to read his expression through the sunglasses without success. My stomach tangled. How close was too close when you're keeping an eye on someone you might not trust?

"You know it's a risk, right?" I held my voice steady. "If Peller suspects anything, if he gets a whiff of what we're doing..." The consequences were too grim to utter out loud. We knew Peller was unstable and very likely dangerous. I let the words hang, hoping he understood what I didn't dare say.

My muscles tensed, my grip on the paddle causing my knuckles to turn white. His own hands were relaxed, his posture easy, as if he didn't feel the same unease, the same thrill of danger. He could simply be a better actor than me. My mind raced through scenarios—Mark being dragged out of Peller's house, me forced to talk to the police, scrambling to explain again. And what if no one caught him? What if he found something that pointed back to me, proof I was insane? I was gambling everything on a man I barely knew, hoping he'd get us through unscathed.

"I'll be careful," he said, but I detected something in his voice, a single-minded focus bordering on recklessness. I wondered if he'd done this sort of thing before, and if so, how many times had it gone wrong?

"What's in this for you anyway?" I asked, dipping into the deep end of my pool of worries.

He paused, his paddle still in the water, and turned to me with a half-smile. "Just helping a friend." His tone casual, words tossed without a second thought, but part of me couldn't rid myself of the sense there was more to it.

We sat in silence, the air crowded with things unsaid. So many questions I wanted to ask, but now wasn't the time. I was too vulnerable, almost literally a sitting duck in the middle of the lake. I sensed his eyes on me through the sunglasses, and I realized how much he saw of my unease, how easily he could guess at my doubts. But I wouldn't back out. If he plotted against me, I'd have no choice but to find out the hard way.

"And what if it goes south while you're in there?" I said, my voice dropping.

He tilted his head, a smirk tugging at the corner of his mouth. "Then you'll have to bail me out," he said. It sounded like a joke, but I didn't know if he challenged me or tested my loyalty. Either way, I wasn't ready to make that promise.

For better or worse, I was in this now. I'd cast the dice, and all I could hope was that I hadn't aligned myself with a stranger's secrets and lies. Whatever happened, I'd see it through to the end, whether Mark was my ally or the one leading me to ruin. The boy's life was at stake, and I needed to do it for him.

"Okay. Tomorrow, then," I said, meeting his gaze. His grin was easy, but I knew better. This wasn't a game, not for me.

Chapter 33

The mustache did it. His slicked back hair, the jacket with the municipal logo on it—I didn't ask how he'd found one of those—and his electronic tablet provided great camouflage, but adding facial hair turned it into a foolproof disguise.

I had to give Mark credit. He took his role seriously. Extensive research filled him in on how to approach the homeowner and what questions to ask. The dry run we performed was surreal and made me wonder who I'd partnered with. With his acting skills, if he knocked on my door and asked to inspect the property, I'd let him in without hesitation. *How dumb am I?*

As he climbed into his nondescript sedan to drive to Peller's house, I wondered if that would be the giveaway. Was Peller familiar with all the cars around the lake? Not likely. Mark had made a mockup of an official municipal placard and placed it on his dash. Would it pass a close inspection? Probably not, but from a distance, most people wouldn't give it a second thought.

What if he didn't come back? The thought struck me hard, out of nowhere, like a rock thrown into still water, leaving me unprepared for the resulting splash. What if Peller caught on and confronted him? What if he became violent? I shook my head as if I could shake away the idea, but it settled into my mind, gnawing at me with every minute that passed as I waited for Mark's return.

I mowed the lawn. I washed the windows. How long could it possibly take? I checked my watch for the umpteenth time, my ears on high alert for any sound of an approaching vehicle.

As I waited, every noise sharpened around me. The caw of a distant crow, the rustling leaves, the faint, endless lapping of the lake against the shore. It all grew louder, drawing out my nerves until I thought I'd explode.

While scrubbing down the porch floor, I heard tires crunching on gravel. Water and suds splashed across the surface as I scrambled to my feet, knocking over the bowl. I rushed around the corner of the cottage and skidded to a stop as Mark climbed out of his car. My gut twisted upon seeing him with slightly rumpled clothing, his face drawn. His usual easygoing posture had stiffened, his expression hard to read, but it didn't show relief.

I stood still, wringing my hands like they held wet laundry, each movement a desperate attempt to release the tension in my body, anticipating his story. He brushed past me onto the newly scrubbed porch without a glance back. The old rattan chair groaned as he lowered himself onto it. A long, weary breath whooshed from his lips.

I opened my mouth, a flood of questions rushing to the tip of my tongue, but no words came out. My throat felt parched, my thoughts stuck in a traffic jam in my mind. Finally, I forced two words past the obstruction. "What happened?"

He ran a hand over his face and took a long breath, staring at something I couldn't see. Finally, he muttered, "It wasn't what I expected." He paused, and my patience snapped.

"How? Tell me."

"He fell for my story once he examined my credentials."

Another excellent job of forgery on Mark's part. Perhaps I should worry about his propensity for crime, but first I needed to know what took place today.

"I started with a walk-around outside. He followed me every step of the way."

I nodded. We'd expected that, but Mark's grimace told me how creepy it made him feel.

"I didn't see anything suspicious. Then we went inside. He answered all my questions, no hesitations." He paused, and my nerves stretched taut.

"There's something else. What is it? Something horrible?" I said, wanting to shake him even as I was afraid of what I'd hear.

"Inside... well, it seemed strange," Mark said, his brow furrowing. "He has a room full of boxes. No labels, no organization. He wouldn't let me near them, just kept telling me to stay on the 'official route.'"

"Boxes?" I said, trying to make sense of what it meant. What would he hide in plain sight? "What do you think is in them?"

Mark's searing gaze met mine. "I think he's moving. The other rooms seemed mostly bare, as if he'd packed them away. But when I asked him point blank if he planned to move, he was annoyed and wouldn't answer."

The idea's significance sunk in. Peller planned to leave, but he didn't want to share that information with Mark. It was a secret, like he wanted to steal away with no one noticing. Why was that? Because he had something to hide, and he'd take it with him. Then we'd never find him... or the boy.

"There are a couple of other things."

My gaze swiveled to Mark, wondering what other bad news he'd share.

"I checked all the property, even the boathouse."

I sucked in a breath. "And?"

Mark gave a short nod. "He has a jet ski, a motorboat, kayaks, and canoes. All the toys."

An image of the jet ski racing down the lake after broadsiding me flashed into my brain. "It was him."

"It could've been. Almost everyone on this lake has one though. It's not definite proof."

"No, but he has access to one." I didn't care about definite proof. In my heart, I knew it was him. I glanced at Mark. "There's something else?"

His expression turned grim. "When I asked to inspect the basement, he refused."

My eyes widened. "Why?"

"He said he had a dangerous dog, and he'd put him in the basement when he saw me arrive. Said it was 'resting' down there."

"A lie."

Mark nodded. "I'm sure of it. I saw no evidence of a dog. No water bowl or food dish, no toys or bones, not even an old dog blanket. Just a closed door."

"And we never saw or heard a dog the times we were there," I said, my mind swirling.

"Which means he's hiding something in the basement."

An unsettling calmness had crept into his voice. He spoke of Peller and his secrets with a hint of satisfaction, as though this were more than just a mission for him. It was almost... personal.

My wandering mind returned to the immediate problem, and my blood ran cold. The basement. Was that where the boy was? "You went through all the other rooms?"

"Yes."

"You insisted on going into the basement?"

"Of course. I told him it was part of the inspection, that he could tie the dog outside while I did it. He refused. Said he'd call the municipality and complain if I insisted. A chance I couldn't take."

No, but he'd taken a lot of chances. Watching Mark's expressionless face, I wondered how far he'd go. The idea rattled me. He'd faked credentials, an entire persona, all for a cause he had no reason to be invested in. What drove him? The child? Someone he'd never seen? Or something else?

My mind leaped unbidden to a horrible image of the boy, huddled alone in the dark, silent basement. Would he know someone was coming to help him? Or would he hear footsteps above and wait for a knock on the door, unsure if it brought help or something more to fear? I tried to push the thought away, but it lingered, grasping at me. We were running out of time, especially if Peller planned to leave and take the boy with him.

"One thing is certain. He's hiding something... or someone. We need to figure out what's going on in that basement," I said, urgency building in my voice. "If there's even a chance the boy is in there, we can't wait for Peller to make the next move."

A thought struck me. "What if Peller realizes we're on to him and that's why he's leaving?" The question hung between us. Mark met my gaze, and in his eyes, I saw the same worry. We'd stirred something dangerous. Would the boy suffer the consequences of our actions?

***

Nothing helped. Not the water, not the birds' chirping in the trees, not the calming sight of a family of ducks sunning on the rocks.

My mind churned with doubts and suspicions, volleying back and forth between Peller, Mark, and Keith. Convinced Peller was guilty of mistreating that boy, my concern lay with whether either Mark or Keith were involved. And if they were, how and why?

Was I paranoid? Seeing threats in every direction? I didn't think so.

I returned and shut myself in my cottage, trying to straighten out my thoughts. As the evening's darkness descended, the light drizzle turned into a full-fledged downpour, pelting against the roof like a train's rumble. Between the noise and my preoccupying thoughts, it took a moment for me to notice the thumping on the door.

I peered through the window to see Mark leaning against the door jamb, clutching his left side, his fingers red with blood.

Chapter 34

A gasp escaped my throat as I wrenched open the door. Mark stumbled and fell against me with a loud groan of pain. I moved to his uninjured side and draped his right arm around my shoulder to support him.

"What happened? Did you fall on something?" I guided him toward the couch and gently lowered him onto it.

"Peller attacked me… I barely got away."

Shock ran through me, but I held onto my questions until I'd run to the bathroom and gathered towels and bandages. I knelt beside the couch and pressed a towel to the wound before I finally looked at Mark's face. It was covered in dirt and scratches. Twigs and leaves clung to his wet hair.

"He came to your house? He attacked you with what? A knife?" I couldn't get the questions out fast enough. "Where is he? Is he still around?" My gaze shot toward the door, realizing it was unlocked, putting us both in danger.

"No. At his house. I went back."

Mark drew a sharp intake of breath as I removed the towel, lifted his shirt, and examined the wound. I was no expert. It didn't look deep, yet it might require stitches.

I shifted my gaze back to his face, needing to hear the rest. "Why did you go back? I don't understand."

"I needed to know. I couldn't get it out of my mind."

"Know what? He caught you? That's when he attacked you? Did you find anything? See anything?"

Mark raised a weak hand to forestall my questions. His words were halting as he shifted on the couch, allowing me better access to the gash. A sheen of sweat coated his pale face.

"I wanted to get into the basement to see if the boy was there." He winced in pain, and his breathing hitched as I pressed a large, white bandage to the cut. "I scouted around the outside, but Peller came at me with a knife."

My hand stilled for a moment before I resumed, my mind racing to imagine the scene he described.

"I fought him and almost got away." His words broke off in a hiss as the antiseptic made contact. "He got me in the side. I had no choice. Jumped in the lake and swam to the next property."

I stared at him, the image vivid—Peller lunging with a knife, the chaos of the struggle. And Mark, bleeding and desperate, hurling himself into the cold, dark lake.

"You swam with that wound? Across the lake?"

Mark's lips quirked into a grim smile. "Yeah, adrenaline does wonders, I guess."

"Where's Peller now?" I asked with another glance out the window, almost expecting to see Peller's sneering face, a bloody knife clenched in his fist.

"I don't know. At his house, I guess."

"We'll call the police." I straightened, intending to get my phone.

Mark grabbed my wrist. "No." His gaze bore into me with the same intensity as the word.

"But he attacked you." Confusion swamped my mind. It seemed logical to have Peller arrested.

"They won't believe me. Not after what happened the other night." Mark released his grip on my wrist, but his tone remained insistent.

"This is different. You know it was Peller. You saw him. You're injured."

"I didn't see his face. It was a man, and it was dark. I can't swear it was him."

I was dumbfounded and didn't hide it. "But you're sure it was Peller. You were on his property. Who else would it be? It doesn't matter if you saw his face."

"I don't want the police involved. Not yet."

Mark's voice was firm, not allowing any room for argument, but everything seemed off. This was our chance to get Peller. Why let it slip away? Yes, I lost confidence in the police after they told me to leave Peller alone, but he'd physically attacked Mark, and he had the wound to prove it.

"I want to let him think he got away with it," Mark said, obviously picking up on my confusion. "Then I'll set him up."

Mark's interest in Peller seemed to border on obsession, almost more so than mine. Why? Was he concerned about the boy, or did he have another reason to get close to Peller? For what end? Did his reluctance to contact the police stem from something else? Maybe this was an elaborate scheme to convince me he was innocent of any involvement with Peller. A ruse? A falling out between partners?

I glanced down at the bandage neatly taped to his side. The wound didn't appear severe. It could be self-inflicted. Yes, he was soaking wet, but was it because of a swim in the lake or from the rain? Was this staged for my benefit?

***

I sat up in bed, my eyes wide, my breathing ragged. My gaze swept the barren room, barely visible in the early morning light. I wasn't in the bathroom, but in my small twin bed with thin covers draped over my trembling body.

I scrubbed my hands over my face, trying to wipe away the dream's remnants. My therapist would have a field day with this one, but I'd never share it with her. The dreams seemed to have intensified. Was that possible? Each one I had was my worst one, so how could they degrade even further? There had to be a limit.

The vivid details replayed in my mind. I was in the bathroom in this cottage, running a bath, even though I preferred showers. I turned to grab a towel and heard a splash behind me. Pivoting to the tub, the water was a dark brownish red, like blood and dirt mixed together. Something floated in the tub. I only saw the tip. Rolling up my sleeve, I plunged my hand into the water and encountered something soft.

I pulled out a stuffed toy. But not just any toy. It was Abby's favorite, a small pink rabbit we'd given her for Christmas one year. It was missing an ear, but she adored it. Now, its eyes and nose were gone, and it had taken on the water's distasteful color. I screamed and threw it back into the tub only to see a child's hand reach up to grasp it and pull it under. But it wasn't Abby's hand. I would know hers anywhere. It was larger, belonging to an older child. A boy?

I awoke with that horrible image in my brain. What did it mean? Was it pointing out a connection between Abby and the boy? Or could it be a connection between Keith and Peller? Was there a connection? Is that why I'd felt a wave of something familiar when I'd seen that old photo of Graham Peller? Or did he simply remind me of someone else?

I needed to clear my head. Coffee should do the trick, followed by a canoe run. A glance out the window told me the rain had stopped, but the clouds hung low and gray over the water. I might be in for a dousing, but I didn't care. Nothing soothed me more than being on the water, no matter how gray. Often, that grayness matched my mood and gave me the sense a close friend accompanied me.

As I turned on the coffeemaker, my thoughts drifted to Mark. How was his injury this morning? Something told me it'd be fine, nothing more than a minor cut. It had seemed painful, but was that an act? I admitted I didn't have any practice with cuts, having experienced nothing more than scrapes and bruises during my childhood and Abby's.

I opened the cupboard to retrieve a mug and squelched a scream.

Chapter 35

Stepping back, I clapped a hand over my mouth. My eyes wide, my heart beat viciously. *How can this be? What's going on?*

I reached out but snatched my hand back, unable to understand what I saw. Backing away until my legs connected with the couch, I lowered myself onto it, never removing my gaze from the stuffed toy that nestled on the shelf amongst the mugs and glasses.

Was I still dreaming? Would I wake up to find myself in the midst of another horrible nightmare? I ran my hands over my legs, up my torso, and across my face. I was awake. This was real. Or at least as real as a weird, almost paranormal experience could be.

Was that the reasoning? Was Abby or some other child haunting me? I didn't think so. Not that I didn't believe in ghosts, but why would it take three years to track me down and find me in this cottage. This place had nothing to do with my past or Abby. There had to be another explanation.

I dragged in several deep breaths, working on lowering my heart rate, hoping my head would function properly. "You can do this. It's just a toy, nothing else. It won't bite."

Making my way to the cupboard, I reached up. My fingers trembled as I grabbed the stuffed animal. Cold sweat trickled down my back, and dizziness washed over me. I glanced around the room as if someone watched me, witnessing my confusion as I wondered if I'd brought the toy here myself in some fit of madness. Had I? My breathing shallow, my heartbeat pulsed. Impossible.

I narrowed my concentration and focused my gaze on the toy, realizing it was an exact duplicate of Abby's stuffed bunny. The same color, size, and look. I turned it over to examine it. Someone had removed the ear, although seemingly cut with scissors. It wasn't wet or dirty like the toy in my dream, nor worn from constant handling with often sticky and dirty fingers. And it didn't look like it had spent a night curled up in a child's arms. It appeared brand new.

As I cradled the toy, I remembered Abby's tiny hands curling around it, clutching it so fiercely that we had to pry it from her grip just to wash it. Abby would tug on its remaining ear, mumbling to it in that special, nonsensical way of toddlers. The memory's raw ache bloomed. Her child's treasure, lost forever, buried with her. But now it was here, a replica in my hands "This can't be real," I said, licking the taste of salt from my lips.

But it wasn't, was it? This wasn't the same toy, not the same object my daughter had held.

A faint splash echoed in my mind, just like in the dream. My head snapped up, eyes darting to the door as if the sound came from somewhere outside. Complete silence. I shivered, recalling the dream's grimy water, the child's hand. Had Abby reached for it? Or was it the boy? I rubbed my palms on my jeans as if to wipe away an invisible stain, but the sensation of wet, sticky residue lingered. My throat tightened. "It was just a dream," I said, trying and failing to reassure myself.

How did this happen? The toy appeared immediately after I dreamed of it. Or did it? How long had it been in that cupboard before I noticed it? Could my subconscious have seen it during one of my hazy grief-stricken sessions and subsequently created the dream?

Or was this a message from Abby? Was she telling me the boy was in danger and needed me?

My brain told me to think logically. I saw the toy for what it was. An object to throw me off, something to drive me crazy. It came close, especially on the heels of the dream, but this bunny was not the one my daughter had cherished. That one was in her arms as they lowered her coffin into the ground.

Someone who knew the effect it would have on me planted this one in my cottage. Someone wanted to hurt me. I needed to find out who.

The same three people came to mind: Peller, Keith, and Mark. My ex-husband headed the list. He knew the bunny. He'd know how it'd affect me, but why would he do such a thing? Did he hate me so much? I couldn't imagine the Keith I knew doing something so horrible.

As for Peller and Mark, the only way they'd know about the toy is if someone told them, namely Keith. This led me back to whether my ex-husband was in cahoots with one or both men to send me over the brink into insanity.

"Why would Keith do this?" I said, pacing. He wasn't like that, not when we were together. But three years of separation could change a person. I'd changed. Why not him?

And Peller? He'd never met Abby, yet I suspected he was cunning and manipulative enough to dig up this piece of my past if he thought it might break me. My mind flashed to Mark, who could have learned about the bunny through Keith and used it in some twisted attempt to connect with me. Did he expect me to run to him for help or comfort? Each possibility seemed more absurd than the last yet no less possible.

I stared at the rabbit, wondering if it meant something I'd missed, a bridge between Abby and the boy I'd yet to save. A feeling I'd failed my daughter crept through my veins, slithering its way into my mind. Was this a second chance to save a child? To undo my greatest regret? I clutched the rabbit, a fierce determination blossoming inside me. I couldn't save Abby, but I could still save him. The thought surged through me, steeling me. I would do whatever it took.

I glanced around the room, remembering I was on my own out here, and no one would burst through the door to help me. I took a steadying breath, meeting my gaze in the dusty mirror by the door. "You can handle this," I said, an intense light in my eyes. "You don't need them. You can do this on your own."

***

After working through the shock, a renewed sense of purpose clung to me. I wasn't crazy. All three men hid something. I was sure of it. For Keith and perhaps Mark, it was to have me labeled as insane, for whatever reason they might have. For Peller, it was the boy, but without proof, I'd get no help. So, I either needed to find proof or find the boy and rescue him.

The morning was still foggy and damp but with no sign of rain. The forecast called for the sun to emerge and burn off the mist that coated the lake. I had breakfast and a relaxed cup of coffee, if only to kill time until it was reasonable to wake up Mark. My gaze focused on the lake, but my mind remained centered on the stuffed bunny that had joined my other treasures in the tin under the bed.

Whoever planted it in my cottage may have wanted to throw me off or scare me away, but I was even more focused on finding the person responsible... along with the boy.

I glanced at my watch and decided it wasn't too early, but it turned out Mark had beaten me to the day. The driveway was empty. I assumed he was off to Victoria for his work, obviously more diligent in that area than I was. Most days, I needed to remind myself I had some sort of employment, the neglected to-do list on my desk a source of shame.

I eyed the canoes lying upside down on his dock. Mark had said I could borrow one whenever I wanted. He didn't say I needed to ask first. The canoe offered an escape, both physical and mental, and right now, I needed it.

With the canoe in the lake, I slipped into my rhythm, the paddle cutting through the water. I followed my usual routine, planning to end with a loop around the island before heading to the cottage. But as the island came into sight, my thoughts converged in that spot where I had a clear view of the dock.

I squinted, scanning the wharf almost instinctively for something left behind. A trinket, a sign, anything masquerading as a message. I knew it was futile. Our bizarre game of gifts ended days ago, but I clung to the irrational hope something, some clue, might still be there.

The property remained eerily still. No movement, no bark of a dog, not even the faintest sign of life. Had Peller moved out during the night after attacking Mark? Had he decided we were too close and it was time to disappear? A lump formed in my chest at the thought.

I started to turn the canoe toward home, the sun breaking through the clouds to warm my back. I anticipated the relaxation, the steady rhythmic lull of my paddling and the water lapping against the canoe.

Then I saw it. A flash. A quick, sharp glint of light that snapped me out of my thoughts like a gunshot. My head swung back toward Peller's property, my breath catching in my throat.

A camera? My gaze darted from tree to tree, expecting to catch sight of Peller crouched in the bushes, binoculars or camera in hand. My gut churned at the thought. Would he report me? Accuse me of trespassing for paddling too close? It seemed like something he'd do.

I saw it again. My eyes narrowed, following the glint to its source. It came from the dock. Not on top but from the side. My heart pounded as I edged the canoe closer, fighting the urge to flee and the equally strong pull to investigate.

What was it?

Chapter 36

My arms plunged into action, propelling the canoe toward the dock, my focus on the shiny thing. Was it a flashlight? Some sort of safety device to guide people to the wharf at night? Was Peller trafficking drugs requiring after-dark movements? Was that what he hid in his basement? Or in those boxes? My imagination ran wild.

When the canoe bumped against the dock, I saw neither a flashlight nor a beacon. It was a mirror, tied to a protruding nail with a short piece of elastic. It dangled and bounced off the wood in time with the waves I'd created.

Glancing around, making sure no one watched me, I moved closer and grasped the mirror. As soon as my fingers circled it, I felt damp paper on the back. My heartbeat quickened as I flipped it over. A note, taped to the mirror, clearly written in ink by a childish hand. The letters, inconsistent in their size and shape, slanted to the left.

Disappointment filled my chest. Wetness blurred the words, making it almost impossible to read.

I carefully removed the soggy paper from the mirror and laid it on the canoe's bottom, afraid to fold it in case I destroyed the rest of the message.

Concerned about being discovered, I hurriedly propelled the canoe to the island and maneuvered it into a thicket of bushes, hidden from sight. I laid the paddle across my lap as I reverently picked up the note and studied it. Few words were discernable, but one stood out as the message's key: HELP.

The boy was in distress, begging for help, and probably counting on me as his savior. My problem revolved around what little else the note told me. Out of about ten words, three were legible: HELP, BOY, GONE. The rest were lost in a blur of messy ink.

It was enough to take to the police, to convince them the boy existed and needed help. I'd gather the other gifts, and along with this note, I'd make my case. Mark would back me up. No matter what other agenda he might have, I was certain he wanted to find the boy and bring him to safety. With his help, the police would follow up and do a real search of the house, from top to bottom, including the basement.

My thoughts tumbled over one another as I raced back across the lake, a sense of urgency driving me. If it hadn't been for my fear of facing Peller alone, I would've shown up at his door and forced my way inside his house. I realized I had to shove aside impetuous ideas and move forward with a real plan, one that involved Mark and the police.

I bypassed Mark's dock and steered the canoe to mine, almost tipping it in my haste to get inside the cottage. Every minute counted. Dashing to the bedroom, I dropped to my knees and snatched the tin box from under the bed. As I opened the lid, the sight of the stuffed toy hit me like a slap on the face, reviving memories both old and new. With a shaky hand, I removed it and set it aside. I didn't want to get into that with the police. It was too painful, too close to my heart. That was between me and whoever put it in the cottage.

The damp note took its place.

I scrambled to my feet and, clutching the tin under one arm, snagged my car keys from the hook, my phone from the table. Gravel crunched under my sneakers as I raced to the car. I slid into the driver's seat, and my clumsy fingers fumbled with my phone as I punched at the screen. Each second dragged on until my GPS finally told me I'd find the nearest RCMP division half an hour away.

The car roared to life, and I hit the gas, the tires kicking up a cloud of dust as I pulled onto the road. My focus was split between the hilly, winding road and the boy's plight. Was he trapped? What condition was he in? And how would I convince the police to act? Especially after the last fiasco.

I pulled into the police station parking lot, found a spot, and slammed the car into park. My fingers hovered over my phone before I typed out a text to Mark.

At RCMP station. Meet me here ASAP. The boy left me a note. I need backup.

I hit send, hoping he'd understand the urgency. Without waiting for a response, I grabbed the tin and pushed the car door open.

The RCMP satellite office occupied a small, brick building next to the post office. No receptionist manned the front desk. If you walked through the doorway, someone showed up to help you. Thankfully, I caught the eye of an officer as soon as the door clicked shut behind me. Unfortunately, I recognized him as a cop at Peller's house that night. To be expected, I guess. They wouldn't have hundreds of officers patrolling the quiet area of Sala Lake and its surroundings.

His raised brows and slight smirk told me he recognized me too, yet he used a polite and professional tone to instruct me to take a seat. I perched on the hard, plastic chair near the door, but my nerves craved motion. Since I didn't dare pace, my legs jiggled at a frenetic rate.

My mind spun with images of the boy and Peller, filled with atrocities I didn't want occupying space in my head. And the note... GONE... what did it mean? What could have happened?

"Ms. Hampton?"

I inwardly cringed. Not a good sign when a cop remembers your name. I faced the same two cops as I did the other night, another bad sign. This might be harder than I expected, a thought that made my stomach flip. My carefully planned argument disappeared from my mind as I grasped the box in a crushing hold.

"Yes...I need to talk to someone about... fresh evidence."

The cop raised his eyebrows. "Fresh evidence against Mr. Peller? You still think he's hiding a child in his house?"

I searched his face for sarcasm, but the officer kept his expression unreadable. "I have proof," I said, offering him the box as if it was the holy grail. He made no move to take it from me, instead turning an almost disinterested look upon it. "Give me a few minutes, please. Wait here."

The two men left the waiting room as I remained seated, my breathing rapid and my hands clasped around the tin. I'd made it over the first minor hurdle. The next would likely be higher.

My gaze flitted between the clock on the wall behind the counter and the door through which the officers had disappeared. I wanted to race from the building and return to the sanctity of my cottage, burrowing under my bedcovers and wishing the world away. I wanted to smack that door and demand they help me save the boy. I wanted someone to stand by my side and help me.

Despite my poor conception of time, only five minutes passed before the younger officer returned and asked me to follow him. I sprang to my feet and scurried to keep up with him, the box clutched under my arm.

He led me to a tiny room about the size of my kitchen and only slightly more modern. A beat-up wooden table sat in the center with four equally used plastic chairs, closely related to those in the waiting area. The walls closed in on me, and the box took on a heaviness, though it weighed almost nothing, its tin edges pressing into my skin.

I didn't hesitate when a cop waved his hand toward a chair, only because my legs threatened to give out on me. The moment of truth was here. If they didn't believe me now, they never would. And then, what would I do?

My gaze swung to the door as another man entered. Tall and heavily built, his gray hair and lined face suggested a superior rank and experience. He introduced himself as Assistant Commissioner James Holt, confirming my suspicions. None of the men sat. Instead, the AC stood over me, his two officers behind him. I didn't know if intimidation was their intention, but it certainly produced that result.

"Dean told me you have new evidence against Mr. Peller," he said, gesturing toward the youngest cop. "Why don't you fill us in?"

Encouraged by his soft and understanding tone, out of sync with his appearance, I recounted my canoe run and how I'd spotted the mirror on the dock, suspecting the boy had put it there.

"Why did you think it was the boy?"

"That's how we've communicated in the past. Using the dock."

Holt exchanged glances with the other cops. "He left you messages?"

Was that a note of condescension I heard? Was he patronizing me?

I drew a deep breath, steadying my nerves. "Not really messages, per se. We've exchanged gifts." I knew the best way to make him understand was to show him. Heat rose in my cheeks as I fumbled with the box lid before finally getting it open.

The men leaned forward and peered into the box as I held it out. Gazing into it, I saw it as they would, and I realized how little I had in there. A feather wrapped in a small piece of paper, a leaf, a scrap of blue fabric, and the damp note, now curling as it dried.

I set the box on my knee, reached in, and lifted out the paper that held the feather and gently opened it. "First, he left this for me."

"A feather." The officer named Dean sounded underwhelmed.

"Yes." My voice rose with desperation. "You see, I left him one, and he gave me one in return. It's a type of communication. And...and he gave me a drawing with it." I unfolded the paper. "See. It's him with a man. And it looks like he's hitting him."

"You can prove this came from a boy in Peller's house?"

"I'm telling you it did."

He nodded but appeared far from convinced. "What else?" said Holt.

"I left him some stones, and he responded with the leaf." As I spoke the words, I realized how weak they sounded, but I couldn't stop there. They needed to know everything. "Then I left him a book, but Peller found it and destroyed it."

A long finger pointed to the box. "I meant what else is in there?"

"It's the note I found today, taped to the back of a mirror." I couldn't suppress my excitement as I removed the note from its resting place with reverent, shaky fingers. This was solid proof. "It got wet, and most words are illegible, but the important ones are clear."

I laid the paper flat on the table, careful not to smudge the writing further. When Holt looked at the soggy note, his gaze flicked upward, eyebrows raised. Was that disdain in his expression? He'd already decided. I saw it in his eyes, a skepticism, as if I'd presented a doodle from a bored child. I wanted to scream, shake him, tell him he didn't understand, but I tightened my grip on the box.

"Where's the mirror?" His tone told me he already knew the answer.

"I left it there," I said, dismayed, realizing my mistake and searching for justification. "I never thought to remove it. He could use it again to send me another message."

"Did you take a picture of it when it was still taped to the mirror?" Again, the knowing tone.

My shoulders slumped. I sucked at evidence gathering. "No, I didn't."

"You remember we didn't find anything the last time we searched Peller's place at your behest?"

"Of course, I remember." The more this man spoke, the less I liked him. He treated me like a young child who'd been caught stealing candy for the second time. "But this is proof. It's a direct call for help. We can't ignore it." My voice cracked on my last words, and I hated myself for it. I thought about the attacks against me, the faulty brakes, the jet ski incident. Was now the time to mention them? Would they strengthen my case? Or would they sound like the desperate ramblings of a desperate woman? Could I prove they were deliberate?

And what about Mark's knife attack? The one he absolutely didn't want revealed to the police?

My mind snagged on that thought as the officer picked up the note and skimmed it again before handing it back. "It's not enough. We've already conducted a search, and there's no reason to suspect Mr. Peller of wrongdoing. You can't even prove this came from his dock." His tone held a finality, an invincible wall.

He held up a placating hand to stop my protest. "We can't chase phantoms without more," he said.

I bit back a retort, and my stomach sank as I clutched the box to my chest. Why wouldn't anyone take this seriously?

My head lifted in surprise when Dean stepped forward. "I could take a run out and speak to Mr. Peller again. Just a kind of follow-up visit."

I held my breath, immensely grateful for the effort but not wanting to move a muscle in case I disrupted the thin veil of tension in the room, making it fall against me. His boss seemed to consider the suggestion, but a knock interrupted him. All heads swiveled to the door as another officer poked his head into the room.

"Mr. Webb is here. Said it has something to do with…" He nodded toward me, and my confidence soared knowing Mark came to support me.

"Send him in," Holt said, any question of Dean going to Peller's pushed aside.

Mark entered, his gaze never reaching me, his shoulders tense, his mouth set in a grim line. His greeting was brief, serious, sending a rush of anxiety through me. Something was wrong. I'd expected him to be eager to support me, to find the boy. The look he finally gave me was unreadable, his face a mask.

"Mr. Webb, what brings you here?" Holt asked.

"Julie told me to meet her. Said the boy left her a note." His hesitation hung there like someone had asked him to defuse a bomb without him knowing which wire to cut. He'd once told me he believed in my instincts, so why the uncertainty now?

"You weren't with her when she found it?" The cop's tone sounded hopeful.

"No, I had business in Victoria. I stopped by her cottage. Shortly after she left, I think."

"So, you never saw the note?"

"Not that one, no." Mark sent me an apologetic glance, as if he'd revealed my big secret, but my brain remained mired in confusion.

"What do you mean, not that one?" Holt asked, a frown appearing on his face, his confusion mirroring my own.

"I found this."

Mark removed a plastic bag from his pocket and slid it across the table. I strained to see what was in it but didn't recognize the folded paper or pen inside. With a quick glance at Holt, I saw his eyes fill with interest. What had Mark found?

Chapter 37

The lake's surface glittered in the fading light, its dark ripples mesmerizing. In the evening's growing darkness, I felt tied to this spot, the water holding me in place, unwilling to let me escape.

A faint sensation of cold and damp eased through my clothing, but I didn't care enough to go inside or pull on an extra layer. Scattered circles appeared on the water's surface, fading away within seconds. Fish captured the unsuspecting mosquitoes who dared to hover close to the water.

I empathized with the bugs. I'd experienced firsthand what it was like to be taken unaware. Why be so trusting that you became oblivious to the danger hiding beneath the surface? Evil could lurk anywhere, even behind a mask of calm and friendliness. You could only rely on yourself.

What had happened? Nothing made sense anymore. I couldn't imagine dropping any lower than this. But I'd said that in the past and look at me now.

After handing that bag to the cop, Mark finally met my gaze straight on. I didn't understand the pity in his look. Not at first, but dread built deep inside me. Why pity?

The officers gathered around, Dean unsealing the bag with efficiency, using tweezers to remove the single piece of paper and hold it up to his supervisor. Holt's brow furrowed as he scanned the words.

"Where did you get this?" Holt's voice was clipped, suspicious.

"In Julie's cottage," Mark said, his voice low.

The world tilted. My head jerked back as if he'd hit me.

"What?" The word tumbled out, disbelieving. Why had Mark been in my cottage? And what did he find?

The assistant commissioner shifted his gaze to me, his voice laced with accusation. "Why didn't you mention this to us before?"

"I don't know what it is," I said as I stood and took a step forward, my pulse erratic.

Dean flipped the paper toward me, giving me a clear view of a handwritten note. The words shocked me.

I'M IN THE BASEMENT. HELP ME.

No missing words, no blurriness, no ifs or buts.

Scrawled in uppercase letters, the handwriting looked like mine. Was it? Had my hand produced that note?

"No." My voice was a whisper, barely audible. My vision narrowed, tunneling in on that damning scrap of paper. My voice rose. "I didn't write that."

"Who wrote it?" Holt's tone turned steely, the soft voice of earlier now gone, replaced by coldness.

I couldn't answer. My mouth opened in a silent cry. My gaze shifted to Mark. His pitying look now made perfect sense, and it cut deeper than anything Holt said.

He didn't believe me. None of them did.

Their silent judgment suffocated me. My mind raced, trying to explain the inexplicable. Fear mingled with a rising tide of doubt.

Mark's gaze lingered on my face, his expression soft with sorrow. It wasn't the look of someone on my side. It was the look of someone who believed I'd lost my senses.

Maybe he was right. They might bundle me into a white van and haul me away to an institution.

Perhaps they should.

Mark cleared his throat and turned to Holt. "I found the pen beside it. Everything was on the coffee table."

Accusation, pity, an overall weariness in having to deal with crazies. It was all there in the cop's eyes. "Did you write this, Ms. Hampton?"

"I... it's similar to... my handwriting, but I don't understand." My voice trailed off. I had no explanation. I wanted to fade into a wisp and disappear. I imagined how I appeared to the four men who towered over me. Confused, defeated, an inconsequential grief-stricken woman who stood on the edge of insanity.

"Did you write this one, too?" Holt asked, pointing at the water-damaged note on the table. "Was this a practice run?"

"No. I swear I didn't. It's not the same writing. Compare them." I desperately tried to defend myself, but pity and frustration filled the gazes of the men before me.

"You sound like the old stories," Holt said, his displeasure apparent. "The Shadow Woman, seeing ghosts where there aren't any."

My credibility sank through the floor with no way for me to claw it back. I tried anyway. I pointed to the note Mark had delivered. "I've never seen that before."

"It was on your coffee table," Mark said again, his tone soft. "In plain sight."

"I left early this morning. I never even noticed it." The argument held little water. I'd already admitted it looked like my handwriting. But I didn't recall writing it.

"Ms. Hampton." The cop's tone resembled that of a father about to chastise his daughter for causing trouble. "You may not realize this, but I could press charges against you for mischief and harassment. This is serious."

"I didn't..." No words existed to describe how lost I felt. I envied mosquitoes. It was a quick and painless death, flying too close to the water their only mistake. No humiliation, no pitying looks, no stern fatherly warnings.

"I suggest you go home, pack your things, and leave the area," Holt said, his voice hard and unforgiving. "I'll keep these items along with my report. Stay far away from Graham Peller's property. Any further incidents, I won't hesitate to press charges. This is your last chance."

I wanted to argue, to fight for the boy, but it was four against one. I wouldn't win this battle.

Mark's eyes avoided mine, his face an unreadable slate. He'd withdrawn, so easily siding with the police officers, leaving me to flounder in the terrifying silence, alone with my untrustworthy memories and their sympathetic gazes.

Something was wrong. A strong case could be made that the problem was me. Certainly, everyone seemed to think so. The police, Peller, Mark, and even Keith. I admitted I should add my name to that list.

But what if it wasn't me? What if someone set me up? Who could it be? The obvious culprit was Mark. He "found" the note I didn't remember writing. Had he planted it or lied about where he found it?

That didn't explain the handwriting. Was it mine? My first instinct was to say yes. It certainly looked like it, but could he have forged it? He'd proven himself proficient at impersonating someone. He'd forged his ID as a municipal officer. How hard was it to imitate my writing, especially in block letters?

And he was the one who'd found "proof" of Peller's past behavior toward his wife and child. Was that concocted, like everything else? If so, then why? How did Mark benefit from this? Amusement? Entertainment? It spoke of his desperation for diversion if he went to this extent. Should I go to a movie, or should I drive my neighbor off the deep end?

Mark was always one step ahead. It made me wonder about his abilities, the ease with which he slipped into a support role. Each doubt I voiced, each question—were they fuel for him?

The problem was I didn't recall writing that note. There had to be another explanation.

My mind shifted to the day of Abby's death when I'd blacked out for hours. The medical explanation was the trauma of losing my daughter, sometimes to blame for blackouts. Had it happened again? Or was it amnesia? Insanity? The last one worried me the most. It brought me back full circle to whether I imagined everything to do with the boy. No gifts, no sightings, no notes. No boy. Just an overworked, overwhelmed, traumatized imagination that got its kicks out of driving its owner crazy, literally.

Now, as I watched the unsuspecting mosquitoes, I thought I didn't have any more battles in me.

If I was insane and imagined the whole thing, it was logical it traced back to Abby's death, which coincidentally, or not, was also by drowning. So, again, why was my imaginary friend on the dock a boy? Why wouldn't I have created a girl, a match for Abby? Good question. Maybe my imagination didn't want to push its luck. I could jump off a bridge, and then it would be bye-bye Julie and, with it, my imagination. My mind could be in self-preservation mode, even as it created the problem in the first place.

Two things were clear. I couldn't trust myself, and I couldn't trust anyone else.

***

So full of life, so precious, Abby had a perpetual smile. And she sometimes used that smile to her benefit. Even though I knew she wrapped us around her finger, I didn't mind. It highlighted her intelligence and tenacity. And to be honest, it didn't happen often.

A special day, I reveled in that charming smile. We were on the mainland, where we'd loaded our bikes onto the back of our car, made our way to Nanaimo, and caught the ferry to Horseshoe Bay. Next, we drove to Stanley Park, unloaded the bikes, and embarked on the trail that encircled the park, stopping to admire the cityscape view.

Our daylong adventure ended with a meal from a shawarma food truck, followed by a dessert from Rocky Point Ice Cream. Happy with our time together, we made our way to the public parking lot to load up the bikes. Concentrating on attaching the bikes to the carrier, I listened to Abby's excited chatter, her eagerness to tell her father about our adventures.

The brief silence didn't warn me. The scream for help did.

I pivoted on my heel to see Abby swept away by an enormous wave. Where did it come from? We weren't beside the water. Abby's mouth was wide open, and the scream should have sounded like hers, but strangely, it didn't.

The blanket tangled around my legs as I surged from the bed, sending me sprawling to the floor. I scrambled upright, chest heaving, and caught the alarm clock's faint glow that showed 2:05 a.m. Its dim digits cut through the pitch blackness, enough for me to get my bearings. I stood rigid as a board in the bedroom, my arms stiff at my sides, like a gunslinger bracing for a showdown. My senses strained, every nerve attuned to the silence.

The wind whistled through the window I'd cracked open earlier, the sound sending chills across my skin. I imagined the Shadow Woman hovering over the lake, her arms open wide, enticing the children to join her. I took several deep breaths, trying to steady myself. Just the wind. Just a dream. No, a nightmare. Yet, it seemed so real.

I padded to the bathroom before returning to my bed. Belatedly, curled under the covers, exhaling slowly, willing the tension from my body, I remembered I hadn't shut the window. Groaning, I tossed off the blanket and swung my legs over the side. Not wanting a repeat performance, I crossed to the window and froze as my hand reached toward the frame.

The sound came again. Not the wind. Not a dream. A child's cry for help.

My pulse spiked. This wasn't the faint, distant sound I'd heard the other day across the lake. No, this was close. Terrifyingly close.

I bolted for the door, shoved my feet into sneakers, and flicked the light switch, frowning when the porch remained in darkness. Swearing at the burned-out bulb, I grabbed a sweater off a chair and dragged it on.

The cool air struck me as I yanked the door open, but it barely registered in my fevered brain. I needed to find the boy. He was near, calling for me.

I stepped onto the lawn, every muscle tense, and listened. The screaming had stopped. Where had it come from?

"Where are you?" I called, my voice trembling with urgency.

Silence.

I wanted to shout in anguish. Why hadn't I moved faster? What happened to him?

Then it came again, a weak cry. "Help me."

I spun toward the sound, my heart hammering. The back of the cottage. I sprinted around the side, the ground uneven beneath my feet, the darkness disorienting me. Clouds smothered the moonlight, concealing everything.

"Where are you?" My voice rose in a shout.

No response.

I tried again. "Where? Tell me where you are."

"Help."

The voice fainter, I followed it, plunging into the thicket behind the cottage. Branches clawed at my arms and slashed my face as I stumbled forward. I swept my hands through the darkness, grasping for anything that would lead me to him.

The wind whispered through the trees and the maze of entwining branches. The sporadic and sparse moonlight created eerie shapes that blurred my sense of direction.

"Where?" I said, increasingly desperate. *Why doesn't he answer me? Why is he weakening? He must be injured, barely able to respond.*

I needed help, or at the very least, a flashlight. "Wait here. I'll be back."

I tripped over a log as I spun toward the cottage. Picking myself up, I scrambled for the back door. A flashlight hung from a coat rack. As I prayed the batteries were fresh, I swiveled to the door. And screamed.

Chapter 38

A man stood on the threshold, outlined by the moonlight that peered from behind the clouds. I raised the flashlight to hit him.

"What are you doing?" Confusion and a touch of fear tinged his voice.

"Mark?" I lowered my arm, relief rushing through me. The welcome prospect of help put my distrust and suspicions on hold.

"What's going on? I heard you shouting."

I rushed forward and grabbed his arm, dragging him around the cottage. He didn't resist, seeming to understand my urgency, running alongside me until I stopped at the edge of the trees. "The boy. He's in the bushes. He must've escaped Peller," I said, shining my flashlight on the trees.

Mark pivoted toward me. "What?"

I ignored the disbelief in his tone. "He's in there, but I can't find him. It's too dark." I shoved past Mark, desperate to get to the boy. "Something's wrong. He must be hurt. We need to find him. Call 9-1-1."

I clambered through the tangled brush again, uncaring if Mark followed me. Knowing he was there as backup was enough.

"Where are you?" I shouted, straining to hear the boy's voice.

My heart knocked as silence answered me. Every time I called, the whistling wind responded instead. I realized, bitterly, Mark would take the silence as more proof of my instability. I pictured him filing it away as ammunition to use against me.

Snapping branches signaled Mark's approach.

"Did you call them?" I asked over my shoulder, my sweater snagging on the thorns as I shoved them aside.

After a moment, it sank in that he hadn't replied. I stopped and turned to look at him.

The darkness obscured his expression, his eyes nearly black as he scanned the bushes, empty of any sign of the boy. Panic surged through me. Did he care if we found him? Or was he here to prove me wrong, to confirm whatever version of "crazy Julie" he'd shared with the police?

"Did you call 9-1-1?" I needed to hear the answer I knew he would utter.

"It's not a good idea." His voice was firm, and even though I couldn't see his face clearly in the dark, I sensed the pity in his eyes.

I wouldn't give up. "We need help. He may be hurt." I heard the desperation in my voice. I had to get through to him.

"Let's find him first."

"You don't believe me."

"Julie..."

Tears blurred my vision. This was the man who presented the police with evidence of my insanity. He wasn't here to help me find the boy. He was here to save me from myself, from whatever evil thing he thought occupied my mind.

I wanted to tell him to leave. I wanted to shout at him to never show his face around here again. But common sense told me to grit my teeth and bear it. I might still need help, and when I found the boy, I'd have the satisfaction of seeing the remorse on his face.

I turned toward the blackness of the woods and directed my attention to the boy. "Answer me. Please answer. Just a small noise, something to guide me. I'm here to help."

Only the sounds of our combined breathing and the rustle of leaves in the wind reached my ears. "Please," I repeated. I desperately wanted to find and help him, but something more sat on the table. I needed to prove to Mark I wasn't crazy, that I hadn't imagined this poor tortured boy.

A nasty sliver of uncertainty insinuated itself into my head. What if I'd just heard an echo? The forest twisted sounds and tricked the mind into hearing cries that weren't there. Or worse, what if I was the only one who heard him? Another lonely voice in my head? Abby's memory flashed. Was I projecting her lost voice onto another child, one who didn't exist?

Urgency surging through me, I ran the flashlight's beam over the bushes again. Pushing through and searching underneath, I hoped to glimpse a sneaker or an ankle. I moved the light over the tree tops in case he'd climbed onto a limb and hid like an owl.

Nothing. No gleam of pale skin. No flash of bright clothing. No sound.

"Where is he?" I whispered.

"He ran away?"

I jolted. I'd been talking to myself, forgetting Mark was behind me. What thoughts ran through his head? The poor, crazy woman imagined another encounter with a nonexistent boy?

I spun around, waving the flashlight in Mark's face. "He was here. I heard him. He cried for help." I brushed past him, fought through the bushes, and stalked to the cottage, ignoring his shout of concern. I slammed the door behind me and slid the lock into place.

A wave of hopelessness washed over me. The boy's voice echoed in my mind, and I wondered if I'd crossed a line, if I'd fallen so deep that I saw no difference between what was real and what my shattered heart wanted so desperately to be real.

I closed my eyes as tears seeped past my lashes. I'd once failed a child I loved with everything in me. Not this time. I'd tear through every branch. If that boy existed, I'd find him. I had to.

***

Sleep evaded me for the rest of that night. I sat on the couch, a light blanket pulled over me, my wide-open gaze staring out the window, my ears listening for the faintest of sounds.

Yet, all was silent. Outside, the lake lay still, and even the birds remained quiet, as though they listened and waited too. My gaze darted to every dark corner, expecting a young face to appear.

I was certain I hadn't imagined it. I heard those cries. The boy begged for help, his distress clear.

At daybreak, I returned to the thicket, hesitating before entering, wanting to memorize each detail. Crushed and broken branches, flattened weeds, and muddy footprints attested to our visit hours earlier.

I bent over and studied the prints, searching for smaller ones, but all I saw were my sneaker treads and the larger imprints of Mark's boots. I examined the trees. The broken limbs were limited to those closer to the ground, probably caused by us or nature's creatures.

No sign of snagged clothing. No sign of a child.

I ventured further, bending to check under trees, behind rocks. I found no clues, making it impossible for me to prove anything.

Every rational part of me wanted to dismiss it, to believe I'd been wrong, that it was just the wind and my exhaustion. But I knew what I heard. The boy's voice was etched in my memory, and no amount of logic or rationalization erased it.

I knew it in my heart and soul. I'd heard him.

My shoulders slumping, my arms hanging loosely by my sides, I pictured Mark's face in the nighttime murkiness. His understanding look, was any of it real? Or was it part of some sick game, carefully crafted to erode my trust in myself? I replayed our last few conversations, scrutinizing every word, every glance, wondering if I'd missed a crucial detail, a subtle clue. Did that understanding and concern hide something darker, something that thrived on seeing me come apart?

Clearly, there'd be no help from Mark or the authorities. I had to go it alone. But first, coffee.

The early morning fog still coated the lake as the first sip of java hit my bloodstream.

"What do I know so far?" I spun from the window and paced across the living room's short length. "I wasn't wrong about the boy. He's in distress, trapped in Peller's house, but somehow, he got out and hid behind my house last night."

Speaking the words aloud made me realize how bizarre they sounded. If he was free and looking for help, why didn't he knock on the door? Why hide in the bush and call?

I conceded it seemed unimaginable. I took a long gulp of coffee, knowing it'd cool before I held it again. Leaving it on the kitchen counter, I exited the back door, heading straight for the bushes. This time, I ignored the footprints and broken twigs. I searched for something else and made quick work of the many remaining branches.

My hands throbbed, stinging where thorns scratched my skin. Mud caked my sneakers, but it didn't matter. I'd shred my hands to ribbons and roll myself in mud if it meant finding a trace of him.

I plunged my arms into the brush again, sweeping them from side to side. I froze when my right hand encountered what I was looking for.

Chapter 39

It was surprisingly small and cylindrical, about two inches in diameter and three inches high, fitting neatly into the palm of my hand. The moment my fingers closed around it, I realized my mistake. I should have bagged it, as the police would have. Fingerprints would point to the culprit, although he'd likely taken that into account and worn gloves. Still, Assistant Commissioner Holt wouldn't be happy. Again.

Whoever planted this in the bushes was one step ahead of me and knew my weaknesses. His goal was to convince everyone, even myself, I was crazy. He'd achieved at least part of that objective, but this find eased my mind. Someone manipulated me.

Hoping to make up for my oversight, I carried it to the house and sealed it in a clear, plastic bag. Then, I examined it. The markings on the bottom clearly revealed it as a Bluetooth speaker. Unfortunately, that was all it revealed. I guessed a remote control matched it.

I recalled a similar, although much larger, speaker we'd had in our old home, also controlled remotely, but you needed to stand within six feet of it for it to function. Had technology advanced far enough since then to extend the distance? Possible, but not likely too much farther. I suspected the person needed to be within a certain range. If that was the case, he'd holed up nearby last night, watching me, controlling both me and the speaker.

My stomach somersaulted. So close. This dangerous lunatic who set out to paint me insane had hidden within feet of me in the dark bushes. I shivered at the thought.

My first instinct was to accuse Peller, until a different, more treacherous person came to mind. Mark.

He was here, helping me search, and quick to remind me why the police wouldn't help. If he was behind this, he'd be the last person to call the RCMP, wouldn't he?

Yet again, what did he have to gain from this offensive against me? Was he friends with Peller? Were they in this together? Some sort of child trafficking ring?

I felt sick. This man had been in my cottage. I'd been in his. I told him everything. My past, my emotions, my suspicions about the boy. He knew how to manipulate me and play on those emotions. What else was he capable of? Apart from getting his kicks out of driving me crazy, did he have another purpose? Did he want to harm me physically, as well?

I took a shaky breath, releasing it slowly, trying to steady the emotions crashing inside me. No one believed me, not the police, not Keith, not even myself on my worst days, but it didn't matter. What mattered was the boy. I owed him. I owed Abby's memory. I owed myself. No matter how deep I had to wade into the darkness, I'd see this through.

I crossed the room and turned the locks on the cottage door. My gaze scanned the kitchen, falling on a carving knife. Its blade glinted under the dim light, almost daring me to pick it up. I reached for it, fingers curling around the handle. It gave me a strange mix of comfort and unease. I gripped it tighter, imagining what I might do if Mark or Peller showed up again.

Images flashed of Mark's intense gaze, Peller's mocking smile. Let them come. Let them try.

I wasn't running. Not anymore.

The best way, the only way, to end this was to find the boy and get out of here. My heart quickened at the thought. I glanced toward the locked door one last time, the knife firm in my grip. A strange calm settled over me. I wouldn't follow in the Shadow Woman's footsteps. I wouldn't collapse under the weight of my grief. The boy needed me.

I wasn't leaving without him.

***

I needed a plan I could carry out on my own. My biggest challenge was getting Peller out of the way. I wasn't a master of disguise, and I suspected Peller would see through it anyway. I needed something else.

Hopefully, Mark was away. I didn't want to worry about him coming upon me and spoiling it. Or worse, killing me and dumping me in the lake with cement blocks tied to my feet.

"I know. I'm paranoid and exaggerating," I said to the table. "But he's proven to be a master faker. I can't take any chances. I need to be careful he doesn't see me."

Ransacking the shed, I hunted for something useful, and as luck would have it, I heard Mark's car pull out of his driveway. He might be off to the corner store to pick up a dozen eggs, or he could be on his way to Victoria for work. At most, I had a full day ahead of me without him, and at the very least, twenty minutes.

I needed to make good use of those precious minutes. Scooting through the trees, I ran straight for Mark's cottage. I knew he never locked his door. Neither of us usually did, although with recent developments, I'd rethought that strategy.

My pulse pounded as I cracked open the door, the quiet click like a siren. If he hid somewhere, tricking me, waiting, I had no way to defend myself. But I pushed forward. I needed to know.

Mark's place had a similar layout to mine, only it was larger, newer, and much nicer. The front door opened into a modern kitchen with beautiful cabinetry and granite counters. Plenty of windows allowed the light to reach the open-concept kitchen and living room. He'd placed soft, white leather couches to allow the best view of the water and the wide-screen TV above the central fireplace.

I knew three bedrooms and two baths took up the rear of the house with a hallway heading down the middle to the back door. One of those bedrooms served as Mark's office. That was my destination. If he was up to something nefarious, I'd likely find it there.

I peeked into the first room to discover his personal bedroom. Basically tidy, with a neatly made bed and some clothing draped over a chair. A laundry basket sat handy for his discarded clothes. Another small television took up residence on the wall opposite the bed.

A picture on the wall drew my attention, making me take a few steps into the room. He'd never discussed his family, and now I saw a younger Mark standing between a tall, handsome older man in a military uniform and an attractive woman in a lovely, blue dress. Mark, sharply dressed in a suit, was obviously part of a formal occasion with his parents. A quick glance around the room told me I'd find little else here.

Not wanting to waste time, I moved onto the next room, obviously for guests, a double bed and a night table the only furnishings. A small painting of a sunny lake view adorned the wall. Sterile and impersonal, the room was perhaps never used.

My search ended in the last room. A twin bed took up one corner along with a small wooden chair. A laptop, printer, and scanner sat atop a desk along with neatly stacked papers and files. A large black chair on rollers was positioned to the side as if someone had recently risen from it and walked away.

The sight of Mark's laptop sitting dead center on his desk sent a jolt of unease through me. If he'd left for work, the computer would likely be gone too. Its presence meant one thing. I didn't have much time.

I jiggled the mouse, and the screen flickered to life, but my relief was short-lived. A login screen glared back at me, demanding a password. I hesitated, fingers hovering above the keys, the seconds ticking louder in my head. I couldn't guess it. Not without wasting precious time. My breathing hitched. This mission seemed doomed.

When I pulled open the first drawer, an unwelcome voice in my mind hissed "invasive," like I dug into someone's private life without permission.

But I ignored it, forcing myself to keep going. My hands shook as I shuffled through the contents, papers crinkling against my fingertips.

Tension tore at my insides. Every rustle of paper echoed in the room.

The documents on the right-hand side of his desk seemed work-related and innocuous. I turned to the left-hand side with little hope, already braced for disappointment.

But then I froze.

Chapter 40

A copy of an obituary.

My pulse thundered as I saw the name, the date, the photo. Ice flooded my veins, chilling me to the core.

Abby.

Her obituary. In his desk.

Dated three years ago, it featured my daughter's smiling face, her front tooth missing. She'd lost the tooth only two weeks before she died. I remember her excitement when she left it for the tooth fairy and got a shiny golden Loonie in exchange.

Now, my pained gaze moved from her smile to the little stuffed bunny she clutched in her small hands, as if she'd never let it go.

The last time she held that bunny, she'd fallen asleep in my arms. Now, its image assaulted me from Mark's desk, proof of a betrayal so deep it cut through me like a shard of ice driven into my heart.

I couldn't breathe. The pain in my chest seemed to constrict every muscle in my body.

Every chilling detail made sense now. That's how he knew about the bunny. He used this photo to disfigure the new toy and make it look like her old one, to plant that terrible seed of doubt. He'd twisted my grief, turned it into a weapon.

All his help, the comfort, the friendliness—it was a sham, a cruel game to him. My skin crawled with the sickening awareness that he knew every raw nerve and exactly how to press each one.

The stories about Peller, the little he'd told me about his own past. could all be fiction, devised to prey on my vulnerabilities. And he'd been so convincing.

The journalist friend, the municipal disguise...was any of it real, or had he woven a false tale, something sure to haunt me? Did he even visit Peller that day? Did he fake his own injury, making me believe Peller had come after him with a knife?

The faint sound of tires on gravel brought my head up with a jerk, making my heart race, ordering me to run. I stuffed the obituary back into the papers, my breath lodged in my throat as I imagined his footsteps drawing closer. Every nerve on edge, I dashed into the hallway. Turning right, I headed toward the back door. As I opened it and slid through, footsteps thumped on the kitchen's hardwood floors.

I gently closed the door until I heard a soft click that seemed like a gunshot to my ears. I ducked into the bushes, the branches scratching my arms as I moved into the tree cover. I watched as his silhouette moved across the office's window, his presence snatching my breath, even from a distance.

Taking the path between our properties was out of the question. He'd spot me in an instant if he so much as glanced through a side window. With a last look toward Mark's house, dread curled in my stomach. *Did I leave anything out of place? Would he discover I was there?* I pushed through the trees to the main road.

The energy that had propelled me through Mark's cottage drained away. My heart was weighed down with questions I couldn't answer and facts I hated to face.

Had Mark ever told me the truth? Every word he'd uttered twisted in my mind.

Entering my cottage, I shut the door behind me with a dull thud. My legs shaky, I made it to a chair and sank into it as my mind churned. Endless images stormed through it. Mark's sympathetic gaze, his encouraging smile, the obituary clutched in my trembling hands. I heard the boy's voice calling out for help, so real it still echoed in my ears.

I pressed my palms to my temples. "What's wrong with you, Julie? You knew. You suspected him. Why does this come as a surprise?"

Yes, I told myself. I'd known something was off with Mark, but within me there'd been a tiny flame of hope that I was wrong, that his intentions were good and pure, and he wanted to help the boy as much as I did. It hurt to see the flame extinguished.

He'd fooled me perfectly, pretending to be my friend, helping me research Peller and search for the boy. Was it all lies? Did Peller even have a son that drowned? Was the online article some elaborate hoax Mark had devised for me? Peller said he'd lost his son, but what were the exact circumstances? Yet Dan had confirmed it, hadn't he? I tried to recall our exact conversation. Had I misunderstood?

All Mark had told me was manipulation. But why? That was the question. What was his motivation? I missed something, but despite it all, a fierce clarity rose within me. The boy still existed, and I wouldn't abandon him. I'd risk whatever it took.

***

Every creak in the cottage sounded like a scream as I spread my makeshift rescue tools across the table. My gaze darted to the windows, scanning, searching. Was someone out there, watching me? Waiting?

A flashlight and first aid kit were obvious choices. But when I returned from the shed, a grim variety of other items joined the pile.

I weighed a crowbar in my hand, testing its heft. It'd make an excellent weapon if I needed it, though I prayed it wouldn't reach that level of violence. My fingers hovered over the box cutter, its blade dulled and speckled with rust. It might prove handy. I threw in the duct tape, only valuable when you didn't have it.

Finding a backpack big enough to hold everything proved harder than expected. I rifled through closets and drawers, my breath coming quicker as the clock raced against me.

"Yes," I said in triumph when my hands came across a bag in the back of a closet. Although battered and dirty, it would do the trick.

The jarring ring of my phone shattered the silence. I froze, so unaccustomed to hearing it ring that it struck fear in my heart. I stood, rooted to the floor, as if the phone itself threatened me. It rang again, each chime shriller than the last. I forced my way forward and picked it up with trembling hands. The name on the screen sent a fresh wave of anxiety through me.

Keith.

What did he want? In my recent experience, a call from Keith wasn't positive.

"Hello." I hated the trepidation in my voice. Why didn't I answer with confidence and strength?

"Julie. What's up? Are you okay? I'm worried about you."

I hesitated, my brows lowered in confusion. What kind of timing was this? "I'm fine. Why wouldn't I be?"

"An awful sense, that's all. Call it intuition or foreboding or whatever. But I feel something's wrong."

Intuition? Foreboding? Who was impersonating my ex-husband? He'd had no intuitive thoughts about me during our entire marriage. Now he got them from a hundred kilometers away? "Why would you think anything's wrong?" My voice sounded stiff and forced, but I couldn't hide my distrust. I wanted to believe this was an innocent call, that he'd somehow changed. But it was too strange.

"I'm in the area. I'll stop by."

Was this concern, or was he playing some twisted game of savior and villain? He hadn't so much as sent a concerned text in years, and now he was checking up on me? Twice?

"No!" I stopped, realizing the forcefulness of my response, but the last thing I needed was Keith's presence.

"I'm nearby…"

"Keith, not today." I tried to remain calm, seem normal, but the urgency slipped through. I didn't need him here, not when everything was about to come together. Not when I was on the brink of figuring out the truth.

Silence blasted between the phones. "You're not yourself, Julie. I want to help you."

Since when did Keith care? This wasn't the man who had shrugged off every plea for understanding during the end of our marriage. And now he called out of the blue, talking about intuition and foreboding? A cold sensation crept up the back of my neck. Was he the one messing with me? Had he somehow gotten a front-row seat to my breakdown?

He didn't want to help me. He wanted to drive me over the edge. Why was he in the area? He rarely came near here. The timing was too convenient. He must be involved or here to witness my downfall. I pictured him, hiding in the bushes with the remote in his hand, enjoying every moment of my torment. Or worse, working with someone else to drive me to the edge.

My mind spun with possibilities, each darker than the last. I couldn't afford to let him inside my head, not now. Not when I was this close to saving that boy and proving I wasn't crazy.

"Tomorrow, okay? That'd be better. I could even meet you in Victoria, if you want. We could do lunch." I rolled my eyes at the madness of my words. I glanced at the crowbar peeking from the backpack, my weapon to take on an ex-military man trained in battle tactics as I breezily proposed a lunch date.

A long silence followed as if Keith saw me standing in the kitchen, a sheen of sweat on my face, my clothing and hair disheveled, and wondered what to do with me.

"Okay," he finally said. "I'll call you in the morning, and we'll decide on a place."

I hastily agreed and disconnected.

Keith's call rattled me, but I couldn't let it break my focus. With no telling what he wanted or who else might show up, I needed to leave now, before anyone else tried to stop me. Before someone stole away my last bit of resolve.

A wave of doubt washed over me, but I braced myself. This wasn't the time to second-guess. I'd go, with or without help. I had the uneasy idea that I might not make it back in one piece. But the thought of leaving the boy, alone and terrified, was worse than anything I could face.

Chapter 41

I stared at my backpack brimming with paraphernalia and realized I was missing something. A plan. I couldn't very well bang around Peller's property and expect him not to notice.

I needed Peller away from his house, leaving me free to search for the boy. My mind scrambled to find a solution before I received an unwelcome visit from my ex. Sometimes he didn't take no for an answer. Despite his tacit agreement, if Keith was in the area, he may show up at any moment.

An idea took form. I booted up my computer, my fingers tapping an unsteady rhythm on the table as the screen came to life. Mark had sent me the file on Peller, but I needed to study it to put my fledgling plan into action.

My legs jiggled as the laptop powered up. I was so antsy I couldn't sit down. Finally, I sifted through my emails. There it was. The file I'd skimmed through without absorbing its full importance. Now, I devoured every detail—names, dates, addresses, anything to help build my strategy.

I straightened and drew several deep breaths. "Calm down," I said to myself, pressing my palms to the table's cool surface. I had no talent for deception, but over the phone, maybe I could fake it. I jotted notes and wrote my script. Each sentence was rehearsed, again and again, until the words flowed naturally. I projected myself into the past when I'd received a similar call and tried to imitate the same tone.

Too bad I couldn't enlist Mark. Clearly, he was better at lying than I was. But I wouldn't turn to him for help. Not ever. He was somehow involved in Peller's scheme.

Thinking about what was at stake bolstered my determination. A boy's life. I may have lost my daughter because of a moment's negligence, but I wouldn't sacrifice another young life. Instead, I'd take action.

I punched the numbers into my phone with clammy hands. I'd never done anything like this before. I knew Peller might see through my ruse, or he'd check with the gas company and have me figured out within minutes. But this was the only way I knew to get near that house without him catching on.

If he discovered me, this could land me in jail with no way to help the boy. But I couldn't let fear of failure stop me. I'd already lost so much, I wouldn't let that child be the next casualty of my errors.

I cleared my throat and dialed the number. My mind screamed at me to stop, to come up with an easier, safer way, but I reminded myself of the stakes. I wasn't doing this for me. It was for the boy.

Peller's gruff voice answered almost immediately, sounding as if I'd taken him from an important task. Good. The more distracted he was, the better.

"Mr. Peller, this is April Dilling from Island Gas under contract with the City of Victoria. Before we begin, I must inform you this call is being recorded for training purposes. Are you presently at your home in Victoria?" I recited the address I'd found in Mark's file.

I hoped the quiver in my voice was barely audible as I tried to keep my tone professional. One slip and he'd be onto me. I reminded myself to breathe, to take it slow, even as I imagined the boy trapped in his basement. *Stay calm, Julie. You can't save him if you panic now.*

"What is this about?" Peller's voice held a tinge of annoyance.

"There's a natural gas leak in your area, and we need to close all the lines and inspect each house to find the source."

"There's no need to inspect my house. I don't have a leak." Dismissive, I feared he'd hang up on me. I might not have the courage to start over with another call.

"I'm sorry, sir, but we have an inspection team equipped to determine that. We'll need to have access to your house."

"That's impossible. I'm over an hour away. You'll have to bypass it, that's all."

I added a note of firmness to my tone. "Sir, if you don't open the door for us, the team will forcibly enter."

"What? Break down the door?"

"Yes, sir. And we won't be financially responsible for the damage."

"You lay one hand on my door, and I'll sue both the city and you personally."

I moved the phone slightly away from my ear to compensate for his raised voice.

"I'm sorry, Mr. Peller. We'll give you ninety minutes to present yourself and give us full access to the house. That should be sufficient. After that time, the team will forcibly enter."

He paused, as if weighing my words. Every second of silence stretched like a rope, ready to snap. I imagined his face, brows drawn low in anger, his cheeks red with fury.

"Dammit! I'll have your hide for this," he shouted before cutting the connection.

"I hope to have yours," I said in a whisper. I released a breath, shaky but relieved.

So far so good. He bought it without question. I considered the risk of him calling the gas company to confirm my story, wishing I'd prepared a second layer of deception. If only I could've looped Mark in, used him as a decoy if things went south, but he was out of reach and untrustworthy.

I shook off that thought, realizing I needed to hurry. Once Peller reached Victoria, he'd catch onto the scam and call the police. Depending on their response time, I had about an hour to find the boy.

I grabbed my keys and backpack, every nerve buzzing with urgency. If I didn't move fast, I'd lose the narrow window of time I'd forced open. My thoughts hammered, imagining the consequences once Peller realized it was a setup.

Scurrying to my car, I flung my backpack onto the passenger's side and slid low in the driver's seat. My trembling hand adjusted the rearview mirror to give me a clear view behind me.

Peller needed to drive past to access the main road to Victoria. I couldn't risk meeting him and making him suspicious, so I'd wait before making my way onto the road. My fingers drummed against the steering wheel as I hunched low in the seat, eyes trained on the mirror. The idea of him slowing down, of those dark eyes landing on me, encased me in a sudden wave of icy fear.

If he spotted me now, he'd know something was going on. He'd turn his car around, and that would be it. The jig would be up, and I'd lose any chance to save that boy. I practically heard the clock ticking in my head, each second drawing him closer to realizing the truth. My heartbeat was deafening in the cramped space.

When his vehicle came into view, my pulse quickened even more. I pressed myself lower, my whole body tense as he crept past, obviously slowing down to look in my driveway. I glimpsed his lips set in a scowl and his narrowed eyes. Each second stretched, filled with the fear he might stop.

The second he left my sight, I exhaled, relief washing over me. But it was fleeting. No time to waste. I straightened, focused, already sensing the importance of my next step, with no turning back.

I started the ignition and slowly backed toward the end of the driveway, giving Peller a minute to navigate the curve ahead. Once on the road, my foot slammed onto the gas pedal and barely let up until I reached my destination.

I bypassed his driveway and maneuvered the car onto the shoulder farther up the road and hiked back, the backpack heavy in my hand. Mark had said he hadn't spotted security cameras on the property, but I knew it was risky. All I hoped for, if they existed, was that Peller wouldn't check his notifications while driving.

As my feet crunched over the gravel path leading to Peller's house, the seriousness of what I planned hit me. The boy's fate rested on this, and I couldn't let myself falter. I pictured his face, the fear in his eyes. Whatever it took, I'd bring him back.

Approaching the house, a chill crept over me. The day's grayness made the house seem even more uninviting. A faint smell of damp soil and wood surrounded me, but under it all was the frightening sense of time running out.

I arrived at the back door and realized my strategy hadn't taken me further than this. How did the boy get down to the dock? Did he come up the stairs and leave through the front or back door? Or had he found another way out? A window?

I circled the house. Blinds shuttered every basement window. Surely, if the boy was in there, he'd open the blinds. What if he couldn't? Restraints? Injuries? My mind flew in several directions, all of them bad.

I hadn't expected the boy to be unreachable, not now when I was so close. Panic tore through me as I searched for any sign of movement. If he was trapped, if he was in there, I needed a way to get him out. And once Peller realized I'd duped him, he'd return, and he'd be dangerous.

I tapped on each window and waited several seconds for a response, keenly aware of time flying by. Peller could've made a phone call to the gas company and realized this was a charade. In that case, he'd be home within minutes, not hours.

My fingers throbbed from the rapping, each window staring blankly back at me. I imagined the boy trapped on the other side, hurt, too terrified to answer.

About to give up and find another plan, I thought I saw a blind jiggle. Was it my imagination? I froze, questioning my eyes. It could be him, desperate and sending me a silent signal. I tapped again. The blind moved, as if someone had thrown something against it. I bit my lip. This was it. The moment of truth. If Peller had a security system, it would sound every alarm.

My breath came in gulps as I removed the crowbar from the backpack, its cool metal giving me confidence. I tapped it against the glass, both as a warning and to steel myself for the impact, knowing the noise could bring more trouble. But I was committed.

I raised my arm and swung with gusto. The impact sent shards flying, and the crackling of glass mingled with my quick breaths. I squinted through the splintered blinds.

"Is anyone in there?" I said, leaning forward, trying to peer through the tiny space. Then I heard it.

Chapter 42

"Yes!"

A small voice, a real voice.

The boy. He existed. Relief poured through me like a dam breaking. He was alive. And I wasn't insane.

Hearing him hit me like a punch to the gut. Relief and fear battled within me, but I couldn't allow the distraction of emotions.

"Are you okay? Are you hurt?" I asked, the tremor in my voice betraying my nerves.

"I'm okay," he said, his voice small but steady. "Will you get me out of here?"

Happiness flooded me for an instant before urgency slammed back. Through the dangling blinds, I saw the metal bars that prevented any escape through the window. My mind raced, searching for alternatives. "Any ideas about how to get out?" I asked. He'd done it before.

"Usually through the garage." His voice wavered. "But he put something in front of the door, and I can't get it open."

I pressed a hand to my forehead, willing myself to think clearly. "Hang tight. I'll be back."

My mind raced. I saw the clock's hands moving in my mind, and now I needed to find another way into the house. Although relieved to not hear alarms or sirens, that was no guarantee. The police could've been notified and were on their way, arresting me first and asking questions later. Meanwhile, Peller would have time to return and hide the boy.

Was there any possibility Peller had left the doors unlocked? Not likely, but I couldn't ignore the idea.

I sprinted around the house, trying every door. The front door, the back patio, and finally the garage door with its keypad that taunted me with its blinking red light. Without the code, it was a wall I couldn't break through. Every obstacle seemed like another layer of his prison, and time was the guard, laughing at me from the tower.

I circled the house, peeking behind flower beds and ornamental shrubs. Finally, I hit pay dirt. A small door built into the house's foundation, obviously leading to a crawl space or the basement, hidden behind a thorny shrub that could tear my skin off. I didn't have a shovel and doubted I had the strength to dig it up. It was large enough to have deep roots.

I dug into my bag and found my rescuer. The roll of duct tape. Working furiously, I wrapped it around the shrub, cinching it into a large gray ball. I suffered minor scratches, but the obstruction became smaller and much less threatening. My instincts were right to throw the tape into the bag, although I'd never imagined using it to tie up a plant.

I turned my attention to the door. It had a latch with a padlock, but it appeared flimsy. Peller relied on the prickly shrub for protection. With that out of the way, I felt the confidence to break through this barrier.

Next up, the crowbar. I wedged the end under the latch, gritting my teeth as I leaned in with my weight. My shoulders burned, my hands raw from the thorns, but I wouldn't stop. No give. The screws were better installed than I'd expected. I turned the bar downwards, placed my foot on it, and jumped.

A loud crack preceded my tumble to the ground, my face narrowly missing my duct-taped plant. But the latch broke from its moorings, freeing the door. My heart soared with triumph. I grabbed the knob and yanked it open, only to have disappointment strike again.

Plywood blocked the opening. Another barrier, solid and unyielding. A groan escaped my lips as I slammed a fist against it. Peller could return at any time. Every moment meant the difference between life and death. For the boy and for me too. I took a steadying breath, fingers tightening on the crowbar. If a way through existed, I'd find it.

My desperation fueled me, lending strength to my swings. The first strike reverberated up my arms, but I didn't stop. Four agonizing blows later, a dent appeared, small but promising. Hope ignited, spurring me on.

The wood splintered and groaned under the assault, and soon, an eight-inch hole appeared. Shining the flashlight inside, I had a view of an almost empty garage. As expected, the car was gone, leaving behind the usual trappings—tires, tools, a workbench, and shelves lined with paint cans and bottles, meticulously neat and clean.

No boy.

Desperation clung to me as I swept the beam across the room. Then I saw it. A steel door on the right-hand side. Did it lead to him? It was in the right spot.

I sprawled onto my back and propped myself on my elbows. Kicking out as hard as I could, my feet connected with the plywood, rattling my bones. With each kick, splinters flew. The rough plywood shuddered but held strong, forcing me to kick harder. It gave a little.

My leg muscles burned, and my feet throbbed, but I didn't stop, not until the wood buckled with a crack. With no time to savor my victory, I grabbed the crowbar and hacked at the remaining barrier until I cleared an opening.

The sharp scent of broken wood filled my nose as I scrambled over the splinters and descended a small ramp into the garage, the backpack swinging from my shoulder.

The flashlight's narrow beam barely pierced the semidarkness. My nerves on edge, I raced to the steel door, taking in the wooden crate placed in front of it. Cursing myself for not packing gloves, I curled my tortured fingers around one board, the splinters piercing my skin, and yanked. It budged a few inches. I braced my legs and summoned my strength before tugging again. This time, about six inches. Three more heaves and I gained enough clearance for the door.

I prayed Peller hadn't locked it. Neither a crowbar, my feet, nor my hands would break through it. Grasping the knob, I turned and almost cried with relief to hear the door unlatch. I pulled it open to reveal a dimly lit room. But that didn't hold my attention. My sole focus was on the boy with brown eyes and dark hair.

Chapter 43

The sight of him, a thin boy with hollow cheeks and a wary look, hit me harder than I expected. Relief, hope, and an odd sense of validation rushed through me. He was real. I wasn't crazy. The moment's magnitude and the look of anxiety on his face almost did me in, but I had no time to process it. That could come later.

I pulled him into a hug, and his arms grabbed me in desperation, a grip that held both fear and trust.

"What's your name?" I asked as I drew back.

"Andrew." He hesitated. "But I like to be called Andy."

I smiled and nodded. "Are you being held against your will?" I needed to ask this question, otherwise it wasn't a rescue but a kidnapping.

"Yes." No hint of hesitation in his tone.

"Is Peller your father?"

His brow furrowed. "Who?"

"Graham Peller, the man who lives here."

"I don't know his name, but I found out he's not my father."

A glimmer of happiness shone in his eyes. He wasn't heartbroken over the revelation.

That was enough for me. We'd work out the details later. With little time for more words, I whispered, "We're getting out. Just stay with me, no matter what. Is there anything you want to bring with you?"

He looked behind him, and I followed his gaze. A tiny room, the size of a prison cell, with a murphy bed that folded into the wall, a small bookshelf that held a few puzzles and paperbacks. Nothing else.

His eyes, wide and distressed, returned to meet mine. "Just this," he said, holding up a small cardboard box barely bigger than a pack of cards, tucked in the palm of his hand.

"Let's put it in here, okay?" I took the box and dropped it into my backpack. "C'mon, Andrew-Andy. Let's go."

I grabbed his hand and led him into the garage and past the splintered plywood. Beside the garage door, the control box required a simple touch of a button to activate the opener. I bounced from foot to foot as we watched its long, slow, upward grind. As soon as we had enough space, we hunched down, and I tugged Andy underneath the door, checking both ways to make sure Peller wasn't lying in wait.

We dashed to the trees, my bulky backpack in my free hand. Fumbling our way through the woods would take longer but presented a safer choice. I couldn't risk being spotted on the road with a child clinging to me.

The forest floor, littered with slick leaves and hidden roots, made each step precarious. Andy stumbled often, his breathing short and panicked. I steadied him, squeezing his hand in encouragement. He mimicked me as I bent low, weaving through the trees, our footfalls muffled by the thick moss.

We'd advanced about thirty feet when I heard a car tear into the driveway. I didn't need to look to know who it was. The crunch of gravel and the sharp slam of a car door sounded far too close. Every instinct screamed for me to find a hiding spot, but the need to escape tugged at me just as fiercely. I didn't dare look back, but I knew Peller was coming.

I glanced at Andy and witnessed the fear on his face. He knew it too. His steps sped up until he almost overtook me. I hurried to keep up, finding myself not as agile as a young boy with a wolf snapping at his heels.

"To the right," I said, keeping my voice low, wanting to send him in the car's general direction. It wasn't the way I'd come in; the terrain was much steeper with dense trees and brush. I watched Andy scramble over logs, his sneakers slipping on the damp leaves.

Meanwhile, I divided my attention between him and whatever activity occurred behind me. A muffled shout reached my ears, followed by a sequence of slamming doors. First the house and then the car. By the time the engine roared to life again, we had almost reached my vehicle, and I needed to decide. Run for the car, certain to be seen by Peller, or hide in the bush until the path cleared.

As the rumble of an engine grew closer, I realized my window of opportunity had slammed shut, the decision made for me. "Andy, stop," I said in an urgent whisper. "He's there. We need to hide."

The boy's terrified gaze swiveled to mine, and I hoped I projected a confidence I didn't feel.

"Where?" His head shifted from side to side, searching.

"Follow me." I spotted a huge, fallen tree and urged Andy toward it. His eyes flashed with fear, but he crouched beside me, his breathing shallow and quick. "Get down there. I'll cover you up."

I guided him to the other side and made certain he wasn't visible from the road before I scurried around and gathered loose branches. I crawled in beside him and tried to bury us on the forest floor. The branches' needles poked and scratched us, but they provided cover.

Our labored breathing competed with my heart's rapid beating. I grasped his small hand in mine and pressed a finger to my lips, meeting Andy's wide, fearful gaze. Every fiber in me wanted to reassure him, to promise he'd be safe, but I didn't trust my voice not to shake. I simply pressed his hand, silently vowing that no matter what happened, I'd protect him.

Any sound could alert Peller to our presence. I hadn't heard a car door slam, but that didn't mean he wasn't searching for us. He'd surely seen my car. It was hard to miss. Logically, he'd hunt for us in the woods.

The sharp snap of a nearby branch made my heart race. My gaze met Andy's, and I'm certain it was as wide-eyed as his. The noise seemed to come from within six feet of us.

Andy's tense body curled tight, trying to make himself smaller. His hand trembled in mine, and I gave it another squeeze. Any movement or sound would give us away.

Another crack. This time, to the left and perhaps farther away. Peller passed us, heading back toward the house but was still too close for us to make a break for it.

The car keys bulged in my jeans pocket, and I imagined myself running with Andy in tow. We'd have to be fast and accurate. Any deviation could spell disaster.

Andy moved. Not much—he probably had a cramp in his leg—but enough to shift some branches. I froze, straining to hear a reaction from Peller. Andy's eyes filled with tears, and his lower lip trembled as he realized his mistake. I shook my head, both to reassure him and as a reminder to stay quiet.

We waited several long minutes. Would my legs hold me when I finally moved? They ached, muscles cramping from the prolonged crouch, but I didn't dare budge. Each second felt like an eternity, my body screaming for relief, my mind locked in a tense standoff between staying hidden and the fear of discovery.

I heard no other sounds from outside our cocoon, but Peller could be standing nearby, waiting for us to emerge. Or he might be several meters away. He'd served in the military. He likely possessed tracking skills, trained to move soundlessly. We were up against a formidable enemy.

A drizzle started, each drop frigid as it seeped through our makeshift cover. The leaves above offered scant protection, and soon the rain soaked through, chilling us both. Andy shivered beside me, but I couldn't pull him into the warmth of my arms. Peller was still out there, prowling, hunting.

How much longer should we wait? We had to make it to the car, a better getaway than on foot. I yearned to peek out of our hideout, but I knew any movement could endanger our fragile cover.

The rain drummed harder, masking sounds and increasing my dread. A soft rustle nearby made me freeze, every instinct honed on that faint disturbance. It could've been the wind, the rain, an animal, or it could've been Peller, approaching us.

My bag sat between us, and I thought about what it held. My hand moved slowly, fingers brushing against metal and fabric, all the while aware of Andy's silent gaze fixed on me. The box cutter's handle was cold, and I allowed myself a single, calming breath.

Pulling the backpack closer, the crowbar peeking out, I leaned across the few inches that separated us and whispered in Andy's ear. "I'll check first, then I'll slowly move the branches aside. Go that way," I said, pointing behind him. "My car is there. It's white and unlocked. Jump in the back and lie on the floor. Don't worry about me. I need a few minutes to do something, and then I'll get in. Okay? Understand?"

Andy's nod lacked enthusiasm, so I gave him a smile and a brief, comforting hug. An image of Peller hiding in my back seat flashed through my mind, but I'd heard him move in the opposite direction. I needed to have faith that this would work. It was our only way out.

I carefully reached overhead to move a crucial branch aside. I signaled Andy with my hand for him not to move as I eased my head through the gap and gazed around. No sign of Peller. Was he far enough away? Or was he waiting a few feet from our hiding spot?

We'd know soon enough, but we needed to be fast.

I shoved aside another branch, trying to avoid making noise. Andy didn't budge, watching me for instructions. When the space was big enough for us to step through, I reached for his hand.

I saw the fear in Andy's wide eyes, the way his breath came shallow and fast. I lowered my voice, willing him to trust me. "We can do this, okay? I'll be right behind you, and I won't let anything happen to you."

His nod was unsure, but he didn't take his eyes off me, as though clinging to my words for courage.

"Remember," I said, "that way. Right behind you. I promise. Jump in the back of the car and lie down." He nodded like a woodpecker tapping a tree.

"Okay. Let's go," I said, rising to my feet and pulling him up beside me. I pointed in the direction of the car, through the forest that created a wall of green.

"That way," I whispered, tracing the line with my finger. I needed him to feel my confidence even if I felt little myself. With a quick glance over my shoulder, I shoved him forward, and like a match to dry wood, his body ignited.

Andy ran like a young gazelle. I raced behind him. If Peller was anywhere near us, I didn't hear him above the sound of our feet, the heaviness of our breath, and the snapping branches in our path.

With relief, I realized we were closer to the car than I'd thought, although it was farther to the right than I'd guessed. Andy spotted it and adjusted his course.

Each step was a gamble. Slick roots, loose stones, and uneven ground threatened to trip us. Andy darted ahead, his feet skimming over the ground, while I followed, branches whipping against my arms and face, my breathing labored as I struggled to keep up.

I couldn't help glancing over my shoulder every few steps, my ears tuned for any sound that didn't belong. Andy sprinted in front, trusting me completely, giving me the surge of energy I needed.

As instructed, when his feet hit the gravel beside the car, he wrenched open the back door. With relief, I saw the car was empty as he slipped into the back seat and pulled the door closed. I let out a quick, trembling breath, the weight of responsibility shifting slightly. Safe, for now.

I had pulled the box cutter from my pocket as we ran, intending to use it as a weapon or a tool, depending on the situation. With no inkling of Peller's whereabouts, I prepared to use it as a tool and hoped I had the strength needed.

Having little experience in puncturing tires, I planned to attempt it, but not at the price of too much time. That, I didn't have enough of, and Andy needed me.

Peller's car was parked several feet behind mine. Seemingly empty. As I raced to it, I cast a quick glance inside in case Peller crouched in the back seat.

All clear.

I knelt beside the front tire. The first stab was awkward, the blade glancing off the rubber. I cursed, adjusted my grip, and pressed harder the second time, moving the short blade left to right in an arc. A hissing sound filled the air as the tire deflated. Just one more, I told myself, even as I thanked my lucky stars Peller hadn't pulled the same stunt on us.

Every nerve screamed to move faster, the sound of air escaping the tires barely louder than the rapid thud of my heartbeat. I stole a glance at my car then the road. We were running out of precious time.

I'd achieved my goal. Or at least enough to slow him down. While the second tire hissed, I raced toward my car. A shout stopped me as my hand grasped the door handle.

The yell cut through the stillness like a bullet, freezing me mid-step. My gaze snapped to a spot behind me, my heart stalling as I took in Peller's figure standing beside his car, only ten meters away.

Time slowed as my gaze fell on the gun, its barrel aimed directly at me. With a cold rush of terror, my mind raced, every instinct telling me to run but knowing it was already too late. Peller's eyes locked on mine.

A thousand thoughts surged through my mind in a heartbeat. If I moved, would he fire? If I stayed, could I reason with him? I gripped the box cutter tighter, as if the small, sharp blade could somehow shield me from danger.

I'd promised Andy I'd be there, that I'd protect him, and I wouldn't let Peller's gun or my fear steal that away. My breath steadied, and I met Peller's hard gaze, hoping to show strength, but only terror filled my heart and mind.

Peller's finger hovered over the trigger, and I knew I had seconds to decide. Shoring up my courage, I stepped toward him.

Chapter 44

What higher power came over me when I faced Peller and that gun? I'd never identified as one of those kickass women in action movies, but turning my back on him and trying to escape didn't seem like a viable option. And if I was killed or injured, Andy would be back in Peller's clutches. Not going to happen.

I called his bluff and walked toward him. Would he shoot me point-blank? He could try, but I hadn't misspent my youth as a tom-boy.

Peller's eyes widened as I steadily approached him, my bravery surprising him as much as it did me. Thrown off by my boldness, I watched his finger relax on the trigger. The gun moved slightly to his right, and my moment came. In one movement, I reached behind my head, gripped the crowbar protruding from the backpack, and flung it toward Peller.

Perfect aim. His eyes widened in shock and pain as the solid metal plunged into his abdomen. He doubled over. The gun clattered to the ground as he landed beside it on his knees.

That was all I needed. I turned and ran to the car, diving in and racing away.

Now, I worried about where he was and if he'd followed us. Of course, he'd have to know which direction we'd taken. He had a choice of three: Victoria, Port Alberni, or through Nanaimo to reach the ferry and the mainland.

I analyzed every kilometer of road, assessing which town to choose. Big city, small town. Where would Peller search first? If I kept us hidden, even for a day or two, it might be enough to get the kind of help I needed, to find someone I could trust.

Putting myself in Peller's shoes, I'd think Victoria or the mainland would be easier to hide in. That's why I rolled the dice and chose the smaller town of Port Alberni.

We left the car in a public parking lot in the downtown area, and I led Andy up and down random streets, constantly scanning the area. His gaze darted over every building and car, his jaw slack with wonder. At times, the honking horns and chatter of pedestrians seemed to overwhelm him, and he flinched slightly each time someone passed too close. A bus rumbled by, and he shrank back instinctively, clutching my hand. These were firsts for him. The colorful shop signs, the people, the life outside the confinement of Peller's world.

I spotted a Dairy Queen. "You hungry?" I said. His quick nod told me we needed to rest and refuel.

Inside the restaurant, the smell of fried food and chocolate syrup filled the air, and Andy's nose twitched as he took it in. He seemed dazed, his eyes shifting from the menu to the other customers devouring burgers, fries, and soft-serve ice cream. Just a kid filled with wonder.

I felt his fear as much as his excitement, and my sense of protectiveness flared. Every stranger a potential threat, I wouldn't relax until we were beyond Peller's reach.

Seated at the table with our order before us, the boy stared at the burger like it might jump up and bite him. He poked it with his plastic fork as if to elicit a reaction.

"Just grab it with your hands and take a bite," I suggested.

"Only ever seen one on television," he said, fascinated. "Never thought I'd eat one in real life."

I didn't know whether to laugh or cry. He'd never experienced so many things I took for granted.

"Watch me," I said as I wrapped my fingers around my burger and bit off a huge mouthful. Andy grinned and lifted his with both hands, holding it like some fragile, alien artifact. With the odor of grilled meat and melted cheese drifting through the air, his expression shifted between awe and uncertainty. His fingers clenched his prize as he took a small cautious bite.

I delighted in his eyes widening as the taste sensation invaded his mouth. Such a simple act, eating a burger. Yet to Andy, it was a marvel. I wanted to cheer, to laugh, but the sadness outweighed everything, knowing Peller had deprived him of modest pleasures for so long. I worried about what he'd eaten over the past several years. My gaze traveled over his frame, thin and pale. Lack of sunshine and fresh air was another obvious failing, something no living being should be denied. Anger, directed at Peller, filled my chest.

We'd driven three hours nonstop, most of it spent in silence accompanied only by the engine's hum and the occasional rustle as Andy shifted to get a better view of the countryside. He seemed hypnotized by the blur of trees, fixated on the view as if he'd seen nothing like it before. And he likely hadn't. As I allowed him time to soak up the scenery, my hands clenched the wheel, my gaze darting to the rearview mirror every few seconds. Each glimpse of an empty road brought a moment of relief, however brief.

How long to change a tire? Fifteen minutes? Add to that the time it took to tend to his wounds, as minor as they were.

During the drive that meandered through endless kilometers of trees and mountains, I'd extracted some information from Andy. He'd always believed Graham Peller was his father, not remembering any other existence. Living a secluded and regimented life within the house on the lake seemed normal to him, knowing nothing else.

Andy awoke every morning at six, made his bed according to strict specifications, and ate a breakfast of porridge and milk. Every day.

On weekdays, Peller homeschooled him. This included a phys ed break that ranged from indoor calisthenics to survival training in the woods. Those were the only times he was permitted outdoors. He spent two hours every evening with Peller in the house's main area. Activities included reading and watching vetted TV programs or movies, mostly military adventures. Andy spent the rest of his time in the basement, where Peller provided him with puzzles and books.

"Andy, one night the police were in Graham's house, and they searched but couldn't find you. Where did you hide?" This question had bothered me for so long. One of those moments when I questioned my sanity.

The boy nodded. "I remember hearing people talking and moving around. There's a secret place in the room, kind of a closet, but hidden in the wall. My clothes are in there. Father... Graham... trained me how to hide when there's an emergency and somebody wants to hurt me. He rings a buzzer upstairs. That means I go in, and I can't move, can't make a sound."

I was stunned silent, imagining this poor boy subjected to Peller's crazy behavior. I caught Andy's quizzical look and struggled to school my expression. This was all he'd known. I didn't want him to think I judged him, but I needed him to understand.

"They weren't there to hurt you. We wanted to find you and see if you were okay."

His crestfallen gaze fell to the burger, and I hurried to switch the topic. "Did you like the gifts I gave you?"

A wide smile lit Andy's face. "I sure did. So cool! I stood on a chair on the bed, and I saw a bit of the dock through the window. I watched you. I'd sneak out when I had a chance, real early."

As I absorbed those images, Andy's gaze frantically searched around us. "Where's your bag?" he asked, a note of desperation in his tone.

"Right here." I pulled it out from under the table. "You want something?"

"The box. You still have it?"

I unzipped the bag and removed the tiny box, setting it in his eager hands. My heart almost broke when Andy opened it to reveal the heron feather and the stones I'd given him, the only items he'd wanted to bring. Nothing from his past life meant as much to him.

I watched his expression dim as if someone lowered a shade over a window. "I saw him find the book. I never got it. That made me really sad."

Reaching across, I folded a hand around his. "I'll get you another one. I promise. Actually, I'll take you to a store and let you pick whatever book you want."

I was painfully aware several challenges lay ahead of us before I could make good on that promise, if ever, but his glowing smile was worth it.

"What type of food do you normally eat?" I asked, changing the subject again as I shifted my gaze between the boy, the door, and the view of the parking lot. I wouldn't let my guard down until I was sure we were safe. Where I'd find that safe place was another question.

"Porridge for breakfast, soup and sandwiches for lunch, stew or pasta for dinner."

The list of foods sounded like a prison menu. Maybe worse. Rage bubbled under the surface. Peller hadn't just controlled him; he'd robbed Andy of everything, even the simplest joys of life. I fought to keep my tone light, not wanting Andy to see my anger.

"Your first French fry?" I asked, pointing toward the carton of fries still untouched beside him.

"They're poisonous. They'll kill me."

I fought to keep my voice calm, but I wanted to strangle Peller for the garbage he'd planted in this boy's head. "They're not poisonous. Admittedly, they're not the healthiest choice of food, but in moderation, it's perfectly fine to eat them." I picked up one and popped it in my mouth. "Plus, they're delicious."

His eyebrows knitted together, suspicion and hope battling in his expression. He'd believed it all, every word Peller told him. But his gaze moved to the food, his trust slowly shifting.

Andy imitated me, picking up a fry by its tip and taking a tentative bite. His eyes widened, and a smile crept across his face. Seeing that innocent joy lit a flicker of hope inside me.

"Good, right?" I said with a smile. "Try dipping it in catsup."

He did. That fry disappeared, as did several others in its wake.

I sent a last, satisfied smile at Andy before turning my head toward the parking lot. And froze. A man strode toward the building, his pace steady, purposeful. My heart kicked into overdrive. I gripped the table, the restaurant's friendly hum fading to a dull roar.

I calculated quickly. Did we have time to leave? Would rushing out attract more attention? My mind whirled, every survival instinct kicking in. We needed a way out, fast.

Andy looked up, his smile fading as he seemed to spot the worry etched on my face. His hand crept toward mine across the table, his fingers seeking reassurance. I swallowed hard, squeezing his hand back, my pulse tripping as the man approached.

Chapter 45

"We gotta go."

Andy didn't hesitate, surging to his feet without asking questions. I grasped his shoulders and guided him to the side exit. The front door creaked behind us, sending a spike of fear through my veins.

"Out, now." My whisper was sharp. We slipped over the threshold, the humid air hitting my face like a slap.

"We going to the car?" His small voice trembled as we ran toward the rear of the building.

"No," I said, my breath coming fast. "Better not. He probably recognized it."

"It's him?"

"No. Someone else. I'll explain later. Keep moving."

Panic washed over me as I spotted a park ahead. "Cut across," I said, grabbing Andy's hand and urging him to run faster.

Andy's legs churned, forcing me to push harder to keep up. My chest burned. The tree-lined park sprawled before us, a haven of hiding places. We dashed into the trees. I glanced back and froze for a heartbeat. A flash of movement. Someone followed us. My heartbeat thudded against my ribs.

"Keep going." I gripped Andy's hand and pushed forward. The faint crunch of leaves behind us grew louder. Footsteps. I pulled Andy deeper into the park. We burst through the other side to face a row of crumbling warehouses.

I yanked Andy around the corner of a dilapidated building, and we pressed against the wall. My chest heaved as I gulped in air, every breath a struggle.

"Who was it?" Andy said, his eyes wide with fear.

"A guy I know. I don't trust him."

The sight of Mark striding toward the restaurant burned in my mind. My chest tightened. He'd followed us. He and Peller worked together. That had to be it. My fingers tightened on Andy's hand. We had to move. Now.

What to do? Returning to the car was out of the question. Mark must've spotted it. Someone might be watching it for him as he searched the restaurants and businesses for two escapees.

We needed to hide. The warehouse, rundown but functional, loomed beside us, massive and dark. I signaled for Andy to follow close behind.

The door creaked. Andy flinched. My breath shuddered. Inside, metal racks of loaded pallets stretched into the dimness. Empty or not, it was our best chance. I pulled Andy in, guiding him between the racks. My heart slammed in my chest. Had Mark seen us slip inside?

The faint whir of a forklift echoed from the far end, which would mask our footsteps, but it added to my sense of unease, the industrial hum both comforting and ominous.

People were in there, but how many? And was it safe? Would they throw us out into the arms of our enemy?

Despite its size, the warehouse's protection couldn't last forever. We needed to keep moving, blending into the countryside. If I could get us to the edge of town, we'd have a chance. But Mark was close behind. Getting rid of him was crucial. We'd hide and regroup until he moved on.

I evaluated the space. The scarcity of employees meant fewer eyes to spot us, fewer questions to answer. But it also radiated a chilling eeriness.

The forklift driver maneuvered a load in the distance, and I saw no one else. This was our chance.

"Come on," I whispered, grabbing Andy's hand. His fingers tightened in mine as we moved deeper.

Stale air met us. I veered left, aiming for the farthest racks, hoping the maze of towering shelves and pallets would offer us a place to hide.

We moved quickly, our sneakers almost silent on the concrete floor. My ears strained for sounds of pursuit but heard nothing above the faint drone of machinery. We reached the end of the aisle, and my gaze darted over the area, searching for a hiding spot large enough for both of us.

Ahead, I spotted a gap between two pallets. Not perfect, but it'd have to do. I crouched and guided Andy toward the narrow space, using quick hand gestures to show him how to edge through. He caught on, his slight frame slipping into the opening.

I followed, twisting my body to fit into the cramped spot. The odor of dust and diesel exhaust engulfed us. Andy pressed close to me, his shoulder brushing mine, his eyes wide in the dim light.

"I'll get you out of here, I swear," I said, my mouth beside Andy's ear. His gaze lifted to mine, wide and hopeful, and that fierce protectiveness swelled inside me again. No one would take him.

Andy's look turned expectant as he spoke in a whisper. "What do we do now?"

It was a good question, one without an answer, but I couldn't leave him hanging. "We'll wait a while. Maybe he'll give up."

"But he knows your car is here, doesn't he? If it doesn't leave, he'll know we're still in town."

Smart kid. "Yeah, you're right. That's why I'll figure out how to leave town without the car."

"Will we steal another one?"

The question surprised me. I'd assumed Peller shielded the boy from knowledge of law-breaking, but apparently not.

"I don't believe in stealing. It's a crime," I said.

"I know, but people do bad things anyway. They steal and murder and hurt people."

"How did you learn that?"

"From the boys."

Chapter 46

"The boys?" My voice croaked.

"Yes. Other boys came, but they didn't stay long." He shrugged and attempted to appear casual, but I heard something in his voice. Sadness? Loneliness? Fear?

"Others? How many?" My thoughts reeled. Was Peller part of a child trafficking ring? Did he kidnap and sell boys to the highest bidder?

"Two."

"How old were they? Were they there at the same time?" My mind raced with questions. I'd never imagined this scenario.

"No." He turned a perplexed look on me. "Didn't you read my note? I told you the last boy was gone, and I needed help."

My mind flashed to the few legible words on the damp note, and puzzle pieces clicked into place.

Boots thumped. I held up my hand to silence Andy. Neither of us moved as we watched denim-covered legs stroll past. It wasn't Mark or Peller, the legs shorter and stockier. The forklift operator? The motor no longer rumbled.

I pressed my back against the cold racking, noticing every thud of my racing heart. Andy's small fingers trembled in mine, and I strengthened my grip, silently vowing not to let him go, no matter what. The smell of grease and rusty metal filled my nose. I held my breath, praying the man wouldn't return and find us.

Each scuff of his boots stabbed at my nerves. Andy's breath hitched, and I squeezed his hand, urging him to stay quiet. The man's footsteps stopped, the sudden silence making my stomach drop. Did he hear us? Would he investigate? My mind spun with escape routes. When the man resumed his trek to the back of the warehouse and was out of earshot, I leaned toward Andy and repeated my questions.

His thin shoulders shrugged. "Different ages. Tony was small, only three, Danny was six," Andy said in a whisper, his gaze unfocused, as if he looked back through a dim window. "Tony didn't talk much. Danny and I… we made up games." A faint smile flickered on his lips before fading, and his shoulders drooped, disappointment and loneliness settling over him again. "Father… him… he kept them in another small room but let us see each other during the day."

I kept my face still, trying to hide the fury swirling inside me, a fierce current that made my hands shake. Each thought of another child suffering at Peller's hands felt like a knife in my chest.

Andy shook his head sadly. "That's how I found out the man wasn't my father. He made the boys change their names and told them to call him Father, but we knew it wasn't true. I started to think he'd done the same to me, but I just couldn't remember."

He paused, and I tensed, not wanting him to stop.

"Then I found some pictures and things in a box in the garage. It was a family, with a baby and two other kids. And there were newspaper stories about a baby boy that had disappeared." Andy lifted his sad gaze to mine. "I knew I was that boy."

"What happened to the other boys? Do you know where they went?" I spoke softly, terrified of the answer.

His thin shoulders lifted and fell in a despondent shrug. "I don't know."

Peller was a bigger monster than I'd imagined. What did he do to those children? I needed to handle my next question with care.

"Andy," I said, peering into his eyes. "Did Peller ever… abuse you?"

"What do you mean?"

His innocent expression made it even more difficult. "Did he hurt you? Beat you, or do inappropriate, scary things?"

The boy's head bowed, and his voice trembled. "He yelled at me a lot, called me mean names. That was scary. When he found out I'd left you the gifts, he hit me with his belt and said I'd get a lot worse if I did it again."

I wrapped my arm around his shoulder and pulled him against me, wondering if that had been the night I'd heard the terrifying scream from across the lake. The mention of the belt sent bile up my throat. I'd imagined worse, but that knowledge did nothing to ease the ache. "No child should ever be scared or beaten," I said, my throat clogged. I inhaled a deep breath to calm my nerves. "I'm so sorry."

The more Andy revealed, the more determined I became. Peller's grip on him was as real and painful as any bruise. As long as I drew breath, I'd make sure that man paid for this.

"You got out of the basement to go to the dock?"

"Yes." His mischievous grin lit up his face, and it heartened me to see his spunk despite all he'd been through. "I figured out how to unlock that door, and I got out through the garage. The man didn't know." He shrugged. "I just wanted to breathe the air and be close to the water."

I smiled, impressed with his resourcefulness. About to ask another question, my mind bursting with them, I stiffened. A bad feeling washed over me. My breath caught in my throat as the sound of footsteps broke through our whispering. It echoed closer, the sound deliberate, calculated. I gently pushed Andy's head close to my shoulder, his pulse surely as rapid as mine.

I had a glimpse of jeans-clad legs, expecting Mark but knew he wore beige pants. Someone else? Was Peller himself here, hunting us down? I imagined him, his gaze sweeping the aisles, searching for us.

A testy voice rang out from another direction. "Hey, what are you doing here? Who are you?"

Chapter 47

"Looking for my son. I can't find him." The sound of Peller's voice made my heart race, confirming my worst fears. What was he doing here? I thought he'd sent Mark to do his bidding. Now they were both in Port Alberni. How could I defend us against two of them? Especially when Peller was armed with a gun.

"Well, he's not in here."

"Are you sure? Maybe someone else saw him. I thought he came in this direction." Peller's voice held a caring desperation that would fool most people, but I recognized it as fake.

"I didn't see anybody."

"This place is so big," Peller said, awed and concerned. "He could hide anywhere."

The two men approached each other until they stood almost directly before us. The same shorter man who'd passed earlier faced off with Peller's taller, leaner frame.

"How old is he?" The stranger's tone softened with concern.

"Ten."

"Ten? What's his name? Just call him. He's old enough to answer if he's in here."

"You don't understand." A trace of annoyance crept into Peller's tone. "He's severely autistic. Non-verbal. When he gets frightened, he hides."

The other man's voice filled with understanding. "Why don't you try anyway?"

Peller half-heartedly called Andy's name several times. I shot a glance at the boy beside me, gauging his reaction to this man who'd robbed him of his family and falsely posed as his father. Wide and terror-filled eyes met mine.

At that moment, I couldn't imagine hating anyone more than the man who stood within feet of us. I clenched my teeth, detesting the gentle tone he used, the way his voice softened, dripping with false worry. I'd heard it before, directed at me. I'd also heard his rage and hate-filled venom. A shiver ran through me as I thought of what this monster was capable of.

"See, I told you he wasn't here," the other man said.

His breath shot out in an oomph. His knees give out before he tumbled to the floor like a bag of flour. A hard kick to his head followed the punch in his gut, and he slumped, unconscious.

To our credit, neither of us made a sound, although my insides froze in horror, and Andy stiffened beside me.

Peller's voice, soft just moments ago, turned cold and jagged. "All right, come out here now. If you don't, if you make it hard for me, I'll make it a lot worse when I find you. I'm already not happy with you after that trick you pulled." The words dripped with malice, and I pictured the predatory look on his face as he swept his gaze over the rows, assessing hiding places. A hunter stalking his prey.

Andy's fingers dug into my hand, his small body pressed against mine. My warning look told him not to make a sound. His tremors shook me. I couldn't fail him now, not after everything he'd gone through.

The shelving vibrated as Peller walked several feet away and shoved a pallet to the floor, the crash of metal and wood hitting cement echoing through the cavernous warehouse.

A low chuckle emanated from somewhere farther down the aisle, and my stomach twisted. "I know you're in here," Peller called, his voice syrupy with something that sounded like glee. "I'm not angry. Just come out, and we'll talk." He barely hid the rancor in his words, and I knew there'd be no talking if he found us.

I crouched lower, forcing Andy's head down as the shelves rattled, each pallet he threw clanging with a force that sent shockwaves through our hiding spot. My pulse thundered, each crash a countdown as he closed the distance between us.

I tightened my arm around Andy's shoulder. We both jumped when another pallet plummeted to the floor. The trend continued, but I exhaled a small sigh of relief when Peller shifted directions and moved farther away. I peered from behind our shelf to see him slip around the end of an aisle, still yelling and still destroying pallets of merchandise.

Andy dug his fingers into mine, the warmth of his shaky breath against my shoulder. I pressed his hand to reassure him, though my own was clammy. "I won't let him hurt you," I said, perhaps more for myself than him.

I knew Peller would empty every rack in this building to find us, and it was only a matter of time before he'd succeed. As much as I hated to leave our safe spot, we needed to move while he continued his path of destruction on the other side.

I climbed silently to my feet and gestured for Andy to do the same and to stay close behind me. I pointed to the right, indicating the door through which we'd entered.

We stepped into the cement corridor, our sneakers soundless. The crashing of pallets that echoed throughout the building masked any noise we made. I used my body to shield Andy from the sight of the unconscious and bloody man on the floor, hanging onto his hand, not wanting to lose contact.

Several feet on, I peered between the racks and saw no sign of Peller. The noise had stopped, and silence filled the warehouse, more frightening than the smashing and havoc. My ears strained, listening for the slightest sound that might give away his position. Only the maddening quiet surrounded us, brimming with danger. We had to move. Fast.

The soles of our shoes barely skimmed the floor, but I couldn't escape the fear any tiny sound would alert Peller. I moved with Andy tucked close, and the door seemed impossibly far, much farther than when we'd come in. *How is that possible?*

Pausing at the end of a rack, I was terrified I'd pass out. We had three more aisles to move past before we reached the door, and I didn't know

Peller's whereabouts. I wished we'd stayed behind the pallets. Someone could have returned from lunch before he found us.

Ready to sprint to the next aisle, I turned to make a sign to Andy, and my elbow snagged a wrench on the shelf next to us.

Chapter 48

The clatter destroyed the silence, making my heart skip. The wrench lay at my feet, screaming our location. I cursed under my breath. No time to freeze, no time to regret. I increased my hold on Andy's hand, every muscle coiling as I prepared to run.

Andy's wide eyes locked on mine, his lips parting as if to cry out, but no sound emerged. He looked at me, frozen. I swallowed the terror threatening to choke me, forcing a steady voice.

"Now," I whispered fiercely, tugging him forward.

The pounding of boots reverberated through the warehouse, closer than I'd expected. I caught sight of a figure charging toward us, closing the distance far too quickly. No time for hiding, no room for error.

"Run!" I propelled Andy forward. His small hand clamped in mine, we tore down the aisles, sneakers slapping against the cold concrete. My lungs burned and fear surged through me like wildfire.

Peller, his eyes blazing, sprang from an aisle, cutting us off. Without thinking, I swiveled, yanking Andy in the opposite direction, my grip like iron on his fingers. We headed away from the door. I had no choice. I banked on circling around Peller.

We sprinted blindly, zigzagging through the maze of towering shelves, our path blocked by broken pallets, spilled metal parts, and shards of glass that crunched under our feet. My mind raced as fast as my heart, calculating routes, searching for a way out.

"Turn right," I yelled, my voice hoarse. I shoved Andy forward, keeping myself between him and the monster on our heels. If Peller caught me, the boy might escape.

With the sound of Peller's boots echoing, desperation took over. Passing a large cart loaded with metal rods, I heaved it over. The crash resonated through the warehouse, an earsplitting racket of clanging steel. I stole a glance at Peller. His face was twisted in fury, his eyes bulging, veins standing out on his sweat-slicked forehead. He grunted and climbed over the obstacle with ease.

Andy was just ahead when I spotted a delay tactic. A fire extinguisher mounted to the shelving. I yanked it free, fumbling with trembling hands to pull the pin.

"Keep going," I shouted at Andy. He hesitated, his small face pale with fear.

As Peller rounded the corner, I braced myself, aimed, and squeezed the lever. A white mist exploded into the air, engulfing him in a blinding cloud. He roared, throwing his arms over his face. I swung the extinguisher with all my strength, catching him square in the stomach. He doubled over with a grunt, and I ran, propelled by fear. I grabbed Andy's hand, and we bolted for the exit.

I saw the open door and prayed we'd make it. A quick glance over my shoulder confirmed my worst fear. Peller's crouched figure emerged from the aisle we'd just left, his dark gaze locked onto us. He wasn't far. If we didn't make it to the door in the next few seconds, we wouldn't make it at all.

Just as we neared the exit, a tall form moved into the light. We skidded to a stop.

Mark.

Chapter 49

For a heartbeat, my mind blanked. Mark, who'd sworn to help me, was here to help Peller. The man I'd trusted gone, his sinister form blocked our only escape. One more threat, one more deception. Two grown men against a woman and child.

"Julie," Mark shouted, his arms extended. "Come here."

He thought I was an idiot. The sound of boots from behind told me they'd surround us in a second. I grabbed Andy and shoved him toward a stack of pallets loaded with metal bars that reached almost to the ceiling.

"Climb." My shout echoed through the vast warehouse.

The boy didn't hesitate. He climbed like a monkey, his thin arms and legs moving at a ferocious speed. I tore my gaze from Mark, and my palms slick with sweat, I scrambled up behind Andy, each climb and jolt adding to the urgency surging through me. This might be an exercise in futility, or it might give us time until someone arrived to help us.

Halfway up, the vibrations of Peller's ascent shook the structure. Each step sent terror up my spine. I glanced down to see Peller's hand snaking up, fingers grasping the air. Too close, only inches from my ankle. The threat of his grip fueled me. I fought against fear, pulling myself upward as if my life depended on it. And it probably did. I shimmied faster until my face was almost even with Andy's feet.

"Go! Go!" I said.

A grunt followed by a thud and moans of pain drew my gaze downward. Mark and Peller were on the floor in a tangle of arms and legs. *What happened? Did Peller fall on top of him?* No stopping. No analyzing. I needed to focus my attention on getting us to the top.

Barely able to catch my breath, we arrived, clinging to the metal rack, and gazed from our lofty perch at the men below us. They were fighting. Peller, strong and fueled by rage, straddled Mark. His fist connected with Mark's jaw with a sickening crack, making his head snap back. Blood sprayed across the floor. Peller pummeled Mark with blow after blow until he collapsed upon the cold concrete.

I watched in horror. Each punch drove a message further into my mind. Mark came to help us. I should have welcomed his presence instead of running from it. His face barely recognizable under the fury of Peller's fists, helplessness twisted inside me. I couldn't watch him get torn apart. I needed to act.

"Stay here," I said to Andy, fixing him with a harsh glare to make sure he understood.

He nodded. I scrambled down the ladder of pallets, trying not to lose my grip and hoping I wasn't too late for Mark.

My feet hit the ground; I swung around to face the men and gasped. Both standing, Peller had jerked Mark to his feet. Mark reeled, vertical only because Peller clutched a fistful of his shirt. Worse, Peller had picked up a metal bar from a pile beside him. He raised it above his head, obviously intent on crushing Mark's skull. "You'll regret helping her. You're both going to hell." Peller's hoarse voice bounced off the metal shelves.

My hands grabbed another pipe, gripping it like the only thing tying me to life.

Peller's attack on Mark morphed into a glancing blow. With trembling hands, I had raised the pipe, outrage overpowering my fear. The vibration reverberated up my arms as it connected with Peller's shoulders. I held firm, putting every ounce of strength I had behind each blow. It was a release, an act of liberation, and revenge. I'd protect Andy, no matter the cost, and this man would pay for everything he'd done.

Peller's grip on his weapon loosened. It fell to the floor with a clang. The man reared back and roared, losing his hold on Mark, who collapsed in a heap.

Peller pivoted to me, and I raised the pipe to strike another blow. His fingers encircled my wrist, crushing my bones. With his other hand, he wrenched the pipe from my hand and flung it down the aisle out of reach.

His eyes blazed with a searing hatred. Those powerful fingers latched around my throat, his grip like iron as he leaned closer, his breath hot against my face. Dark spots danced across my vision. Desperation made my limbs thrash in panic.

"No one can save you now. Or the boy." His voice dripped with evil.

"No!" Andy lunged and grabbed Peller's wrist, trying to tear his hand from my throat. He'd ignored my instructions and followed me down. I was both thankful and filled with terror.

Peller loosened one hand long enough to swat the boy heavily across the face and send him sprawling to the floor. The hand quickly returned to its task as I tore at him, trying to eek a breath through a throat dangerously close to being crushed.

Andy recovered quickly, and I saw him clamber onto a pallet. From there, he leaped onto Peller's back. Andy's eyes, usually wide with fear, now held a fierce strength. Not a frightened child, but my partner in survival.

Seeing Andy risk himself for me sent a sharp pang through my chest, equal parts pride and panic so sharp it hurt. My instincts screamed to shout for him to run, to hide, to get as far from this nightmare as possible. Too late. He was here, and together, we needed to end this, Mark beyond helping us.

As Peller maintained his grip on my throat with his left hand, his free hand dropped to his waistband. A chilling realization ran through me. The gun.

I clawed at his arm, my nails digging into his flesh, but his grip was like a vice. My vision blurred at the edges. If he accessed the gun, it'd be over.

Andy, still clinging to his back, yanked his hair and dug his small fingers into the man's eyes. Peller roared, momentarily loosening his hold.

I gasped in air and acted on instinct. With every ounce of strength, I drove my knee up between Peller's legs. A sickening grunt escaped him, his body jerking in pain. His hand fumbled, yanking the gun free from his waistband, but the impact threw off his aim.

The shot exploded through the warehouse, deafening me. The bullet shattered a fluorescent light overhead, sending down a shower of sparks and glass.

Blinded by pain and rage, Peller staggered. I seized my chance. I lunged, grabbing his gun hand, pointing it toward the floor. He squeezed the trigger again. A second shot ricocheted off the concrete. Shards pelted me.

Andy barreled into Peller from the side, knocking him off balance. Peller fell against a metal rack. The gun flew from his hand, skidding across the floor.

I dove for it. My fingers closed around the cold metal. Rolling onto my back, I raised the gun as Peller lurched toward me.

"Don't." My voice was raw, my throat wracked with pain.

He stopped, chest heaving, his eyes flicking between me and his weapon now aimed at him. For the first time, I saw something in Peller's expression I'd never seen before.

Fear.

Chapter 50

His scream echoed through the warehouse. I lunged to my knees, grabbed Andy, and wrapped his trembling body in my arms.

The snap of bone had been unmistakable. My blood ran cold even as relief washed over me. Peller crumpled to the floor with a thud. I barely resisted the urge to collapse beside him.

The pipe clattered on the concrete beside the man's feet. His swing unerring, he'd connected with Peller's leg, bringing the monster's reign to an end.

Amidst the chaos and terror, I hadn't noticed his approach, but the forklift operator had clearly decided to seek vengeance for Peller's attack against him. His timing couldn't have been better. Despite having a loaded gun in my hands, I wondered if I would've been capable of pulling the trigger. I'd never so much as held a gun in my life. But I'd never had so much at stake before.

I pressed my forehead against Andy's as we both trembled from head to toe. "We did it." The words quivered on my lips. "We're safe."

Another pained groan caught my attention. I spun to see Mark rolling onto his hands and knees, his face bloodied, his body beaten.

Meanwhile, Peller yelled, swore, and threatened us as he writhed in pain on the hard cement floor. I spared him only a glance as he grasped his broken leg. Part of me wanted to feel satisfaction. But as I held Andy close, all I felt was relief.

"Cops are on their way," the man said as he leaned against a shelf for support.

I remained by Andy's side, not willing to let him out of my sight. Not until we were well and truly out of Peller's reach.

"Thank you. We'll need an ambulance too," I said with a glance toward Mark, Peller's injuries low on my priority list.

The trembling of Andy's thin frame matched my own. As Peller's curses echoed faintly in the background, a strange sense of peace settled over me. It was over. For now.

***

Once again, another holding pattern in a hospital after a traumatic event.

Heat stifled the waiting room, harsh fluorescent lights reflecting off the pale green walls, creating a sterile, impersonal glow. Coughs, sniffles, and whispered conversations filled the air, interrupted occasionally by a nurse calling a patient's name, each sound grating on my already harried nerves. Andy's hand clung to mine, his knuckles white, a shudder running through his small frame as he leaned into me. His wide-eyed gaze absorbed the sight of weak and tired-looking elderly people, teenagers accompanying an injured friend, and crying babies in strollers or parents' arms.

Every time someone moved past us, I flinched, my body still in fight-or-flight mode. I surveyed the room, my mind replaying the ordeal in the warehouse, every instinct focused on keeping Andy safe. When the nurse called his name, Andy looked at me with frightened eyes, refusing to move unless assured I'd stay with him.

The doctor approached us in the examining room, but his kind face only made Andy press himself closer to me, his fingers twisting in my shirt as if to make sure I couldn't slip away. "It's okay, I'll be right here," I said. His gaze remained fixed on me, as if analyzing every word I said for truth.

I understood the struggle in his eyes. Broken trust and endless rules had taught him not to let go of the one person he thought might protect him.

The child had been through so much in his brief lifetime. And the only adult he'd ever known turned out to be a criminal, a man who, at the very least, kidnapped children. His other crimes were yet to be revealed.

I sent him a small, reassuring smile. I was there, and I wasn't going anywhere.

Now, we waited. Each passing minute stretched endlessly. Mark had fought for us, even when I doubted him. I glanced toward the hallway, willing someone to emerge with news, my stomach in a jumble as memories of his bloodied face flashed through my mind.

In the warehouse, within minutes, the wail of sirens had filled the air, getting louder with each second, drowning out Peller's threats. Flashing lights painted the warehouse walls in rhythmic pulses of red and blue. Paramedics and police officers poured from their vehicles.

Peller tried desperately to drag himself toward the door. He didn't stand a chance of making it, and none of us offered to help. Instead, I pulled Andy's trembling body toward me and sheltered his gaze from the gruesome sight. He'd already seen more than enough.

The authorities quickly secured Peller, even though he no longer posed a risk to anyone. Despite his weakness, his shouting and threats continued. Obviously unhinged, he'd finally revealed his true character.

The police read him his rights as the ambulance technicians bundled him onto a stretcher amid loud screams of pain. Even strapped down, his face twisted with fury, shouting curses and promises of revenge, his voice hoarse and feral. He looked as if he'd claw his way free if he could, even as pain and weakness kept him down.

They quickly examined the rest of us on site. Andy and I had fared the best of everyone, but the ambulance transported Mark and Harry, the warehouse employee, to the hospital after we gave a brief statement to the police. They tucked Andy and me into the back of a patrol car.

With hard seats and the faint stench of disinfectant that didn't quite mask the smell of stale smoke and some other unidentifiable odor, the patrol car nevertheless gave me a sense of security. My body decompressed, knowing the threat was gone and we were on our final sprint.

Andy's gaze swept around him, his wide eyes filled with wonder and a trace of fear. I didn't blame him. I'd never sat in a police car, which was commendable, considering my recent run-ins with the cops. I put an arm around the boy's shoulders, sensing his anxiety as we drove up to the looming hospital.

"It's okay. They'll just check us out."

"Where's Graham and the other guys?" I heard the slight quiver in his voice, despite his best efforts to hide it.

"They're here, at the hospital, but Graham can't hurt you anymore," I said, squeezing his shoulder. His small, tense nod told me he wanted to believe it.

Inside the examining room, the doctor's gloved hands moved over Andy's arms and legs as his small fingers dug into mine. He kept his eyes pressed shut, as if retreating into himself was the only way to get through it. I held his hand tighter, murmuring quiet reassurances, even as my heart clenched. Likely, he was rarely touched in kindness by another human being.

I watched the doctor's face closely, searching for any hint of concern. What if deeper wounds existed, invisible scars? They'd find the obvious signs of injuries here with examinations, tests, and x-rays, but the emotional and psychological scars could take years to uncover and were much more difficult to treat.

A meeting with two RCMP detectives ensued, along with Assistant Commissioner Holt, who reprimanded me for not contacting the police before or after rescuing Andy from the house. I politely reminded AC Holt that any efforts I'd made to convince the RCMP a boy was trapped in that house were met with disbelief and even threats. He had the grace to apologize before moving on to the most important reason for the meeting.

As expected, they needed to hear Andy's story. Their voices remained calm, almost soothing, but I noticed Andy's tension. Each question seemed to tug at some buried memory, his answers clipped and uncertain as he tried to piece together his childhood. I placed a hand on his arm, trying to ground him.

As it unfolded and became apparent he was a kidnapping victim, the detectives set into motion a series of questions and tests, including taking a

DNA sample. They determined Andy, never having known any adult besides Peller, was probably abducted as a very young child, perhaps even as a baby.

When he told the men about the other boys, their questions intensified. His small voice echoed in the quiet room, speaking of names and faces I didn't know but feared for. My heart twisted with each word. Andy couldn't give any more details besides their names, approximate ages, and a guesstimate of when they were in Peller's house. What happened to them after they left remained a mystery.

The police promised to assemble a photo compilation of missing children of the same gender and age for Andy to identify. Hopefully, it'd help.

By the time they finished, Andy looked drained, his eyes dull and hazy. I pulled him close, letting him lean on me as we left the room. Together, we walked down the hall, away from the fluorescent lights and sterile smell.

Now, as we waited for news about Mark, I looked down at Andy's thin, tired face. Peller's reach might be over, but the consequences of that reach would take time to heal.

"Who is this guy anyway?" Andy's small voice cut through the silence.

A good question. And one that could take many conversations to figure out, but I'd try to simplify it for a child's sake.

"A friend," I said. "Someone who wanted to help us."

"Then why did we run away from him?"

Such perception in such a young child. "Because I didn't know he wanted to help us. I made a mistake, and I'm really sorry about it."

Andy patted my arm, his expression earnest. "That's okay. I make mistakes too."

I smiled at him as tears welled in my eyes. What a sweet boy, so undeserving of all he'd suffered. I hoped and prayed he'd reunite with his family.

The minutes dragged, punctuated only by the coughs and cries of patients waiting to see a doctor. Andy sipped at his juice box in silence, his small hand clutching it, the plastic crackling slightly with every shift of his fingers as he took in everything with a quiet fascination. In his other hand, he clutched a cellophane-wrapped cookie, still untouched. His intense study of the treat suggested he'd either never tasted a cookie, or cellophane was a new discovery.

I tried to sit still, but my leg bounced, a traitorous sign of my inner turmoil. Guilt and misgivings overwhelmed me. Fractured thoughts and regrets circled in my mind, always leading back to Mark, how I'd doubted him, mistrusted him when he was probably just as lost in this nightmare as I was.

Paranoia had been my constant companion, tripping me up, clouding my judgment, and warping everything Mark did into a threat. My suspicions, fueled by fear and bad experiences, hit back at me as I realized how blind my distrust had made me. Because of it, I'd risked my life and that of a young boy. Unforgivable.

A nurse emerged from a side door, her gaze zeroing in. I straightened with anticipation when she made a beeline toward us. News about Mark.

Chapter 51

"Ms. Hampton, you can come with me now."

Andy tucked his cookie into his pants pocket and accompanied us through the door into a maze of pale green corridors with metal railings lining the walls. An antiseptic smell invaded our nostrils as we marched down hallways and around corners to arrive in a low-lit area with cubicles separated by blue curtains. The emergency ward.

The nurse led us to a corner bed and smiled as she allowed us to pass. My gaze locked on Mark as she closed the curtain behind us.

With a white bandage encircling his head and one eye swollen shut, he resembled a character from a horror movie. Concerned, I glanced at Andy, whose gaze traveled over Mark's face with open fascination. I watched him absorb every detail, cataloging the scene as only a child might, as if understanding these marks would somehow help him understand the strange adults protecting him.

"Hey," Mark said through puffy lips.

"I want to ask how you are, but I guess it's obvious."

"Feel nothing now. Great painkillers." His slurred words and unfocused gaze spoke to the medication's strength.

I put my hand on Andy's back and urged him closer. "I don't think you've met. This is Andy." I glanced down at the boy. "Andy, this is Mark. He helped me look for you. We wouldn't be here without him." The child glanced up at me uncertainly before turning to Mark with a solemn nod.

"Did it hurt when he hit you?" Andy asked, his eyes fixed on the purple bruising around Mark's eye. The question's bluntness startled me, but Mark's lips twitched into a slight smile, wincing as his split lip stretched.

"Bet I look pretty scary, eh?"

Andy blinked at him, a smile forming as he replied, "You look like a knight who fought a dragon... and almost lost." The three of us shared an awkward laugh, breaking the tension, if only for a moment.

"I'm sorry for what happened," Mark said, his voice soft, eye downcast. "I wanted to believe you, but I was busy creating conspiracy theories. I should have trusted you." He met my gaze, his face filled with regret. "I followed my agenda without considering the effect it had on you and the boy if you were right. And you were. I was wrong. I'm sorry."

I was momentarily stunned. My apology to him had been teetering on my lips, waiting for the best moment to deliver it. Nothing prepared me for his words, not understanding what he meant about his own agenda. Were the drugs talking for him? I was the one who held onto a healthy helping of guilt, and I owed him the truth. After everything he'd been through, he deserved to know my trust had waned.

"I thought... I thought you were in cahoots with Peller, that you were part of this." My voice was barely a whisper, but I held his gaze.

I felt Andy's questioning look as Mark's good eye widened. Hurt flashed in his gaze before he looked down at his clenched hand, as if bracing himself against my words.

"Why? Because I doubted you?" His gaze lifted to mine again.

I smiled slightly. "In part. Also, you had access to my house," I said, counting off my suspicions on my fingers. "The strange note materialized because of you. You're a talented actor, as proven by your excellent performance as a house inspector. And you have experience with bikes."

Mark seemed to absorb my words and slowly nodded. "Yeah, I guess that'd do it."

"Remember the night I heard the boy calling to me from the bushes?" His brows lowered as he nodded. "I found a Bluetooth speaker in there. I suspected you'd put it there."

Mark's lips twisted in a grimace.

All or nothing. Drawing a deep breath, I continued. "I also kind of let myself into your house one day when you were gone." I watched that one good eye widen again. "I found Abby's obituary there. You'd done your research, and it convinced me that you'd manipulated me, tried to make me think I was crazy."

"That was all it was, I swear." His words came out in a rush. "Just research. I wanted to know everything about you and your past. My obsessive nature, I guess." He ended with a wry tone.

I didn't mention my concerns about who had fed information to Keith. But the memories of living with the specter of insanity hovering above my head created a clump of powerful emotions. My fingers found Andy's shoulder, centering me as I searched for the right words, everything inadequate for what we'd both endured.

"It worked, you know." My voice lowered in sorrow. "I considered the possibility I was crazy. But even that couldn't make me stop. What if I wasn't? What if there really was a boy in that house?"

Andy leaned into me, his small hand clutching my arm. Mark's gaze fixed on us, his expression softening as he watched the boy nestle against my side. In that moment, our scars, both visible and not, seemed to fade, and for the first time since this nightmare began, I experienced hope.

I smiled at Andy and received a wide, uninhibited smile in return. I saw Abby in his eyes, that same spark, that same joy, and I was happy I'd helped put it there. Tears filled my eyes, and I wrapped him in a strong hug. My gaze met Mark's, and I noticed a wetness in his good eye. Our shared guilt felt like something we could overcome together. We'd all suffered because of Peller's games, but now, we could heal.

Chapter 52

The cottage seemed oddly empty, its creaky floors and drafty windows appearing more conspicuous now that I was alone again. Even the once-cozy corners seemed haunted by memories of Andy's laugh and quiet footsteps. Outside, the leaves rustled in the chilly breeze, a quiet farewell as nature readied for its seasonal shift, just as I readied for my own.

A profound sorrow filled my heart, an unexpected result of the past few days. I expected joy, pride, and fulfillment. Sadness was a selfish emotion. But I needed to wallow in it, so I could toss it aside and carry on.

I had one week left in this cottage. One last week of forced isolation and self-pity, followed by the turning of a page, or perhaps several.

After an eventful, eye-opening, scary summer, now, as the first leaves changed color, taking on the season's warm reds, yellows, and oranges, it was time to evaluate everything gained and tally up my losses.

The biggest, most heartwarming gain was Andy's reunion with his parents, Dylan and Emily Fielding. Peller had snatched the seven-month-old from a stroller in Winnipeg, the family's hometown, shattering their lives and plunging them into a horrifying nightmare. Andy's parents never stopped searching, never stopped believing they'd find their son, Max—his real name.

When the DNA test came back with a positive match, they joyfully caught a plane to Victoria to reunite with their child. We did our best to prepare Max for the moment he'd meet the family he didn't remember. He was cautious, curious, his small face unreadable as we explained his real mom and dad were coming.

When Dylan and Emily entered the police conference room, they brought with them a tidal wave of happiness. Emily's sobs broke the silence as she dropped to her knees, her arms open wide, trembling. Dylan stood behind her, his hand gripping her shoulder, tears streaming down his face.

"Max," Emily whispered, her voice cracking.

Max hesitated, looking up at me. I knelt beside him, gently placing a hand on his shoulder. "It's okay," I said. "Go say hi. They love you."

His hand slipped from mine as he stepped forward, tentative at first, then quicker when Emily gave a joyous laugh. She scooped him into her arms, and Dylan crouched beside them, his arms encompassing them both. Their sobs and laughter mingled, filled with relief, love, and overwhelming joy.

Tears poured from my eyes, but I wasn't alone. Not a single person in the room remained untouched by the scene. Even the officers present turned away to discreetly wipe their eyes.

Max's face lit up when he met his older brother and sister. They hugged him like they'd known him forever. He laughed freely, his loneliness and fear melting away in the warmth of this family who'd never stopped loving him.

As I watched from across the room, a bittersweet ache settled in my chest. I'd physically passed a precious torch to this ecstatic young couple and taken a step back, happy but excluded.

The feeling didn't last. When the police chief introduced Mark and me to the Fieldings, we received warm, grateful, and tearful hugs. Emily clung to me as if words alone couldn't convey her gratitude.

"You brought our son back to us," she said with an emotion-choked voice. "You'll always be a part of his life. Promise me that."

Dylan nodded, his voice firm but warm. "We owe you everything."

Their words settled over me like a soft blanket, soothing my emotions. I didn't need further encouragement. Andy, or Max, had found his way back to where he belonged. And in some small way, I had too.

***

More discoveries followed. The brave young boy was instrumental in helping to identify the other boys who briefly roomed with him. The RCMP searched every inch of Peller's property and found traces of DNA that had yet to be identified.

Unfortunately, despite the strides they made in the investigation, Peller remained uncooperative. He admitted to one charge of kidnapping and denied everything else. His reasoning for kidnapping Max was that he needed a replacement for his son, Nathan, who'd drowned ten years earlier. Obviously insane, he believed himself justified in taking Max since he was childless, and the Fieldings had two others.

His kidnapping charge alone carried a life sentence, but Peller seemed determined to hang on to whatever other lives he had and wouldn't confess to any additional crimes. That two other families were not yet granted the same wish as the Fieldings broke my heart. I'd left that case in the capable hands of the RCMP. Hopefully they'd resolve it quickly, but I was terrified the other boys hadn't met a good end.

Thus, part of the reason for my sadness. The other part stemmed from Max himself. He'd given me new life. He drove me to care about what went on around me, to set aside my problems and help another human being. Shortly, he'd leave with his family, who still lived in Manitoba, not wanting to leave the place they'd last seen their precious son. It was unlikely I'd ever see him again, despite the heartfelt pleas of his parents. I was smart enough to realize he'd take up a life with his family, make new friends, attend a proper school, and grow up with little memory of my brief involvement in his life.

I pictured him running through a schoolyard, his laughter mingling with friends' voices, his life unfolding in ways I'd never see. One day he'd barely remember Sala Lake or the strange woman who helped him find his way back. It was how it should be, and yet, I couldn't help but experience a deep pang of loss. I'd lost my heart to Max the first moment I'd seen him on the dock.

My sadness was self-indulgent. I felt deep joy for him, but I'd miss him terribly, and my future veered toward the emptiness I'd had before I came to the lake.

I also couldn't ignore the guilt that clung to me, a persistent reminder of my doubts about Mark. How had I let myself get so wrapped up in paranoia? And yet, it wasn't only paranoia. It was survival instinct, honed by too much grief. As I prepared to re-enter my "normal" life, I hoped I'd keep this new sense of purpose rather than sinking back into isolation and distrust.

The thought of a new apartment seemed surreal, detached from the life I'd led here. The walls would be empty and new, devoid of the memories and tension that had filled this summer. But that's what I needed, a clean slate, a space I could mold into my own. Maybe I'd get a dog. A living being to talk to instead of random pieces of furniture. A pug would be nice.

My new apartment would be the first fresh start. I decided I'd throw myself back into my career and perhaps build another one with a renewed interest in nature photography. And I wanted to volunteer my time to help others. I'd scouted out an organization that interested me, The Compassionate Friends, which provided peer support for families grieving the loss of a child. Fortunately, they had a chapter in Victoria.

But before I fully committed to this new life, I had one last wound to confront. The truth about that horrible, fateful day sat like a stone in my heart. I wasn't sure how Keith would react, or if he'd even want to hear it after all this time, but I needed to unburden myself, to truly start anew.

Chapter 53

I took a deep breath, inhaling the fresh air, staring across the lake that shimmered in the sunlight. In a few minutes, I'd face Keith to tell him what I'd kept buried so long. After that, I'd step into the unknown, hopeful that whatever came next might finally bring me peace.

The sound of footsteps caught my attention, but they didn't frighten me. I'd expected him. As Mark lowered himself into the rattan chair beside me, I turned to look at him. The swelling had disappeared, and he now had two functional eyes. The bruising had morphed into a shade of yellow that made him appear jaundiced. But his genuine smile cheered me.

We'd taken long strides together. Mark made his own confession the day of his release from the hospital. I'd driven him home and, while I tidied his kitchen, I heard him clear his throat behind me.

Sensing he wanted to say something, I faced him. His battle scars had lessened little since the incident in the warehouse, but the decrease in medication had improved his focus, and his eyes appeared clear and steady. Wariness also lived in them.

"What's wrong?" I said, dread creeping over me.

"I have something to tell you, and you won't like it."

I smiled, hoping this was a lead-up to a joke. "Try me."

His gaze moved to his clenched hands, and I knew there was no punch line to this speech. "My helping you wasn't entirely selfless. Something else motivated me." He lifted his head to look at me, seeming to gauge my reaction. So far, all I felt was concern.

"Go on."

"I have a bit of history with Peller," Mark said.

My breath froze. Had I been right all along? Peller and Mark as a team?

Mark raised his hands in defense, correctly reading my expression. "It's not what you think. It's nothing to do with kidnapping Max or trying to drive you crazy." He hesitated. "But I wanted to get into his house somehow. And since you seemed to have the same end goal, I used you to help me."

I lowered myself onto a kitchen chair, unsure if my legs would hold me. What was he getting at?

"I need to go back several years." He paused. "My dad was in the military and served under Peller."

I recalled the photo of Mark and his parents, his father in uniform.

"Dad didn't like Peller, thought he was a little off, too intense." He gave me a you've-been-there look. "Dad started snooping around, asking questions, and word got back to Peller, who concocted a plan to set up my father with false accusations and have him thrown out of the army with a dishonorable discharge."

His voice deepened in anger toward the end of his tirade, and a wave of pity for both Mark and his father filled me. More of Graham Peller's victims. *But how do I figure into this drama?*

"It destroyed my father. He was dedicated to the military, through and through. He never got over it. He started drinking, my mother left him, and now he's rotting away in a retirement home, feeling sorry for himself. My sister and I tried everything to help him, but nothing stuck." He drew a deep breath, as if steeling himself, before releasing a flood of words. "I admit it. I became obsessed with this monster who destroyed our lives. It festered inside me and grew over the years to the point that even my wife couldn't take it anymore. She left me. Another family torn apart because of him. At least that's how I looked at it. I was desperate, wanting to find something to use against Peller to force him to clear my father's name."

Understanding dawned. "And you latched onto the fact that he may have killed his only son and kidnapped someone else's."

Mark's head drooped. "Yes. When I realized Peller and I both had places on this lake, I wanted to get close to him. And your discovery seemed heaven-sent. I had a chance to vindicate my father and get revenge. I wasn't sure how, but I certainly had something to work with."

"And someone."

"I'm sorry. I jumped onto your cause to help my own. And that's why I didn't want to call the police when he attacked me. I wanted to take him down myself. I needed that satisfaction." His tone was dispirited. "If it's any consolation, I really was afraid for the boy, and I sincerely wanted to find him. I attached a GPS to Peller's car. That night when he stabbed me. I had several reasons, but mostly I wanted to find him if he tried to leave with the boy. It led me to the warehouse." His wry expression acknowledged that his appearance at the warehouse may have created more harm than good, at least for him.

I studied him for a long moment before asking him a question that had been eating away at me. "Why did you turn on me? The note... at the police station. You believed I'd written it."

He flinched as if I'd hit him. "At that moment, I did. I admit it. I'd seen the effect Peller and the boy had on you. I'd watched you fall apart. I was worried you'd staged the note in a last-ditch effort to convince the police, maybe without even realizing you'd done it. I could've let it play out, let the cops search the house again. But... what if... ?"

He didn't need to finish his sentence. I understood. What if they didn't find the boy? What would it have done to me? To my mental health?

I couldn't meet his gaze. I stood and strode to the window, staring out at the lake that had seen so much of our stories over the past weeks. It had helped and hindered me, protected and attacked me, but I would never stop loving it. It brought Max back to his family and me back to life.

I'd made mistakes, too many to let this one ruin my life or anyone else's. I swiveled to face Mark.

"I understand. I wish you'd been upfront with me and told me your story earlier, but I understand, and I won't hold it against you. If its forgiveness you want, then you have it."

So many emotions crossed Mark's face in that moment—relief, happiness, gratitude, and maybe something else.

Now, sitting on my porch, the wind shifted, and it was my turn to seek forgiveness.

"Still working up your nerve?"

"Yeah, kinda." I'd confided in Mark, lessening the weight on my shoulders, but it wouldn't disappear until I spoke to Keith.

"When does he get here?"

I glanced at my watch. "Any minute."

"Want me here? Moral support?"

"Thanks, but I'm good. I'm a big girl now."

"You always were. Don't forget it. You rescued that boy and took Peller down on your own."

"Andy helped me." I still thought of the boy as two parts of a whole. Andy before and Max after. "He's quite the kid," I said.

He reached over and folded his warm hand around mine, knowing how much I missed Max.

Releasing me, Mark eased himself from the Adirondack chair. "I'll leave before Keith arrives. If you need me, holler. I'll keep an ear open."

"I'm surprised you're up to doing battle again so soon."

He grinned. "I was just practicing on Peller. Keith'll be easy."

Mark bent over and gave me a hug. I noticed the kiss he gave me on the top of my head before he strode off toward his cottage.

I hoped my "hollering for help" days were over. Although the events over the summer had lifted me out of my gloom, I didn't want to live through another adventure like it, fighting for my life and a child's, questioning my sanity at every turn.

The police investigation revealed so many things, and likely many more would come to light, but several put my mind at ease. Peller had indeed attempted to push me to the brink. He'd been a client of Keith's. We'd met at a function years ago, and he knew Abby's story, had followed it in the news. He contacted Keith when he realized I was his ex-wife. He dug for information, feeding Keith some about me in return.

He'd orchestrated everything, from the bike's failed brakes to the jet ski attack. He hid the speaker with the recording of Max's voice in the trees and hovered twenty feet away, controlling both the device and me with delight.

He accessed my cottage when I wasn't there and set up the stuffed bunny in the cupboard. He also forged my writing and planted the note, hoping I'd find it and wonder about my mental health. Instead, Mark discovered it. An even better scenario from Peller's point of view.

Mark no sooner disappeared than I heard the crunch of tires behind me. I stood and watched Keith climb from his car. For once, he appeared uncertain. I'd told him I needed to talk to him about something but offered no other hints.

"You're a famous lady. Your picture is all over the news," he said as he approached, his tall, lean form so familiar to me.

I shrugged, attempting to look casual. My fifteen minutes of fame.

"Can I get you something? A beer? A glass of water?" I was suddenly nervous with this man I'd married twelve years ago. We'd almost become strangers. But something intense hung between us.

"I'm good." He settled into the chair Mark had vacated as I took the other one. "This is a nice place. Bet you'll find it hard to leave."

"Yes and no. It's beautiful, and it certainly was adventurous, but I'm ready to get on with my life."

"Glad to hear that, Julie." His voice rang with sincerity, and I knew I had his full support, unless things went downhill after this conversation.

The early evening sun gleamed on the lake, reflecting the kaleidoscope of sunset colors. The quiet between us grew thick, mingling with the pleasant, earthy muskiness of decaying leaves. I traced the peeling paint on the Adirondack chair with a finger, focusing myself as I summoned the strength to speak. He looked at me expectantly, seeing it for the segue it was.

I'd spent three years convincing myself I could live with the lie. But it festered, a hollow ache that swelled every time I saw Keith, every time I looked in the mirror. I wanted to blame him, almost needed to, and hated myself for it. Now, as he sat across from me, his face etched with lines I hadn't noticed before, the truth dragged its way up my throat, demanding release. I clenched my hands, my knuckles white against the chair's wood, willing myself to find the words.

I drew a deep, shaky breath. "I need to confess. I'm not proud of it, but it needs to be said. I can't move on without it."

He remained silent, waiting.

"That day." There was no need to explain. Only one "that day" existed for us. "I told you to keep an eye on Abby before I went inside."

Keith's flinch cut through me. I knew the expression well, the way his shoulders stiffened, the way his gaze dropped as if looking at me was too painful. He'd heard my accusation before and seen it in my eyes a thousand times. He expected me to accuse him once again of letting our daughter drown.

For a moment, I was back there. The way Abby's laughter faded with each step I took toward the house. The thud of the back door closing and the finality of it. I didn't look back to see if Keith was watching.

"Two things. Two terrible things." My voice cracked, fighting my need to get the words out. "I saw Abby get off the trampoline before I went in the house. And I knew you didn't hear me."

"What?" Keith's gaze snapped up to mine, his eyes wide and confused.

I swallowed. "I knew you were concentrating on that lawnmower, and I knew how you got. I told you I was going in, but even as I did it, I realized you probably didn't hear me. And I'd seen Abby get off the trampoline." My shoulders trembled as I spoke, words spilling out like water from a broken glass. Tears welled in my eyes, blurring his shocked expression. "I should've stayed outside. I should've watched her, warned her to stay away from the pool. I could've brought her inside with me. So many things I could've done. But I didn't. It was my fault, not yours." My voice broke, and I covered my mouth with trembling fingers.

Keith sat frozen. His mouth opened, but no sound came out.

"All this time," I said, forcing the words past the lump in my throat. "I blamed you. I needed to because if it wasn't your fault, then it was mine. And I couldn't live with that."

A dark silence fell, broken only by the distant cawing of a crow and a whisper of a breeze. Keith's eyes glistened. When he finally spoke, his voice was low and unsteady. "I always thought..." He stopped, shaking his head as though trying to clear a fog. "I thought you hated me for not saving her. I thought you were right to hate me. I spent years replaying that moment, thinking if I'd just looked up..."

"I don't hate you." The words tumbled out before I could stop them. "I hated myself for not making sure you heard me, for not being there, for failing her. But I couldn't admit that. Not to you, not to myself."

"We both failed her." His voice cracked. "But we loved her. And she knew that. We can't change what happened."

I sobbed, unable to hold anything back. I'd done the same when I shared my confession with Mark. He'd held me and let me cry. Then he told me I needed to tell Keith. I had to absolve him of his guilt and share the blame, even though neither of us were to blame. It was an accident. But I'd never get over the trauma of losing Abby if I didn't rid myself of this burden that crushed me.

And it did. Not one day passed that I didn't hate myself for what I'd done to this man. He hadn't deserved it, but I'd needed to lash out, and he'd been the closest person, the only person.

My hands covered my face, my head bowed. I'd done it. Confession might be good for the soul, but it was terrible for my heart.

A warm hand with calloused fingers gently gripped my forearm and urged me from the chair, holding me steady. I braced myself for his anger. Anger I fully deserved. When he pulled me into his arms, the tension that had hounded me for years collapsed, leaving me lighter. We cried together, clutching each other close.

"Ah, Julie, you caused yourself so much pain."

I leaned back to look at him. "You mean I caused you pain."

Keith shrugged. "Yes. But why did you hold it in so long? You should have told me right away."

"I was too ashamed."

"The pain of losing Abby crippled you. It destroyed both of us. We could have held each other up. Instead, we struck each other down."

"I did it."

"We both did. Yes, I always knew I was partially to blame for what happened, but I also knew we each had a part in it. This type of thing happens far too often. One parent thinks the other is taking care of a child and vice versa. It was an accident. A tragedy. But you didn't need to create another tragedy. That's what you did. You cut yourself off from everyone for three years. You've paid your dues. It's over."

"Yes, it is." I rested my forehead against his chest, my energy sapped.

We walked in silence to the dock, the lake stretching out before us, serene and beautiful. Keith stood beside me, our past lying heavy between us. Then he exhaled, as if letting go. I watched his reflection ripple in the water, as if the last traces of that day slipped away.

"Can we be friends now?" Keith said.

"I think we already are."

Keith glanced over my shoulder, lifting an amused brow. "And what about the guy lurking in the trees? Should we invite him over?"

I turned and saw Mark hovering near the edge of his property, half in shadow. A laugh sprang from my throat, the sound catching me off guard. It felt strange and good.

"Mark," I called, waving him over. "You don't have to stay over there."

He hesitated, then stepped forward, his expression uncertain, as if not sure where he stood in all this. But I knew.

I held his gaze. The ache in my chest, that hollow space Abby left, was still there. It always would be. But it wasn't the whole of me now. For the first time in a long time, I wasn't just treading water.

I was ready to swim.

Acknowledgements

The idea for this novel came to me as I was (you guessed it) kayaking. From there, I needed a setting, and what better place than Vancouver Island? Some of the spots referenced in this novel are real, including Victoria, Port Alberni, Vancouver, Stanley Park and many others. However, Sala Lake is fictional.

The Kwakwaka'wakw people are located in the northern and central parts of Vancouver Island. They are a First Nations people who have profound traditions related to mourning, including the "sała" ceremony, which involves specific songs and dances to honor and release the spirit of the deceased. I chose the name to match the overriding theme of conquering grief and loss.

In their language, Kwak'wala, the word "Namima" means kinship or a clan group. That is the name I gave the fictional nearby village where Julie learned the story of the Shadow Woman. The story is also fictional. As far as I know, there is no legend or local lore about the Shadow Woman.

Very near the end of the novel, I mention an organization that Julie plans to volunteer for, The Compassionate Friends. This is a real organization that helps families deal with grief, and they have a chapter in Victoria, B.C.

I hope you enjoyed this novel, my first foray into psychological thrillers, and probably not my last. Of course, I needed a team to bring it to you, and that team includes the wonderful folks at Black Rose Writing. I thank them for their help and encouragement. But it doesn't stop there. I had an excellent editor in the form of Mary Ellen Bramwell whose invaluable input filled in the gaps and helped me polish the final draft. I also had helpful insight from members of a writing and reading group I participate in, including Gail Olmsted, Cam Torrens, Bob Stowe, Lucille Guarino, Ruth Stevens, Deborah Heim, and Peggy Williams.

And last but not least, I thank my family, friends, and you, the reader, for your support.

About the Author

The award-winning author of crime fiction, A.J. McCarthy is always on the lookout for new ideas. Her friends and family are cautious, concerned they may become a victim in her next novel. Those who are more adventurous offer up ideas and are willing to sacrifice certain family members for the cause. A.J. bides her time, waiting for the right moment and the perfect victim. She hides behind a quiet façade, and few know what she's really thinking.

A.J. grew up reading Agatha Christie, Sidney Sheldon, and many other masters of mystery and suspense. A lifelong love of the genre evolved. She's a member of Crime Writers of Canada, Sisters in Crime, and International Thriller Writers. When she isn't writing, chances are she's reading.

Other Titles by A.J. McCarthy

A Charlie & Simm Mystery series

Faux Friends

By the Book: A Canadian Crime Novel

Cold Betrayal

Legacy of Fear

Note from A.J. McCarthy

Word-of-mouth is crucial for any author to succeed. If you enjoyed *The Boy on the Dock*, please leave a review online—anywhere you are able. Even if it's just a sentence or two. It would make all the difference and would be very much appreciated.

Thanks!
A.J. McCarthy

We hope you enjoyed reading this title from:

www.blackrosewriting.com

Subscribe to our mailing list – *The Rosevine* – and receive **FREE** books, daily deals, and stay current with news about upcoming releases and our hottest authors.
Scan the QR code below to sign up.

Already a subscriber? Please accept a sincere thank you for being a fan of Black Rose Writing authors.

View other Black Rose Writing titles at
www.blackrosewriting.com/books and use promo code
PRINT to receive a **20% discount** when purchasing.

9 781685 137434